IOSI, THE REMORSEFUL SPY

IOSI, THE REMORSEFUL SPY

CONFESSIONS OF THE FEDERAL AGENT WHO INFILTRATED THE ARGENTINE JEWISH COMMUNITY.

LOVE, DEATH, BETRAYAL, AND COVERT OPERATIONS.

THE BOMBINGS OF THE ISRAELI EMBASSY AND THE AMIA.

MIRIAM LEWIN
and
HORACIO LUTZKY

Translated by FRANCES RIDDLE

SEVEN STORIES PRESS
New York ✳ Oakland ✳ London

Copyright © 2015 by Miriam Lewin and Horacio Lutzky
Translation copyright © 2025 by Frances Riddle

All rights reserved. No part of this book may be reproduced, stored in a retrieval system, or transmitted in any form, by any means, including mechanical, electronic, photocopying, recording, or otherwise, without the prior written permission of the publisher.

Seven Stories Press
140 Watts Street
New York, NY 10013
www.sevenstories.com

Library of Congress Cataloging-in-Publication Data

Names: Lewin, Miriam, 1957- author interviewer | Lutzky, Horacio author interviewer | Iosi interviewee
Title: Iosi, the remorseful spy / by Miriam Lewin and Horacio Lutzky ; translated from the Spanish by Frances Riddle.
Other titles: Iosi, el espía arrepentido. English
Description: New York : Seven Stories Press, 2025.
Identifiers: LCCN 2025000900 (print) | LCCN 2025000901 (ebook) | ISBN 9781644214572 trade paperback | ISBN 9781644214589 ebook
Subjects: LCSH: Iosi | Undercover operations--Argentina | Jews--Argentina--Politics and government--20th century | Jews--Argentina--Politics and government--21st century | Spies--Argentina--Biography | Argentina. Policía Federal--Biography | LCGFT: Biographies
Classification: LCC HV8080.U5 L4913 2025 (print) | LCC HV8080.U5 (ebook) | DDC 363.2/32--dc23/eng/20250326
LC record available at https://lccn.loc.gov/2025000900
LC ebook record available at https://lccn.loc.gov/2025000901

College professors and high school and middle school teachers may order free examination copies of Seven Stories Press titles. Visit https://www.sevenstories.com/pg/resources-academics or email academic@sevenstories.com.

Printed in the United States of America

9 8 7 6 5 4 3 2 1

To Josef, my father, who continues to inspire
me with his transparency.
To my children and to Daniel.
To the memory of the victims.
To the memory of Sebastián, most of all.
—ML

To the memory of my parents.
To my children and to Andrea.
To those who refuse to accept impunity for the powerful.
—HL

CONTENTS

The Spy Who Brought Us Together 1
Me, the Spy 11

PART I 17

The Kid from Flores 19
Hidden World 22
Elite Training 26
Filters 32
Laura, My Handler 35
Young Zionist 37
Undercover in La Tablada 43
The Argentine Eli Cohen 44
First Steps 46
The Fortress 51
Jativá, More and More Connections 52
Women, My Weakness 56
The Keys to AMIA 62
Romantic Entanglement 65
A Leader is Born 66
Alternative 71
Her 76
The Female Agents 84
Last Minute Change 91

PART II 97

A Call. 99
Strange Guy. 100
Doubts. 102
Drop by Drop 105
Trial. 109
Spokesperson 112
The Elevator Operator 117
Mysterious Flight. 119
The First Hearing. 123
The Feds. 126
Glitch. 128
Garré, Out the Window. 130
Charging Garré 132
Court on Trail 136
Israel's Role 138

PART III 143

A Surprising Story 145
Regrets. 148
Lockbox. 149
Nazi Hunter. 150
The Combative Lawyer. 151
Horacio, Confirmation. 154
The First Lady 155
Stisuo, the Legendary Spy. 157
A Foreign Documentary. 160
Childhood Friends 162

PART IV 167

   Watched. 169
   Warning Signs 173
   July 18th. 176
   Kabat. 186
   Safeguarding AMIA 191
   Zionist Leader 193
   Suspicion and Exile 197
   The Entre Ríos Office. 202
   Side Gigs 204

PART V 207

   Attempt in Washington 211
   New Role. 218
   Undercover Reporter 220
   Displacement. 224
   No Time to Lose 225

PART VI 231

   Last-Ditch Effort 232
   The Big Leagues 234
   Someone Else. 237
   Dashed Hopes 239
   The Trap. 241
   Internal Affairs. 242
   Péres with an "S" 245
   An Unbearable Buzz. 247
   Back in Buenos Aires 248
   Working for the Minister 250

Wrong Time............................ 254
Money, Money, Money 256

PART VII 261

Exit Strategy............................ 262
Messaging 264
Blind Faith............................. 267
Testifying Without Nisman 272

PART VIII 281

Defenseless Witness 283
Adrift................................. 287

EPILOGUE 291
GLOSSARY 297
BIBLIOGRAPHY 305
ACKNOWLEDGMENTS 309
PHOTOS................................ 311

THE SPY WHO BROUGHT US TOGETHER

Neither Horacio nor I expected, at the very start of the twenty-first century, to find ourselves trapped inside a spy movie: a tangled web of love, hate, complicity and betrayal, corrupt judges and politicians, lies and illicit dealings. A story that included over a hundred deaths across two terrorist attacks, tampering with evidence, bribery, and cover-up. There was a long list of vulnerable witnesses and, the cherry on top, a prosecutor, whom we didn't fully trust, found dead inside his luxury apartment. Although, looking back, each one of us had already been trapped inside that movie long before meeting Iosi. Because we live in Argentina, where truth is stranger than fiction.

Both Horacio and I are Jewish and middle-aged. We are both journalists. Horacio is also a lawyer. But Argentina has a large Jewish community and the community of journalists is wide-ranging and diverse, so we'd never met until an undercover federal agent introduced us. We were brought together one afternoon in 2002 by a mysterious character plagued by remorse. A thin, dispirited man, who in no way resembled the stereotypes of the Hollywood spies. He looked like the saddest man in the world. A remorseful spy, tortured by demons. He was haunted by the victims of one of the bloodiest attacks in the history of Argentina, the bombing of the Asociación Mutual Israelita Argentina, the AMIA. Iosi, as he called himself, suspected that, as a member of the Federal

Police Intelligence Service, he had inadvertently facilitated the terrorist attack through his reports. When Horacio and I met Iosi eight years later, there were still eighty-five families awaiting justice. And they are still waiting.

I'd covered the AMIA bombing as a TV reporter that winter morning in July 1994, arriving at the immense and still smoldering mound of cement, marble, metal, and glass shortly after the explosion had occurred. I'd also been at the Israeli embassy, microphone in hand, as a novice street reporter, two years prior, when it was bombed, killing twenty-two people inside the diplomatic headquarters and surrounding buildings. Standing in front of the police barricade, I saw stretchers roll past carrying mutilated bodies. I am the daughter of Polish immigrants, totally assimilated into Argentine society and with little Jewish education within the community, but from that day forward I began to feel more Jewish, more connected to my people. Perhaps a result of the danger, the threat, that was something I'd never felt before, not even when I was sequestered by pro-Nazi military officers during the dictatorship.

A popular local adage holds that all anti-Semites claim to have "one Jewish friend." In Argentina, hatred and distrust of Jews is not overt. Instead, it is a low-level anti-Semitism that simmers just underneath the surface. But eventually, it boils over. It might be graffiti, an anonymous sign on the street, the vandalism of a cemetery, a beating, an angry call to stop Israeli soldiers from vacationing in Patagonia.

As a Jewish community, in terms of size, we are the largest in Latin America and the fifth largest in the world outside of Israel. Our social and cultural integration into Argentine society has been solidified over several generations; the waves of Jewish immigration to Argentina from Eastern Europe and other areas where we were persecuted or mired in poverty mainly took place before the Second World War. Horacio and I, for example, both define ourselves first as Argentine and then Jewish.

Our religion can be practiced freely in this country, and it is no longer a requirement that the president of the nation be Catholic. There are Jewish senators, government ministers, legislators, and judges; we have a strong presence in academic spheres as well as in business. In the area of diplomacy, where until recently old prejudices remained intact, a well-known Jewish journalist served as foreign minister and ambassador to the United States.

But, in the armed forces and the police, on the other hand, there are almost no Jewish officers at all. A nucleus of anti-Semitism remains, and picking out a Jew among them is like finding a needle in a haystack. Some say anti-Semitism is the very DNA of the nation's military, although that's a debated topic. Someone once said that the lack of Jews among the military ranks was due to the fact that "the Jews aren't interested in defending the nation, because they don't consider themselves Argentine." This type of reasoning reveals prejudices based in ignorance.

Horacio and I are descendants of immigrants, like almost everyone else in this country. I come from a leftist Polish family linked to the Labour Bund Party, which my father defined as a Socialist political movement born in the late nineteenth century in the Russian Empire. The Jews from that party who emigrated to Argentina, several of my relatives among them, formed the ICUF, Idisher Cultur Farband, a network of Jewish cultural institutions, leftist and non-Zionist, linked to the Communist Party. A group of idealistic youth formed in the ICUF, in its clubs and schools, joined Argentine guerrilla organizations in the 1970s, resisting the military dictatorship that took power in March 1976. As a member of one of these organizations, a leftist Peronist, I had to go into hiding. My friends and peers were falling like flies, kidnapped by paramilitary commandos and never seen again. We heard tales of unspeakable torture. I left my home, my university, and my job. I was eventually illegally arrested on the street, at age nineteen, by one of the task forces, a hidden arm of state repression.

I immediately understood that these men, who had placed a hood over my head so I couldn't see their faces, held anti-Semitic values rooted in conservative Catholicism. In a clandestine detention center run out of an old house in Buenos Aires, I was interrogated by Air Force Intelligence and tortured with electric shock, asphyxiation, Russian roulette, and beatings, and kept in a tiny cell with a swastika carved into the wall above my cot. I was held there for over ten months. One young soldier brought me the New Testament and tried to convert me to Catholicism. A leader of the torture squadron asked me what period of history I would've liked to have lived in, and I said France, in the Second World War, to fight against the Nazis. "We'd have been on opposite sides no matter the period," was his response. On national holidays, I heard my repressors swear oaths of loyalty to God and the Nation. In Jesus's name, these state-sponsored terrorist commandos murdered, raped, and robbed, dressed in civilian clothing and under the cloak of night.

At the detention center, in addition to the military men, there were officers of the Federal Police, the same force that sent Iosi Pérez, the spy protagonist of this story, undercover in the Jewish community, which they deemed to be a threat.

Horacio Lutzky's great-grandparents emigrated to Argentina at the end of the nineteenth century and beginning of the twentieth, from Kishinev and other small *shtetls* or villages populated by Jews in the Russian Empire, escaping starvation and pogroms. His maternal line settled in the province of Mendoza, his father's side in an agricultural colony near Carlos Casares, in the province of Buenos Aires. This was one of the settlements founded by the Jewish Colonization Association, the philanthropic entity created by Baron Hirsch to aid the resettlement of thousands of Jewish families fleeing persecution. Horacio was born in Buenos Aires and raised in a small apartment where his bubbe, Magdalena, a school principal, talked to him about Émile Zola and that Jewish French officer, Capitaine Dreyfus, accused of treason, about whom *The Dreyfus Affair* was written. Horacio studied law like his father. At university, some of his professors were openly anti-Semitic. One of them, Walter Beveraggi Allende, talked about the Andinia Plan, a supposed Jewish conspiracy to take over Argentine and Chilean Patagonia, accepted as an undisputed fact in the institutions that formed the nation's security forces. On a steep staircase inside the university, the young Jewish student passed the neo-Nazi professor flanked by two boys who looked like a walking advertisement for the Third Reich. Horacio considered pushing the man to his death, an act of reparation for so many Jews exterminated during the Holocaust, even if its occurrence was denied by Nazi propaganda.

In the book *Prisoner Without a Name, Cell Without a Number* by journalist and businessman Jacobo Timerman, the author states that the Argentine security forces, during the military dictatorship, aimed to wipe out the Jews. While interrogating the enemy was a chore, torturing the Jews was a pleasure, a moment of entertainment for the soldiers, their loathing of the Jews expressed in a visceral scream, a guttural growl, their entire being given over to hate.

During the dictatorship, however, the Delegación de Asociaciones Israelitas Argentinas, or DAIA for short, which served as the political leadership of the Jewish community, was cautious to a point that bordered on complicity. They never stepped in to defend Timerman or other Jewish business owners who were kidnapped so that the government could appropriate their assets. DAIA did not speak out in support of the Jewish soldiers harassed by their superiors during the Malvinas War in 1982, or when faced with the evidence that a high percentage of the forcibly disappeared persons were Jewish; their families' demands were ignored. Jewish leadership tried not to anger the military government, minimizing the gravity of the situation before international entities. The Jewish Movement for Human Rights, the *New Presence* newspaper, and Rabbi Marshall Meyer were the lone voices of dissent within the community.

Horacio was furious at every new instance of DAIA's inaction, especially since, decades prior, the DAIA had boldly taken on neo-Nazi groups in Argentina. Alejandro Lutzky, Horacio's uncle, was the secretary general for DAIA in 1962 when they called for the resignation of Federal Police Captain Horacio Green who defended the Tacuara organization and the Nationalist Restoration Guard, two groups that carried out constant and violent attacks on Jewish religious, cultural, and educational centers. When a young university student, Graciela Sirota, was attacked and a swastika carved into her chest, the head of the police denied the veracity of the claims and blamed the Jewish institutions and the "Communists" for having provoked a disturbance to the public order. DAIA, at the time, called for a total cessation of activities among the Jewish collective in protest of the anti-Semitic attacks and the complicity of the Federal Police. Hundreds of businesses and institutions displayed signs reading "Closed in protest of Nazi aggression in Argentina." The general mobilization led to Captain Green's resignation.

After the fall of the military dictatorship, in 1983, Raúl Alfonsín, the newly elected center-left president, appointed Jewish politicians to his cabinet. This action generated renewed anti-Jewish campaigns from ultranationalist sectors. It was in this period that Horacio began to feverishly gather information and collect magazines, flyers, pamphlets, and all variety of documentation on neo-Nazi activity in Argentina. He aimed to add that perspective to the defense of human rights that was beginning to emerge in our fragile democracy. Horacio Lutzky founded a Jewish community TV station and became head editor of *New Zion*, a newspaper read by activists, politicians, and intellectuals who admired the publication's socialist spirit, its criticism of Israel's right-wing government, and its defense of human rights. The newsroom, under Horacio, was a utopic, anarchic space that harbored the marginalized, iconoclastic, and nonconformist. In that environment, no one was suspicious of a guy who would sometimes stop by to visit his girlfriend (Horacio's young assistant), an ever-present figure committed to the security of the building where the newspaper offices where housed. This was Iosi.

It's often said that Peronism, the massive political movement born in the mid 1940s that has governed Argentina on several occasions, has sometimes harbored certain Nazi sympathies. But this is a very controversial statement. There is plentiful historical evidence that disproves this affirmation, but other facts could be seen to support it.

The fact that I, as a leftist Jewish woman, have been a Peronist activist, could seem contradictory given that General

Juan Domingo Perón himself allowed high-ranking Nazi commanders to take refuge in Argentina, but it is not. Peronism is a broad movement that encompasses many different, sometimes opposing, branches of political ideology. Members of the Tacuara Nationalist Movement, right-wing Catholics accused of anti-Semitic attacks, for example, joined Peronism; but so did leftist militant Marxists.

And there is evidence that it was not only Argentina that harbored Nazi refugees, many of them war criminals. The United States, among other allied nations, opened their doors to hundreds of German scientists who had cooperated with Hitler's regime and did not feel safe in post-war Europe. The new enemy was the Soviet Union, so past disagreements could be set aside to add anti-communist Nazi brains to the equation.

Some notable Nazis reached the port of Buenos Aires and lived out the better part of their existence in Argentina: Adolf Eichmann and Josef Mengele, for starters. Both lived at the same time in Vicente López, a zone of comfortable mansions outside the city where numerous Germans settled. Eichmann, after moving to a house in another area, was captured by Israeli intelligence, without the Argentine government's knowledge, and transported to Israel, where he was tried and condemned to death. Mengele owned a carpentry workshop, where he sold agricultural machinery that his family fabricated. He was once incarcerated for a matter of hours for performing illegal abortions (he partnered in a laboratory dedicated to specialized medicine), and he eventually fled to Paraguay and then Brazil. It has to be admitted that many Nazi higher-ups and other war criminals received refuge in Argentina: Erich Priebke, Josef Schwammberger, Eduard Roschmann, Friedrich Rauch, Milan Stojadinović, Erich Schroeder, Fridolin Guth, Gerhard Bohne (head of Hitler's euthanasia program), Pierre Daye, Jacques de Mahieu, Wilfred von Oven (private secretary for the Nazi minister of propaganda Joseph Goebbels) and Walter Kutschmann (who died in a Buenos Aires hospital as the paperwork for his extradition to Germany was being processed). Kutschmann's wife went on to found, in the suburbs of Buenos Aires, a sinister program that promoted the use of gas chambers to kill dogs which was exposed by Horacio at *New Zion* and on the Jewish community TV network.

In 1998, the same year that my uncle first told me, crying, that several members of our family who had stayed behind in Białystok had been murdered, I traveled to the beach town of Santa Teresita to interview Nada Sakić, wife of Dinko Sakić. Dinko was a Ustasha, a Croatian Nazi in Hitler's service, the last boss of the atrocious Jasenovac concentration camp who had been identified by the team of the program I worked for, *Telenoche Investigates*.

In a mansion on Ninth Street, a bony little woman with an entirely inoffensive appearance opened the door and peered out at me. She looked so innocent, but she had led the female prisoners to their execution site when the camp was closed, according to a witness. The Ustasha top brass had all fled to Argentina, starting with the Croatian genocidal dictator Ante Pavelić, the former Croatian ambassador under Hitler, Branko Benzon, and commander Ivo Rojnika, along with Dinko Sakić and his wife. Sakić, in the 90s, had participated in clandestine arms trafficking to Croatia for the Balkans War, orchestrated by the government of President Carlos Menem. Dinko and Esperanza, the name his wife adopted in Argentina, were both extradited to Croatia. He was charged and died in prison; she was allowed to walk free after three months.

Horacio and I both publicly condemned anti-Semitism.

Horacio, from the team at *New Zion* and also as a lawyer committed to obtaining justice for the victims of the two attacks on Jewish entities in Argentina. This is why Iosi, the secret agent tormented by regret, chose us to accompany him on his long road to revealing the truth, a journey that still remains incomplete.

One night in January 2015, the body of the DA leading the investigation into the AMIA bombing was found in a pool of blood inside a luxurious apartment in Buenos Aires. The mysterious death of Alberto Nisman, to whom Iosi presented his testimony in July 2014 before entering witness protection, is just one of the milestones on this dramatic odyssey. Iosi has been forced to disappear, to live in hiding from the enemies who would try to silence him. Horacio and I have been attacked, unjustly accused, and have seen attempts to silence us as well. The truth can be annoying, especially when some victims supposedly out for truth and justice become involved in the cover-up, whether consciously, in exchange for political or economic gain, or unknowingly, through naivety or submissiveness.

Iosi's entrance into our lives was destabilizing. For Horacio, it meant the emergence of new fears. For me, the resurrection of terrors I'd long since buried. On one hand, it showed that we Jews were vulnerable and persecuted: it proved that we lived in a country where the security forces were watching us. Obsessed with Iosi's secret, which we couldn't share with anyone except each other, we lived with the disquieting fear that anyone who passed us on the street could be an intelligence agent. We also felt that Iosi's safety—his life—was in our hands. This led Horacio and I to develop a blind trust in each other, something that still persists. We have identical ethics and values, even in dangerous situations. Together, we have gone up against forces of power, seen the indifference or ill-will of people we've approached in search of help for Iosi to safely testify. We have confirmed that the Jewish community leadership was committed to protecting those responsible for the bombings. Government officials have now been tried and charged with cover-up and the intentional mishandling of the investigation, but that serves as little consolation.

Iosi became tangled in a web spun by Argentine government officials, with support from the US and Israeli embassies, that aimed to blame Iran as uniquely responsible for the terrorist attacks, without investigating the local connection. Anyone who aims to challenge that version of events is unwelcome. And so Iosi's story remains largely ignored, as the pact of impunity and silence continues to prove much stronger than any desire to expose the truth of a tormented spy and the two Jewish journalists who believed him and decided to help him.

ME, THE SPY

They call me Iosi. Short for Iosef, the Hebrew version of José. A large part of my days I was Jewish and participated in political and cultural activities within the Jewish community of Argentina. But that is not my true identity. No: I am an agent of the Federal Police Intelligence Service.

In reality, I was both things at the same time: from 1985, my job as a federal officer consisted of infiltrating different groups within the Jewish community to obtain information and report back on their activities. The main objective of my covert operation was to uncover a Jewish plot to occupy a swathe of land in the Patagonia and create a new Jewish state, as laid out in the so-called "Andinia Plan." As well as any other machinations brewing inside these mysterious, impregnable circles. This was the mission my bosses had tasked me with.

I did my job better than anyone. I mastered Hebrew and gained solid knowledge of Jewish religion, culture, history, and traditions. For almost fifteen years, patiently, skillfully, I infiltrated various Zionist organizations; I organized activities. There was not a single Jewish institution that I was not able to access—sometimes armed—without being questioned, even after the bombings of the Israeli embassy and the AMIA. I waved to acquaintances as I walked the halls of the embassy, the same halls walked by the mythic Mossad agents. I was able to do all of these things because I was, and am, Iosi.

It was a job without regular hours or days off. As they say in "the collective," it's not easy being Jewish. But we'll get to that later. For the first few years, I fulfilled my duties without any personal conflicts or spiritual afflictions, and I rose so quickly that my mentors couldn't believe it. I remember their expressions of satisfaction when I was invited to join the team of directors of an important organization within the Jewish community. I gained access to every space I aimed to infiltrate, and I grew to fully understand the collective, its desires and fears, its good side and its bad side, its struggles and sufferings, and its infinite internal debates. I led student organizations, and at some point—I'm not sure when it happened—I began to feel fully at home in that community, where my entire life took place. I hadn't uncovered any dark conspiracies, nothing of what was warned by the anti-Semitic texts that my reporting officers referenced. There were some negative elements, as in any group of humans, but no turbid plot against Argentina.

I blended in so well, integrated so fully into the collective, that I fell hopelessly in love with a Jewish girl. An immeasurable, forbidden, secret love that I threw myself into body and soul. I couldn't stop it from happening: she was the love of my life. I'd never felt a love like that and I know I never will again. We married in secret and even attempted my conversion and an escape to Israel.

When the bomb hit the Israeli embassy, shortly before I was about to leave for a meeting there, I began to wonder if the information I reported in secret to my superiors might have been used to carry out the attack. After a second bombing, at the AMIA, I no longer had any doubt. They'd asked me for details about the building; I'd drawn my bosses a floorplan, reported on movements, names, responsibilities, and schedules.

In order to ease my conscience, I joined the community defense league trained to provide security for Jewish organizations, clubs, schools, and synagogues. I stopped giving my bosses accurate details on things such as last names and training locations for the security teams. They began to grow suspicious of me and ultimately relieved me of my duties. I was transferred to another province, assigned to bureaucratic tasks, separated from my wife. It destroyed our relationship. On visits back to the Jewish community in Buenos Aires, I was treated with admiration and respect. I had convinced everyone that I'd been called away on some secret mission to help the community so that they wouldn't ask questions about my long periods of absence.

I began to fear that my bosses might want to have me killed. I recorded a video, stating that if I was found dead they should look to the feds. I saved evidence of my work, documents, credentials, reports. I sought out two people who I felt I could trust: a Jewish lawyer who was the editor of a Jewish newspaper, and a Jewish journalist. I contacted them timidly, afraid they might shun me or even turn me in for being an accomplice to the two bombings. But they both wanted to help me. They tried for years, through all means possible, to find a way for me to testify outside the country, where I'd be safe. The Argentine justice system's complete unwillingness to uncover the truth about the bombings had led us to the conclusion that testifying in the local courthouses would be futile. In their long and Kafkaesque searches for support, they ran up against indifference and complicit silence. Sometimes, after some initial eagerness to help, contacts would simply fade away. They knocked on every door they could think of, from the Simon Wiesenthal Center to the Inter-American Commission on Human Rights in Washington, DC, to the office of then First Lady Cristina Fernández de Kirchner, and the influential American Jewish Committee. I have to admit, I sometimes doubted myself along the way, afraid of losing what little I had left. I'd already lost my wife, now I could lose my son and my aging father as well.

For over ten years, I faithfully fulfilled the duties I was ordered to carry out, to serve my country, so they said, to protect our newly restored democracy. I completed every task asked of me, efficiently, completely, sacrificing my family life and all personal plans; until I realized that the information I provided was being used to harm the people I was spying on—people I had grown to love, who I wanted to protect and defend.

The faces of Riqui, Carlitos, Silvia, and other people killed in the AMIA bombing flash through my mind. The people whose lives were destroyed with the help of an intelligence report which I, Iosi, unknowingly turned in. But there's more—much more. So I have decided to tell my story, from the heart and without holding back, as if I were talking to a close friend. So that everyone will understand how I was able to transform into Iosi, the intelligence agent who infiltrated the Jewish community, and everything that happened after that.

PART I

I was always afraid that my worlds would one day collide. What happened was much worse: I have been exiled from both. I live now in witness protection, in hiding, concealing everything I know. The prosecutor who gave my order for protection, Alberto Nisman, was found dead in his home. I don't know what to do. My heart is in shreds. I can no longer sleep without pills and even then I'm plagued by nightmares of blood, mutilated bodies, wails of pain. My heart races wildly and a buzzing sound echoes through my head with increased intensity every night. The anxiety eats away at me. I can't take it anymore. I'm going to lose my mind here in this tiny, forgotten town, so far from my family, without a friend in sight, no one to talk to. I go out every morning to jog the back roads in hopes of calming my nerves, kill time in cafés and shops, but it's hopeless. As soon as darkness settles in, panic takes over.

I'm a ghost who cannot leave any trace of my existence. I'm a protected witness and no one can know where I am.

"Protected witness." It sounds important, but I feel like a miserable fugitive. I'm not supposed to have much contact with the locals, because I'd have to lie about my life and my identity. I could easily do so, but I don't want to live a lie any longer. I built a false existence before, with false friendships, false loves. I was under orders, but that false existence gradually took over and became very real. All of that has now been destroyed and I no longer know who I am.

There are many people who don't want me to tell my story, which involves espionage against the Jewish community and government involvement in the 1992 and 1994 massacres in Buenos Aires that left more than a hundred people dead. These souls weigh on my conscience. Because I formed part of the structure that made those massacres possible.

I'm here, in the middle of nowhere, looking out for myself like I've been trained to. But no amount of security is infallible, evidenced by the disappearance of Jorge Julio López, a witness for the prosecution in a trial against the police and the military. Mysterious deaths are not uncommon in Argentina, as proven once again by the death of Alberto Nisman, the prosecutor who ordered my placement in witness protection, even if he was never truly interested in what I had to say.

I am not a criminal, but I live like a fugitive, and in my dreams I am fleeing.

I feel, like never before, a sensation of extreme vulnerability. My life is worth nothing.

If something happens to me, my secrets will go with me to the grave.

It's too much solitude for one man to bear. Too much of a burden to continue carrying in silence. I want the truth to come to light. The whole truth. That's why, from this rathole where I'm forced to hide, I will take all the time I need to recount my life and leave this written record with people who will know how to put it to good use, when the time comes.

THE KID FROM FLORES

I was a regular kid like any other. I was born in 1960. I grew up in Flores, a quiet neighborhood of small houses in Buenos Aires, where we could play in the streets. I went to public school. I wasn't lacking for anything, but I was far from spoiled. My father worked on ships, as a sailor. My mother was a homemaker. I had a happy childhood, you could say.

The soda man came by to replace our empty siphons on a horse-drawn cart that he would let us climb onto when he finished his rounds. We rode our bikes to Parque Avellaneda or Parque Chacabuco. We played in the trenches the electric company dug to bury the power lines. We gathered branches to make bonfires on the corner to celebrate San Pedro and San Pablo. Summer vacations were spent at my grandparents' house in the country or in San Clemente, on the coast.

I didn't come from a family of police officers. I did have one uncle who was a noncommissioned officer, but he had nothing to do with my career choice. We didn't discuss politics. We respected the officer posted on the corner who lived on our block. We asked him for permission to play ball in the street and we left our bikes for him to look after.

I played sports from age seven. I swam some but mostly played baseball at the DAOM Club, near the cemetery. A neighbor who worked for the city had gotten me a membership. In 1972, the Summer Olympics were held in Munich and, like all the kids at that time, I followed the games on television. I was horrified when the members of Black September killed eleven Israeli athletes, shocked that the terrorists would do such a thing during this sacred sporting event. I couldn't understand how the world didn't come to a standstill, how the Olympics were not suspended, how they kept going on as if nothing was wrong. I felt angry and helpless.

I had Jewish friends growing up; it was never something that I differentiated. In my group of friends there were two guys from the collective. They went to the Weitzman School, on Varela Street. I lived five or six blocks from there and one of them played baseball with me, at the club.

When my mom went to withdraw my father's salary, which was deposited at the Banco Nación branch on the corner of Varela and Eva Perón—which at the time was called Avenida del Trabajo—or to pay an installment at the clothes shop that sold on credit, she would leave me sitting on the steps of the synagogue two blocks away, so that I wouldn't get into trouble. It was a safe, familiar place, where the people would pat my head as they went in to pray.

There was nothing unusual about my life. In 1976, I was attending the Belgrano Technical high school, on the corner of Cochabamba and Deán Funes. There were three main concentrations to choose from: the most popular were electronics and construction, but I chose to study optometry. As teenagers we would go to the movies, to the Rivera Indarte Theater or the Pueyrredón Theatre; and after the movies, which we would watch three of in a row (often a James Bond), we would go for slices of cheese pizza and fainá with Coca-Cola.

One of my friends lived on Avenida Escalada near the Ricchieri Highway. It was in a little neighborhood of police housing, but I wasn't sure exactly what his father did. One day when I was having lunch at his house, the phone rang, and his mother answered. She was silent for a minute or two, like she was paralyzed, then she suddenly fell to the floor. Someone had planted a bomb in the cafeteria of the Federal Security building where my friend's father worked. He was a commissioner and managed to survive by chance. The floor of his office had been stamped onto the roof, desk and all. It turned out he'd been away when it happened, but no one knew whether he was dead or alive until late that night. It was then that my friend began to explain the kind of work his father did. He told me that he was fighting "terrorism," referring to the guerrilla groups resisting the military government at that time. He didn't provide any further explanation; it wasn't necessary.

At school there was a lot of political activism. You probably won't believe it, but I felt most in synch with communism. Since I played baseball, the ideology reached me through the sport, because the most famous baseball players, after the Americans, were the Cubans. I went to the Cuban embassy and rang the buzzer so I could read *Granma*, but I was only interested in the sports pages. I even went to a few Communist Party meetings, always keeping a low profile. I never liked to stand out.

Time went by and I graduated technical school as a licensed optician. I had a girlfriend, she got pregnant, we got married and had a baby, but we separated a year later, even though at the time divorce wasn't yet legal. I earned just enough to cover my personal expenses and help support my child by working at a glasses wholesaler. I wasn't sure what I wanted to do with my life; I thought about opening an eyeglass store. Around that time I ran into my old high school friend who I had lost touch with. He was working in the Computation Department of the Federal Police. His father had gotten him the job.

I went to visit him, and he told me that his dad could get me into the Intelligence Department. This was 1983 or 1984. It sounded interesting, awakening a certain adventurous but also idealistic spirit in me. The man had been chief of the anti-terrorism division. He asked me if I knew what "intelligence" referred to. I said that I did, but that I only knew about it from movies. I told him that I went to see spy films, but I didn't like them for the same reasons as everyone else—I liked to see how the agents operated. The man smiled; he must've thought I was so naïve, but he didn't let it show. He explained that they worked to "counteract terrorism," and also to "safeguard domestic security."

"We're like the FBI," he told me.

All I knew at the time was that I wanted to fight terrorism. I didn't care which side the violence was coming from, the right or the left. I'd seen, for the past seven years, a war playing out on the streets of Argentina between the military, who I saw as trying to defend the Western Christian order, and others, who wanted to impose foreign ideas on us. But in reality I had grown up with that version of the story and that was only one side of it, the side of those in power. That was my reason for wanting to join the Intelligence Department of the Federal Police of Argentina.

HIDDEN WORLD

I began my incursion into a world that was invisible, reserved, hidden, directly at the Intelligence Academy, across from the Ramos Mejía Hospital, on Urquiza Street, above the police station. The course lasted five years.

The Federal Intelligence Service began in the times of Perón, initially headed by Coronel Jorge Manuel Osinde, who became famous after the Ezeiza Massacre in which a right-wing government faction, along with members of the armed forces, shot, tortured, and killed people who had gone to meet their leader, Juan Domingo Perón, at the airport. After that event, the Intelligence Service was created, with armed agents following the model of the Nazi SS Intelligence Services.

Osinde was a falconer; he kept a bird on his desk and when he met with his agents he told them: "You guys are going to be my falcons, you're going to go out hunting for me." They say he tortured and detained many people, and this was one of the reasons Perón was overthrown in 1955. During the time of the military dictatorship, known then as the National Reorganization Process, the Intelligence Service worked very closely with the military government. They had the power to determine whether the people they detained would live or die. Once democracy was restored, fierce internal disputes erupted; from there, the custom of calling us "feathers," insultingly, instead of "falcons."

The Intelligence Academy instilled in us a strong sense of belonging right from the start, with very strict rules. Agents weren't allowed to use their real identities; we had to go by false names even within the Academy. Mine, within the service, was always Jorge Polak. They advised us to distance ourselves from our friends. I couldn't tell my family anything about what I was doing. I had to reduce my social circle to as small a group as possible. I had to be almost a hermit. Those were the orders, as outlined by decree no. 2263 from the times of Onganía in 1967, and orders had to be followed.

The professors had fake names too. There was one we were all afraid of, who we called Barzola. He was fat, with blue eyes. We knew he was capable of anything because he had been a heavy hitter in the time of the military dictatorship. He'd cycled through several positions. He went overboard in interrogations. He also went by the name Barreiro. When he left the force, he went to work for the Techint Group. In security, I heard.

Only one of the teachers was critical of the Service. He told us that in the future we would be the ones, through our reports, who would determine what processes would be carried out, and he inferred that in past times it was these reports that determined who lived and who died. He had us watch a movie, *Brazil*, directed by Terry Gilliam, where a fly trapped inside a typewriter changes a single letter and that alters a person's entire fate.

Other teachers told stories about mistakes that had dramatic consequences. Mixing up names, addresses, human error. To the point that, on one occasion, they went to a house on the wrong side of the street and ended up at the home of a military official. When the guy saw a group of armed civilians closing in, he assumed they were guerillas and started shooting. The front of his house was left looking like a colander and meanwhile the true target got away. They must've made a thousand mistakes, arresting people based on some misunderstanding. But no one showed any remorse. No one cared.

At the Academy we studied civil and penal law, political history, the history of terrorist organizations, psychology. It was ironic that we learned the laws and then they taught us how to commit crimes, for example what they called "surreptitious incursion into a domicile," which meant obtaining access to someplace, getting what you needed, and leaving everything exactly as you found it so that no one would ever know you'd been there. And, at the same time they taught us what the punishment would be if one of us was found on private property. You learned the rules and how to break them.

The textbooks were the same ones that had been used during the dictatorship. We weren't allowed to leave the Academy with them. Everything was secretive. One of the professors had said that if any of us had a particular skill or specialized knowledge we should work to hone it because it could prove useful. For example, if someone was a good tennis player they could travel the world in that role, under that cover, from tournament to tournament, and in reality be a spy, an intelligence agent. They could traffic information without arousing suspicion.

I was familiar with the Jewish settlements of the Entre Ríos Province because my family was from that area. Basavilbaso, Villa Clara, Domínguez, Sajaroff. That part of the province was full of Jewish settlements, and I knew about the different waves of immigration, could list off many of the last names. I knew, for example, that the settlers of the Avigdor Colony were German Jews, survivors of the war, and that they were the last community to settle in the region.

So I prepared a presentation on Zionism in which I talked about how the decision to create the State of Israel had originated in Europe. I don't know if this was for the class called Antidemocratic Activities or a different subject. My report was so thorough that two of my classmates, who were sons of military officers, started to tease me, insinuating that I knew too much. That maybe I was Jewish, a double agent. It was ridiculous, because before accepting me they'd investigated everyone down to my grandparents. The truth was, I think, that they'd expected me to base my report on the conspiracy theories surrounding the Jewish collective, their supposed desire to take over the world, and the accumulation of power and influence. That halo of mystery, that secret plot which, later on, when I went to live my daily life within the community, I proved to be a fraud, nonexistent.

When I received my grade for that report, which was very good, my classmates asked me: "Are you from the Mossad or Shin Bet?"

"Well, I don't know, you tell me," I answered.

Who knows what kind of stories they'd made up in their heads about me. I think that report must've been for Antidemocratic Activities, because they thought that Zionism was dangerous, a true threat to the nation. And the story I have to tell has a lot to do with that.

ELITE TRAINING

You don't get to choose your destiny. I'm not talking about destiny in general, I'm not trying to be philosophical, I'm referring here to your place within the agency. I suppose it's clear. When you read my story, you'll understand.

When they send someone undercover, they select you based on your abilities. They mark you; they watch you in action. And they also take into consideration your needs, your history. In the Academy, an experienced agent would approach you, and in general, it was someone who had been working there since the dictatorship, which they referred to as "the other times." Almost all of them had a dark past.

When you were selected to go into the field, they told the rest of the class, your cohort, that you'd dropped out. The excuse could be anything. That you had fallen in love with a girl and gone to live abroad, that you had family problems, that you were sick, for example. That's when you started to lie like you were going to have to lie for the rest of your life. The first step was fooling your classmates. You had to disappear, never to be seen again. You began to live in total secret. Your file was retired and locked away in some unknown location, a strongbox, so that no one could access it.

The next step was a rigorous training, super specialized. An elite training. This took place at the Special Forces Training Center. There were two instructors, one of them, a man by the last name Dib, was totally anti-Semitic. Anti-Jew to the core. During the dictatorship, the Special Forces Training Center had been called the Center for Anti-terrorist Training, but when democracy was restored they changed the name to make it seem like it was different. But the culture was the same because the structure and ideology stayed exactly the same. Now it's called the Federal Special Operations Group, but the new name is no guarantee that the instructors have changed. They may try to camouflage themselves, but they're still the same in the end.

There were two buildings near Puente de la Noria where they trained us. We had dorms there, a little auditorium. It was a small group, around ten to fifteen of us. There were no women, not because there were no girls in intelligence, but because after a certain point they trained them somewhere else. The course lasted twenty days and it was pass/fail. You had to pass no matter what.

At the Training Center we received instruction on clandestine activities: tailing, losing a tail, sabotage, infiltration, explosives. They taught us to be disciplined, methodical, patient. They took away our watches, and they sent us out at all hours to do physical strength training. They'd asked us to bring fatigues, but since I didn't have any I wore my coveralls from technical school.

They took us to Campo de Mayo to experiment with explosives. We learned to use detonators, wires, we made bombs. If I wanted to explain it now, I wouldn't be able to, because I don't remember anymore, but I must have my notes from those lessons hidden away somewhere. If I had them, I'd still be able to build something efficient, impeccable.

We also practiced following people. If someone caught us doing something strange and we were detained, we had to let ourselves be taken in to the station, then from there ask them to communicate with our bosses. We didn't even carry ID. We didn't know whether the targets we followed were one of our guys, someone from a different area of the agency, or a true target, some activist, student, or union leader.

We also simulated interrogations with supposed terrorists utilizing techniques created by the Americans. One afternoon they made us watch a video about it. The girls were still with us at that point, before they split us up. The women and a few of the guys couldn't stand to watch; they got up and left. It depicted the familiar forms of torture along with everything else the human mind is capable of imagining. Standing up and leaving meant quitting, admitting that you weren't cut out for the job, that you were soft.

For the first practical exercise they took us to the auditorium. There were seats facing a stage. In the back was a two-way mirror where the instructors could observe us, like a Gesell dome. They sat us down and they brought in a guy, handcuffed with his head covered, and a suitcase. They told us that he was a terrorist and that, supposedly, the suitcase contained information about a bombing. We had to extract information from the detainee. We had to open the suitcase and then interrogate him. But the suitcase was booby trapped so when you opened it there was a small explosion. We looked at the papers, which had been singed a little, and we confirmed that he was planning to carry out a terrorist attack. We had only half an hour to stop it. The supposed bombing was going to take place at a nursery school, no less. And it wasn't a coincidence that all of us were fathers with young kids, even babies, nursery school age. They were evaluating us. We were exhausted from training, under a lot of psychological pressure. There was a huge clock on the wall. No one said anything, but we knew they were evaluating us as a group, so we had to work together.

When there were fifteen minutes left and the guy still wouldn't talk, we started to bring out the techniques they'd shown us in the video. They'd left some tools for us on the table, a hammer, for example. I don't want to say any more about it . . . We didn't know if the guy was an actor or what. I don't think he was. If we'd broken a finger, a knee, or even cut off a toe, no one would've reported us. I was twenty-five years old, and the others were younger, except one guy, Luis Falco, who much later was discovered to be the one responsible for kidnapping human rights activist Juan Cabandié and he ended up going to prison for it. He was older, from another class. The instructors all came, like I said, from "the other times," even the police chaplain who tried to convince us that we were going to war with the devil, fighting evil. The instructors were watching to see who would take the initiative in that situation. In the end the supposed terrorist confessed, and we all rushed off to stop the "bombing." And yes, we pressured him. If we hadn't had any tools on hand we would've pulled some cable out of the wall, found some way to make him talk.

Do these kinds of exercises take place in all of the intelligence services? Yes, we were not the exception. They pushed us to the limit, always right to the edge. There was tremendous psychological pressure, unbearable, constant. There was an ambulance parked outside when we did certain exercises. For example, we had to jump off of a building from a height of fifteen yards using a repelling rope, while carrying FAL rifles. "The other day they had to take a guy to the ER at Churruca," they said, like it was nothing. One of the guys was too scared to jump. If something happened, if someone wasn't brave enough, if they hesitated, there would be a bus waiting to take them away, and we would never see them again.

Everything was designed to destabilize you. They ordered you to put on a suit and took you to a vacant lot to do resistance training, to run five kilometers or crawl across the ground. Or they told you to put on gym clothes and took you to lose a tail in the business district. You never knew what was going to happen; nothing was predictable. They were measuring your ability to adapt and react.

I suppose that the people who saw us running around Puente de la Noria, escorted by officers, must've thought it was strange. Everyone all dressed different; a mishmash, because the clothes were whatever we could each scrounge up. Behind the campus, there was a shantytown. One time, during nighttime shooting practice, we were using blanks and some of the neighbors from the slum took off running because they thought we were shooting at them. We practiced with live ammunition too, but at Campo de Mayo.

At the end of twenty days we finished the course, exhausted but happy.

The last test was to make a full lap around the racetrack. I don't know how many kilometers it was, but it wasn't too much for us at that point. By the end of training we could run between five and ten kilometers per day. We were pure muscle.

When the test was completed they took us all to the auditorium, where there was a rosary on each seat and a blue beret with the Special Forces Training Center logo on it. It's a fist with a phrase in Latin: *vincere malum in bonum* that means "do good by combatting evil." They took some liberties with the translation of the verb *vincere* as "combat," but that didn't matter. In reality, when I looked into it, the true Latin phrase—which comes from Saint Paul's *Epistole to the Romans*—is *vince malum bono*, meaning: "overcome bad with good," which is a very different idea.

The room was dark. When we sat down the stage suddenly lit up. The chaplain came out and blessed us, it was very emotional. That guy had taught one of the classes, I don't remember if it was Professional Ethics or Religion, but I do remember that he'd constantly encouraged us.

The lights went out again and they began to project videos of our families: "I love you," "I miss you so much," "You're my hero," things like that from our wives and kids. They didn't film my family, they'd only selected a few, but they'd achieved their objective. We graduated ready to eat the world.

The priest had personal advice for me: "You don't need to be so self-critical. Because if you are, you're going to have problems in the future in your career," he told me. It was unusual, I always remembered that. Because he only spoke to me, he didn't say anything special to the others.

On more than one occasion, during the lessons, the professors had said to me: "You're not Pérez with an "S" are you? You're not Jewish?" They said it to mess with me. "You're not going to make it to the end of the course," they told me, because they thought it impossible that I knew so much about the Jewish community without being Jewish.

Behind my back they were suspicious of me and talked about how I'd done a report in the Academy about the World Zionist Organization. They were all pro-Nazi. It wouldn't be the first or the last time I received such accusations. But I didn't care. I wanted to fight terrorism. I was determined to make it to the end of the course. Supposedly anyone who passed was going to have a perfect service record, because the tests were so hard, psychologically and physically, that not just anyone could pass. And I passed.

FILTERS

Within intelligence, there were three categories: A, the operatives; B, analysts; and C, the doctors, lawyers, and accountants, in the department referred to as infrastructure. Within the A category, the filters, the infiltrators, were the elite. Not just anyone could be a filter. One requirement was not having relatives within the agency, no one could have the power to identify you. It was a matter of security, survival. You also couldn't be seen entering any of the known police buildings, you can imagine why. It was a matter of life or death.

When I finished my training they sent me to the main offices of the Intelligence Department, at 1417 Moreno Street. There were other offices as well, such as the one above the Precinct 46 station. There was the Intelligence Academy, located on the top floor of the Precinct 8 station, and the Technical Department above Precinct 9. Although there were also "caves" everywhere, around the city, where you'd least expect them.

I wanted to be part of the A squadron, I felt that I met all the requirements. But, I have to emphasize, this wasn't something you could decide for yourself. You could put in a request but the bosses had a ranking based on merit.

Intelligence encompassed many areas, for example, Student Affairs, Cultural Affairs, Foreign Affairs. My first posting was in Labor Affairs, which was nothing at all like Human Resources. The department was divided between Company Affairs and Union Affairs. On the Company side, we would go to meetings of business associations and visit plants and factories, identifying ourselves as Federal agents, but with assumed names, and we would ask the owners and managers for information on union problems that they might have, internal employee organizations, or political activism among the staff.

The other area, Union Affairs, had two branches. Some of us went to meet with the union leaders, who would provide information on activists and delegates. And then there were the intelligence assets who had infiltrated the unions, posing as regular workers and attending union assemblies, delegations, and meetings.

I had been assigned to Union Affairs, and I had three or four unions that I visited. There was the Construction Workers Union, the Tilers Union, the Musicians Union, and I don't remember the other one. I used a false identity, and I would introduce myself, saying: "I'm an assistant to Commissioner So-And-So at the office on Moreno and San José."

At first I thought, naively, that they were going to ask to see my credentials. But as soon as I would show up at the union headquarters they would let me right in to see the secretary general, who received me with open arms. "Come in, kid, your boss was just here the other day," they'd say and pat me on the back. They were ready with the information, saying things like: "I have this delegate at such-and-such plant who's a leftist piece of shit."

I took note and passed it all on to my superior. I never entered intelligence headquarters, I met my boss at a café two or three blocks away. No one could ever see me entering the union offices and then the intelligence headquarters on Moreno.

I spent a few months in that position, then, after I took my first vacation days, they transferred me to Social Work, which was also located above the Precinct 46 station in Retiro but in the left wing of the building. It was a boring administrative position, but it could only be done by intelligence staff. It was mostly processing retirement and medical leave for active personnel. That office has now been moved to the 900 block of Caseros, in a nondescript glass building that also houses the doctors' offices for intelligence staff and their families. None of us can go to the Churruca Hospital, where the rest of the Federal Police Force receives medical treatment; intelligence has separate healthcare since no one should see that the agents or their family members are linked to the force.

I didn't stay at that position for very long. I must've been there two months and then they transferred me to another sector, also above the Precinct 46 station but on the right side.

"Wow, you must have some good connections if they're sending you to the other side," my coworkers said. But the reality was that I didn't know anyone, I didn't have any leverage or receive any special treatment. I supposed it was because my notes had proven useful or some aspect of my personality stood out. That office on the other side was another area of intelligence, what was called the Meeting Center. They posted me in the security booth, which controlled the cameras and spotlights. My job was to watch the monitor and make sure everyone signed in. Of course, not just anyone was allowed to go up. We had pistols, rifles, machine guns, everything. We worked in shifts and we didn't have any connection to the police officers at the precinct downstairs; it functioned like a fully separate building. There was a back stairwell that led to the morgue and holding cells. At that time they weren't in use but they had been during "the other times." It was scary to go down there, I can assure you. There was no natural light at all and only very dim artificial lighting. The iron doors had large bolts on them, like in some medieval castle. It was sinister.

LAURA, MY HANDLER

There, working in security, is where I met Laura, or Red, as they called her. I wasn't part of any team, but I knew that the officers coming and going were all operatives, heavy hitters. It was a goal of mine to become one of them, but I didn't know how long it might take before that happened, just that I had to do a good job, even if it was boring, and not make any mistakes. My task was to guarantee the building's safety, which was not nothing. One day, I had just finished my shift and was walking to catch the bus right as Red was coming out with her car.

"Where are you headed?" she asked.

"To Flores," I said.

"Get in, I'll take you," she answered.

Laura was pretty and elegant with red curls and green eyes. She was some ten years older than me. The car was filled with the smell of her perfume, but it never crossed my mind to try to seduce her. It was clear that was not an option. She was a superior.

"So you're interested in the issue of the Middle East?" she said, leading me. "You think you'd be brave enough to go undercover?"

"Where?" I asked.

"The Zionist groups."

I paused before answering. It was an opportunity I couldn't let pass me by. It meant that they'd noticed me, they'd chosen me, that they believed I was capable. I took a deep breath. "Well, I'd have to prepare for it. I'd have to start studying," I said.

Laura didn't waste any time. "Perfect," she replied, and she sped up. "We'll talk to the boss first thing tomorrow. We'll evaluate the options, and you can stop coming into the office."

Something that represented a dramatic change for me was an everyday thing for her. What would've happened if I'd said no? Where would I have ended up? Maybe somewhere else, infiltrating some political party, factory, or student center. Maybe, if I'd refused, they would've found some way to get rid of me, because the bosses suspected that I was really a Jew. It might have confirmed for them that I was a Mossad spy or something. But the truth is that what I'm telling you now wasn't what I thought in the moment. I was simply obeying an order, something I couldn't question. If they were sending me to spy on the Zionists there must be some good reason for it, I thought.

They never suggested that I was going undercover to look

out for the collective. They didn't think that they were vulnerable, not at all, the truth is that they thought just the opposite. They thought like the Nazis. They wanted to know what the Jews were doing, what they talked about, what their plans were. My bosses were fully convinced that there was a real danger, a threat to the Argentine republic. I still have, stashed away somewhere, a report they gave me with a timeline of the history of the Jewish people in Argentina, detailing all the anti-Semitic attacks that had occurred. I remember that it mentioned the attacks carried out by the far-right Tacuara organization, which bombed Jewish organizations in 1965. There was no condemnation of these crimes, just a list, point by point.

YOUNG ZIONIST

That night I couldn't sleep. Luckily I was alone. My parents had moved to the country, and I had the house to myself. There was so much to think about, so much to plan. I knew that the next day things were going to change for me, dramatically. This was what I'd trained for, but I had no idea how it was going to affect me.

I went into the bathroom and stared at the medicine cabinet mirror reflecting my image in three parts. How many ways could I divide myself, how many different personalities could I have? There was the boy from Flores who wanted to be a federal agent but whose career had been cut short due to personal problems, now working some routine office job, which is what I'd told my classmates when I was called into the field as the instructions for my cover indicated. Then there was the intelligence officer who had passed his elite training, determined to go as far as possible. Then there was the complex identity I had to create from this moment forward, that of a young Zionist Jewish man, charismatic and born to lead, trustworthy and brave.

I turned on the light and studied every inch of my face. My skin was dark, like so many Sephardic Jews or "Turks" as they were often called in Argentina. I had brown eyes and dark wavy hair, almost black. Could I pass as an authentic Jew? I looked at my nose in profile, my mouth, my full lips. Anyone would believe I was a true Sabra, as they called those born in Israel. I could easily pass a superficial examination. My name wasn't Jewish but instead of changing it and trying to procure false papers, I could say I was the son of a mixed couple. That my mother, daughter of immigrants to the Jewish settlements in Entre Ríos, had married a pure blooded criollo, a Pérez.

My face and my name were the façade. I had to convince everyone that it was real, but I also had to convince myself. There couldn't be a single crack in my story, it had to be impeccable. The first line of defense against suspicion would be my knowledge of the history, religion, and language. I was going to have to study until my head hurt, to immerse myself in the traditions, celebrations, the food, to not simply be one of them, but the best, the most Jewish of the Jews.

I was going to work for the greater good, to follow my calling. I'd never seen the Jews as a threat. But what if we truly had to save the world from Zionist domination as laid out in *The Protocols of the Elders of Zion*? That text read:

> Our government, following the line of the peaceful conquests, has the right to substitute for the horrors

of war less noticeable and more efficient executions, these being necessary to keep up terror, which induces blind submission. A just but inexorable strictness is the greatest factor of government power. We must follow a program of violence and hypocrisy, not only for the sake of profit but also as a duty and for the sake of victory.

A doctrine based on calculation is as potent as the means employed by it. That is why not only by these very means, but by the severity of our doctrines, we shall triumph and shall enslave all governments under our super-government.

Supposing that Nazi propaganda was true, that the Jews were scheming to submit gentiles to their will, it didn't feel wrong for me fool them in order to foil their plans to take over the country. I wasn't a hypocrite, I was a soldier for justice. That's what I'd been taught anyway. *The Protocols of the Elders of Zion* served as the philosophical and political framework for the Andinia Plan; that couldn't be argued. As much as they might deny it, the Jews wanted to establish a second Jewish State in the world, in the Americas, in the Patagonian region of Chile and Argentina. The plan was clearly laid out for anyone who wanted to read it, and it could be used to interpret step by step what was happening in Argentina: waves of immigration, accumulation of enormous capital, Jewish activism in leftist political parties and organizations, the repression, discrediting, and weakening of our armed forces, the corruption of politicians, social chaos. It all seemed undeniably true. There were pieces of the historical puzzle that seemed to be paving the way for Zionist supremacy, or at least that's what they were trying to convince me. Herzl, Marx, Trotsky, Einstein, Grinspun—President Alfonsín's minister of economy—a long list of influential, powerful, and diabolical Jews haunted my superiors. This was what I had learned, what I'd been taught in the Academy.

The next day Laura took me to meet with our boss, the Commissioner. There must've been some informant in the Federal Police Department because intelligence officers weren't allowed to show our faces at the station downstairs, we couldn't set foot in there. Everyone who worked for the Federal Police reported to the Commissioner, who had the Commissioner Inspector above him, then the Commissioner Major. That was the chain of command.

There was a certain tension between the regular federal officers and intelligence, as I explained before, which was a holdover from the other times. During the dictatorship, intelligence had worked closely with the military, and, for that reason, intelligence had a lot more power than rest of the police force. The military brought intelligence operatives into their work groups. We had a very good relationship with Army Battalion 601, with the Air Force Intelligence Service, and with Marine Intelligence, excellent. There was even a chaplain who worked for the Marines and also for the Federal Police, who during the dictatorship was in charge of trying to convince people sequestered by the military government to give in, to tell the truth. When democracy was restored, and the Federal Police took control of security from the military, that's when the internal rivalries emerged.

The boss met with Laura and me, or rather first with her while I waited outside, and then they called me in. The guy stared me down and he said: "I was talking with Laura here, and she told me that you have what it takes to go undercover. I support it. I'll go on the hook for you. But if you make any missteps, I'll rip you to shreds."

They never said "we'll fire you," it was always "we'll rip you to shreds." Threats were common currency. Because "I'll rip you to shreds" meant literally that. It was not a metaphor.

The Commissioner told me that from that moment forward Laura was going to be my only contact and that I had to follow her orders. I would deal with her exclusively, he stressed. She was going to be my handler, my boss.

The only other person who knew that someone was going undercover in the Jewish community was the head boss, the Commissioner General, because they'd informed him. And supposedly the minister of the interior Antonio Tróccoli, too, because at that time the Federal Police Force answered to that ministry. And I say "supposedly" because that was the protocol and we were under democracy, but everyone knew that in reality nothing went higher than the Commissioner General, it stopped with him.

When Enrique "Coti" Nosiglia took over as Commissioner General years later, some agents shook their heads and said: "To think that I tailed this guy." Because he was a member of the Radical Party and they were considered leftists, a threat. We even had people undercover in that party, which they called the "Radical Synagogue," a term that had been created in reference to prominent Jewish members such as Bernardo Grinspun and Mario Brodersohn, minister of economy and secretary of the treasury, respectively, and also César Jaroslavsky, Enrique Mathov, and Jorge Matzkin—even though he was a part of a different party, a Peronist. They said they were all Zionists.

So, you can imagine, everything stayed there. They didn't notify the government about anything. The boss gave me his telephone number so that I could call him for anything I needed. Then, Laura and I went to a café where she gave me a series of instructions. She was used to handling assets; she was tough as nails. She was one of the first women to ever go undercover herself. She was a spy, and she handled other filters, up to as many as twenty agents at a time, me among them. In "the other times," during the dictatorship, she was pregnant and working undercover as a journalist for a very important human rights organization. She could handle anything, no matter the pressure. You'd never know by looking at her: super feminine, always wearing a skirt, high heels, pantyhose. But when she narrowed her eyes, it was terrifying. She was stone-cold, you got the impression that she could cut off your head without getting a hair out of place. I feared her, for sure. Feared and respected her. That was our relationship.

Once a month, or every two months, all the undercover agents who answered to her would meet at the restaurant La Isla, which was in Retiro, in the same building as the offices of the marines healthcare provider. In the afternoon between lunch and dinner service, there was hardly anyone around, so we could have coffee and each give a brief oral report. No one was allowed to write anything down, only Red took notes. There was one guy who said he was undercover in a branch of the Radical Party under orders from Commissioner General Coti, a Korean spy in the Chinese community who was studying the language. I told them I was undercover in a Zionist group, but I didn't give the name. The majority of us had infiltrated leftist organizations: political parties, student associations, unions. But there were a few who were undercover in right-wing organizations that distributed Nazi literature. There must've been interest in the movements of the far right because of the uprisings of the right-wing extremist Carapintadas group.

UNDERCOVER IN LA TABLADA

One of us was undercover in the far-left Todos por la Patria Movement. He'd shown us photos of Jorge Baños, the human rights lawyer from the Center for Legal and Social Studies, who was also a member of the movement. The group attempted a takeover of the La Tablada Army regiment in late January of 1989, supposedly to prevent a military coup. The group had gathered with the guerilla leader Gorriarán Merlo, and our guy didn't show up to the meeting that day. He was a young guy with a young son who had gotten sick, and he'd stayed home. That's why that day, the 23rd, Red was crazed, because he wasn't at the meeting at La Isla and she thought that he was inside the regiment, so she'd started to organize a squad to rescue him.

He hadn't given any warning of the attack because none of the members knew about the plan ahead of time. They'd found out that same day in the meeting with Gorriarán. And even if he could've sent warning, no one was going to stop it. That's the way things were. They would've told him to go in and then they'd try to get him out later, which would've been chaos, because our guys would've had to go in without identifying themselves, and the soldiers defending their base might accidentally shoot them. It would've been a bloodbath. But that's how things go in intelligence.

Eventually, I don't remember when exactly, the guy managed to send word that he wasn't present at the attempted takeover. Later I found out that they sanctioned him for it. We felt sorry for him, because if he had been there he'd have been killed. If he'd gone in with the guerrilleros, he would've had to shoot at the soldiers. How could he explain to them that he was undercover? Impossible.

Around then is when I heard of Alberto Nisman for the first time. He was a prosecutor in the Morón District Court where the La Tablada case was tried. Nisman investigated two of the four cases of guerrilleros who were captured in the attack and were later disappeared. He accepted the soldiers' version of events that claimed the men had been taken as prisoners and escaped, and he closed the case.

Sometimes these kinds of dilemmas occurred. You know that an attack is going to happen and you report it, but your superiors let it happen even if people are going to die, because acting on it would blow your cover and they'd lose their informant. It's a calculated loss, so you could be more useful inside in the future.

THE ARGENTINE ELI COHEN

I identify very closely with Eli Cohen, the Israeli spy born in Egypt who infiltrated the Syrian community of Buenos Aires in the sixties as a business owner, and from there moved on to Damascus, to the Baath party's inner circles of power, close to President Hafez al-Assad, who he'd met while working as military attaché at the Syrian embassy in Argentina. He obtained extremely valuable, strategic information that he transmitted by radio from his apartment, where he received visits from members of the regime, the minister of defense, the minister of information. He got too arrogant and they found him out. His boss in Israel had warned him not to risk himself, to be careful, and that they needed to establish some limits to ensure his safety. He'd discovered a Nazi, Franz Rademacher, who lived under an assumed identity in Damascus, a man who had been right up there with Adolf Eichmann. But his superiors told him that he wasn't there to find old Nazis, that he was on a much more urgent and important mission.

Israel was able to occupy the Golan Heights region thanks to information that Cohen provided, and he was condemned to death for it by the Syrians. They say he had been about to be named vice minister of defense for Syria. Who knows. Who knows how far I'd have been able to go if what happened hadn't happened. I always say that I'm Eli Cohen but the other way around. For his mission, Cohen, who had been born in Alexandria and spoke Arabic, but not with a Syrian accent, went as far as to study with a phonetics teacher. But first he studied the religion, in depth. He went to mosques in the Arabic neighborhood of Jerusalem, learned the prayers, read the Koran at length.

I started out by going to the Library of Congress. It was open twenty-four hours, but I went at seven or eight in the morning and asked for anything related to the religion and history of the Jewish people. I sat and took notes until my eyes stung. There was one book that explained everything: the holidays, the Hebrew calendar. There was a particular story that fascinated me, and I wanted to learn more. It was the siege of Masada, the desperate defense of a Jewish village in the hills against the Roman troops. That sacrifice, that display of heroism, really moved me. I felt like I had been there, as if I was the reincarnated soul of one of the men who had defended that fortress and had chosen to die over surrendering to the Romans. The truth is that I'd never been convinced that what they taught us about the Jewish community in the Academy was real. Maybe because I hadn't been raised that way, from childhood, with clear prejudices against people who were different. I had always had a visceral rejection of lies based in ignorance. I always say that the worst anti-Semite is the ignorant one. I never thought for a moment that the Holocaust was a lie, just the opposite, I was horrified by it. I considered Nazis to be the enemy. It was only natural that, because of the persecution the Jews have suffered for the entire history of humanity, they wanted to gather in clubs, temples, in order to maintain their traditions, customs, and identities; to continue the path of chosen people of the Old Testament, which meant those chosen to safeguard their culture, not to take over the world.

FIRST STEPS

To me, infiltrating was a professional challenge, a goal to achieve and nothing more than that. I didn't tell my bosses that I doubted what they were telling me, but I was not going to lie to confirm their hypotheses. My job was to transmit the information I obtained; they could interpret it however they wanted. At the time, the only thing that made me suspicious was that the Jewish collective had their own security apparatus. I didn't understand why they didn't just let the state protect them like the rest of us Argentines, especially since we were now living under democracy. Over time I changed my thinking on this.

Most people don't know the difference between ethnic identity and nationality, and that's why they consider the Jews to be foreigners, or they wrongly assume that Judaism is a race. I started going to Hebraica, the Argentine Hebrew Society, on Sarmiento Street. It was a totally open institution, very large and absolutely secular. It was easy to get in.

Until the attack on the Israeli embassy there were absolutely no security measures in place. They asked to see your ID at the entrance, but if you told them you'd forgotten it, they'd let you in anyway. Also, you could access the library via two entry points: through the club, or through the auditorium, where there was a stairway with a glass door. I would go there regularly to read the Jewish community newspapers: *Israeli World*, *New Zion*, and others.

This was 1986. I had already begun creating my new identity. People at the library started to recognize me, everyone said hello as I walked by. It was mostly old men who went to read the newspaper for free; I think I was the youngest one there. I supposed that the agency had sent someone to tail me, to keep tabs on what I was doing, but I moved with total freedom. To all the regular officers of the police force, a filter was a lazy bum who didn't really work. I had to prove to them that I wasn't like that, that I was no lazy bum. And that I was going to be the best.

I used my real last name, Pérez, when I went undercover. It wouldn't be a problem because anyone born to a Jewish mother is Jewish, no matter their father's religion. And my mother, supposedly, was Jewish. Although the more Orthodox branches didn't accept this. Someone might say: "Jaroslavsky is Jewish." And I would answer: "No, Fernández is more Jewish than Jaroslavsky because his mother is Jewish and Jaroslavsky's isn't." And I'd start to talk about the times of the Inquisition, about when the Jews had to change their last names to protect themselves. They called themselves Mendoza, Córdoba, they passed themselves off as Christians. Wherever I went, I had to explain myself, like my own personal hasbara. Why didn't they just give me a new ID with a last name like Goldman, or even Polak? Because we were living under democracy now and there were certain things that the agency didn't dare to do, such as falsify documents, for example.

At first, they wouldn't let me leave town, not even to see my parents, because they had to set up a team to travel with me in case my cover was blown. They couldn't just inform a branch of the Federal Police in say, Córdoba or Rosario that they had a mole that needed protection. If something happened with the people in the community there, if I made a misstep, how could they explain my presence? Who was I, why was I there, who'd sent me?

Going to the library, I never had to give any explanation, they never asked me any questions. I soon found out that a university group met at Hebraica on Fridays. And since my objective was to connect with a group of that type, I decided to start attending. At that time, the people in charge of security at Hebraica weren't part of the collective. You'd greet them two or three times and then they'd recognize you and let you right in, simply because your face looked familiar. I could move around the entire building, and I even drew floorplans: the layout, the access points. On Fridays you'd show up and let them know you were going to the moadon for the student organization, and they'd let right you in. They met in one of the basement rooms. There was another room down the hall, which at some point had served as a shooting range.

The kids in the university group asked me questions, because I was new. I told them that I was the son of a mixed marriage and that I wanted to meet girls my age because I had the intention, in the future, of starting a Jewish family. Everyone knew that this was the main purpose of university organizations, right? There were no security issues, I just had to make sure that there was no one from Entre Ríos among them because the Jewish community in that province is small and everyone knows each other. I'd have to always be careful about that, it was my weak spot. I told them that my mother's last name was Jacob. Later, I ended up changing it, but at that time that's what I said. A while later, when I joined the Zionist Organization of Argentina, my ID read José Pérez Jacob. Even, just a little while ago, that's the name that figured in their registry.

I started going every week, never missing a meeting. I told them I was studying to be an eye doctor in the College of Pharmacy and Biochemistry, because I was already an optical technician and I understood how it worked. Practically every night there was some political, cultural, or social event that we all went to. It was a group of around twenty or thirty guys and girls. When whatever activity ended, we usually went out for a drink, or sometimes I just went home. After a while a guy from Mapam, a branch of the Israeli Socialist Party, came to give a talk on the conflict in the Middle East and he mentioned some Zionist university groups. A lightbulb went off in my head, because that was my broader goal: to get into those groups. I was still getting the lay of the land, I didn't yet have a "who's who" of the Argentine Zionist movement. He mentioned Tzavta, a Jewish Community Center, which he told us was located at 250 Junín Street. I wrote it down, thrilled to have more leads. One day I got up the nerve to go. I went in and said that I wanted to subscribe to one of the two Spanish-language magazines that came from Israel for the Latin American audience, called *Rumbos* and *Aurora*. They were both brought over by *New Zion*, the more progressive Zionist newspaper. I continued receiving those magazines for a long time, although I don't remember what address I gave them. I lived at first in a boardinghouse in the Constitución area and then I moved to an apartment at Anchorena and Mansilla.

I started to look for work, because I had to be able to explain how I made a living, beyond the fact that I was a student. I landed an office job with Del Valle Cider company, as a low-level employee. They had a bottling plant in San Fernando, but the offices were at Castillo and Humboldt near the Juan B. Justo Bridge. All of us in intelligence, mainly the operatives, were authorized to have a second job, because that way we could justify how we supported ourselves, since obviously we couldn't tell the truth. I spent three or four months at the boardinghouse and when I got the job I moved into an apartment because it was more normal for a Jewish college student to live in an apartment building.

I was a soldier at the time. I didn't have a girlfriend; I was on my own. I had to call the office four times a day from a public phone. Someone would answer, whether it was my handler or the operator. Whoever answered had to register my call. In my case it was four calls per day, I don't know how many the others made. I had to find a place to meet with my handler that was open twenty-four hours a day, and I had to use all counterintelligence measures possible on my way to the meeting. I even started to limit visits to my son, who lived with his mother in Barrio Norte, to minimize the risk of someone seeing me.

Meanwhile, I continued going to the moadon at Hebraica. We were all between twenty and twenty-five years old, students or recent graduates. The group had no specific political orientation, most of us were there to find partners. There were often guest speakers at the meetings, where someone might come to talk about economy, for example, or issues related to history or current events. Some of the talks might have a specific political leaning, such as when the guy from Mapam came to give his speech and explained the Socialist Party's position on peace with the Palestinians.

THE FORTRESS

I'd read in a newspaper article that Sojnut, the Jewish Agency for Israel, was located in the same building as the Zionist Organization of Argentina, and I knew that I had to get in there somehow. I decided to try. The imposing, nine-story fortress was on Perón Street between Larrea and Azcúenaga. Right next door was the Natan Gesang Jewish School, which had hardly any security, just a guy who stood guard as the students came and went.

The security measures at the Sojnut headquarters, however, were as good as at any Israeli embassy. The Head of Security was a top-ranking, highly trained Israeli military officer, and his staff was trained either locally or in Israel. I rang the buzzer and walked through the bulletproof door into a closed antechamber. I placed my ID into a metal receptacle, and it was whisked away by a person I couldn't see behind a mirrored window. They asked me what I wanted. I said I was the son of a mixed couple, and I wanted to know how to get in touch with my roots. It was such a naïve excuse, it could've easily gone wrong.

Then someone with an Israeli accent spoke: "I'm going to ask you some questions. What year are we in, on the Jewish calendar?"

I answered.

"And what's the next upcoming holiday?"

"*Pesach.*"

"Go up to the eighth floor," the person said, and they let me through a second door.

Up on the eighth floor, they sent me from office to office, everyone listening to me politely, until a girl finally told me to try at Tzavta, the Jewish community center where I'd gone to subscribe to the magazines. Because in that fortress they were all stricter, more conservative groups, less tolerant to mixed marriages with non-Jews, so they thought I'd have better luck connecting with my roots at the more secular community center. This was not unexpected, and my real objective was just getting into the building to explore. I started walking around the eighth floor, where the Sojnut offices were located: the aliyah office, which helped people who wanted to emigrate to Israel, the student department, and the finance department. Outside in the hallway were some shelves with brochures and flyers; I took one of everything. Suddenly, an announcement on a bulletin board caught my eye: the Moadon Aliyah group for youth who wanted to emigrate to Israel met at such-and-such time. I wrote it down.

JATIVÁ, MORE AND MORE CONNECTIONS

I had started studying Hebrew, I'd enrolled in a course on Paraguay Street, at the headquarters of the Argentina-Israel Institute for Cultural Exchange. But the aliyah department of Sojnut taught the language as well. It was much cheaper, and the classes were held at the Rambam School, named after the wise Maimonides. It was on Ayacucho Street between Tucumán and Viamonte and people studying to become Hebrew teachers went there. It was convenient for me because the agency gave me a limited budget to work with. But in addition to the fact that it had an accessible price, it also allowed me to meet people who planned to emigrate to

Israel, who were taking classes there for that reason. I'd be able to build more and more connections, growing my network within the Zionist movement. That would create opportunities to gradually enter other places that were off limits to the general public, restricted areas.

Why? Because the bitajon, the Jewish community security force, differentiated between people who were friends, acquaintances, or enemies. Based on these categories you were either accepted or rejected. Let me clarify: a friend is allowed in directly, there's no danger; an acquaintance says they know so-and-so, who comes, vouches for them, and they're allowed in; a guy who doesn't know anyone is considered an enemy. That's the criteria that the bitajon uses. So the more people who knew me, the more chances I had to access those restricted areas.

One afternoon I arrived early to the moadon in the Sojnut building on Perón and Larrea. The seats were empty. I sat down and took out my Hebrew textbook. A girl came in and took out her books too.

"Are you studying Ivrit?" I asked, feigning shyness.

"Yes," she answered.

"Are you going to make aliyah?" I asked.

"Yes, are you?"

"No, I don't know yet. I'm just now getting reacquainted with the community because I'm the son of a mixed marriage."

The girl seemed to like my answer. "Oh, I have just the place for you! I'm Tamara, nice to meet you. I'm in a student group, you should come."

It was Jativá, a Zionist student organization with more conservative leanings. She told me that on Fridays they celebrated Kabbalat Shabbat. I explained that I was the son of a non-Jewish father, and that I hadn't had much religious education.

"Don't worry, you'll be my guest," she said.

The girl turned out to be the president of the group, no less. I got lucky, the velvet rope was lifted. But first, I reported to Red, of course.

"Say yes and see how far you can get," was Red's response.

So I showed up to a Friday meeting. Beyond what I'd read and studied, I felt lost during the ceremony. Luckily, as Tamara's guest, they didn't ask me any questions.

I'd never in my life been to a Kabbalat Shabbat. No one was dressed special for the occasion, except for the men, who put on their kippah, the cap used to cover their heads in a sign of respect to the Creator. They lit candles. Up to that point I'd only been inside two synagogues: one very Orthodox, on República de la India Street. I'd been walking by and since there was no security out front, I went in. Inside, there was a box with a bunch of kippot. I picked one, put it on, and sat down like anyone else. I didn't understand a word because the prayers were all in Hebrew, but I stood when they stood and bowed when they bowed. The second visit was to the Libertad Temple, where I also walked in without being questioned. I just put on a kippah and sat down. But there the ceremony was in Spanish. I had the sensation that beyond the differences between the Old and New Testaments, it was a reading of the Bible, like in a Catholic church.

My objective in Jativá was to find out what was behind that university group, what they did. There were cultural activities, mostly ideological talks. They were organized into teams. One team was focused on integration or absorption, called klitah in Hebrew, taken from the term that describes integrating into Israeli society after making aliyah. Then there was the hasbara team, responsible for explaining Zionism, and the bitajon team, security. The teams took turns organizing the Friday activities. There were about fifteen or twenty regular members in total and many more sporadic participants. Each team was made up of three of four students with one leader for each.

The security team worked hardest when there was some outside activity, such as *Yom Ha'atzmaut*, the celebration of Israel's Independence Day, which always meant a massive event. The bitajon team was the group's link to the community defense apparatus. The bitajon team never set up presentations, that was not their role. When there was an event or a majanot, a camping trip, or we went to Macabilandia or Córdoba, the bitajon team made sure that no one from outside the group could join us or even approach us. All the teams reported directly to the president, Tamara.

When I joined Jativá, the first team they sent me to was integration. That meant I had to help others with the same process I'd been through when I'd joined. It was mostly just getting to know them and having a little talk with them. Shortly thereafter I ended up as the leader of the ideological team. I had the feeling of being a Formula One driver. Everything was happening too fast. My responsibility there consisted of giving talks on Zionist formation and commitment, the State of Israel as the center of the Jewish world, the duty to return to the motherland, to make aliyah. My previous readings had served me well, but I had to learn more.

In general, I arrived at the meetings early to look around for any material I could take to have photocopied. In one of those incursions, I found a list drafted by DAIA—the Delegación de Asociaciones Israelitas Argentinas—which named all Jewish persons forcibly disappeared during the dictatorship. It had information on all the Jewish people who had been sequestered by the previous military government and the circumstances under which they'd been detained. It was thousands. I reported the list to the subcomissioner, Osvaldo Canizzaro, who later on rose to become second-in-command under Rubén Santos as head of the Federal Police. Santos has now been charged with the deaths resulting from police repression in the December 2001 protests of the financial crisis. Canizzaro was the one who told me how to get the list out and share it with him, through an asset by the name of Pereyra who took it to the offices of the Ministry of the Interior, at Moreno 1417, so it could be photocopied and then returned to me. I'd then take it back in and leave it where I'd found it, without anyone ever noticing it was missing. And that's what we did.

WOMEN, MY WEAKNESS

The routine of going to Jativá was followed by movies, plays, and dancing after Kabbalat Shabbat. The women of the group were all between twenty and twenty-two years old; I was older and came across as a natural leader. They often seduced me and . . . what could I do?

I started dating one of the girls in the group. This was the way things were supposed to go, since pretty much everyone wanted to get into a relationship and build a life in the Jewish community here in Argentina or in Israel. Her name was Dafne and her father owned a clothing shop at Rivadavia and Carabobo in Flores, my old neighborhood—who'd have thought. She was my first girlfriend in the community. But, in truth, I wasn't that committed to her, I had my eye on Tamara. I'd expressed my interest, because we were almost always together, but she rejected me very diplomatically. Tamara had a boyfriend, so even though I couldn't take my eyes off of her, I didn't make another move. At least not for a while.

Women were my weakness. On the one hand, they were a good source of information. I could write full reports based on conversations with them. It allowed me to have lots of eyes, since I saw not only what I viewed personally, but also what, innocently, the girls told me. I threw out my hook and they bit, it was easy. But, later on, it became a problem.

Every team in the student group had a leader, and each of those leaders was a member of the board. All of the Zionist university groups received funding from Israel, which was distributed by the Sojnut Student Department. The funds arrived in dollars and were exchanged into pesos. Each group had an account and from there they could draw the money to finance their activities, such as paying a speaker, organizing a machane, buying materials, paying for travel. When I was named leader of the jinuj (education) team, and joined the directive team, I was added as one of the title holders for that account. Two or three signatures were required to cash a check, and one of them was mine.

I always used my legal ID for everything, because my true file had been retired and locked away in a safe in the Federal Police Central Headquarters. It had been replaced by a new file, which contained my false information that listed my mother's maiden name as Jacob. The officers who worked there inside the headquarters at Moreno and San José were under strict orders: "If anyone asks for this information, blow your whistle, sound the alarm, fire shots, and let us know." Because if someone was asking for it, that meant they were checking up on you. Never, in my entire career within the community, did anyone ask for my file. They would've showed them the false one, of course, with the information that matched my cover, but it would've meant that someone was suspicious of me, and I would've been alerted. It would've meant that they were looking into me. Because within the community there were people at the DAIA and the AMIA who could pay the Federal Police to obtain restricted information or even a passport in twenty-four hours. There was a guy from the Zionist Organization of Argentina who even said to me: "I have a friend at the precinct who can get you a passport in two hours."

Later, when I found out, I made sure to pass along the names of the guys who were part of that racket within the Federal Police. I revealed the community's carnal relations with the force, because to me, the pig is just as guilty as the farmer who feeds it.

I don't know what ever came of that, but I passed on all the information I received about the feds who took money in exchange for favors. That's when I first began to understand, as I later confirmed, that there were business dealings between certain Jewish community leaders and the police. That knowledge might've been the reason that they moved me, in 1998, when Adrián Pelacchi left his post as general commissioner and was named secretary of security.

But back to Jativá, I don't want to get off track. I'd become one of the leaders authorized to manage the funds sent from Israel. If I'd stayed undercover long enough, I swear I could've become president of the Zionist Organization of Argentina. At that time I was going out with Dafne, but I was attracted to Tamara. I don't know if it was because she was so athletic, because she was the boss, or because she had such a talent for leadership. One day, we organized a camping trip to a machane in Chascomús, at a campground run by the Automotive Club.

There were couples' tents and tents for girls and for guys. Since I hadn't brought my sleeping bag, I went to sleep with Dafne. That made our relationship public. I don't know if that's what made Tamara look at me in a new light. During a game, we found ourselves alone, and we exchanged some furtive glances. That's when I knew something was going to happen and, in fact, it did.

Back in Buenos Aires, she left her boyfriend at 10:00, I left Dafne at 10:30, and we met at 11:00. At that time, I was in touch with the people from Jativá seven days a week, in addition to my job at Del Valle Cider. My personal life played out almost entirely within the collective.

When I traveled, I had to notify my handler that I was leaving and that I wouldn't be able to make my four calls per day. By that time I no longer needed protection when I left the city. When I got back I had to write everything down, because all intelligence reports were written out by hand. I wrote one report daily, detailing my complete schedule, what I did, who I saw. In one of the meetings of undercover agents, before Laura arrived, one of the other assets said to me, "Hey, man, slow down with your reports, you're making us all work harder." Because I filed seven per week. And, as if that weren't enough, at some point every day, usually in the morning or around lunch, I met with Laura in one of three cafés downtown. I'd chosen them according to the rules; they were open twenty-four hours and had a fair amount of movement. One was on Florida Street at the corner of Paraguay and had an entrance on both streets, the second, on Florida between Paraguay and Marcelo T. Alvear, and the last at Córdoba and San Martín. If one of the two of us missed the meeting, we moved on to the next place and so on, progressively. When we couldn't meet, a cycle of phone calls was initiated, one in the morning and another at night.

In the periods when I didn't have Red as my handler, when she was on leave or vacation, her replacements never took such good care of me. They put their own comfort first. They'd ask me to meet them at the Railway Workers Hospital so that they wouldn't have to go far and sometimes even asked me to meet above Precinct 46 where, as an undercover agent, I couldn't be seen. I had one handler who called himself Julio and the others were Osvaldo Mercader, Fernando Shapiro, Eduardo, and Rubén.

I didn't provide any analysis on what I reported, I simply shared the facts straight up and it was other people's job to interpret them. I sometimes had to translate Hebrew words in the margins, but the rest was raw material. I didn't know exactly what they were looking for, so any detail could prove useful, I thought. Red gave me total freedom, she didn't lead me, she didn't tell me what information she was interested in. We were in the preliminary stages, I was getting settled, gaining ground, gathering information. But they constantly reminded me: "Never touch anything you're not authorized to." I couldn't enter a place unless I had been expressly given the key, I couldn't just steal a key and break in. If they gave me a key, then I could go in and take what I wanted or needed, a document or whatever, without raising suspicion, because I had permission. I don't know if there had ever been a filter in such a delicate situation, they never gave me any examples of previous experiences.

There was an officer on the Federal Police Force who had a Jewish last name and who was never promoted in rank for that very reason. They didn't trust him. He was one of the informants that the DAIA (Delegación de Asociaciones Israelitas Argentinas), used to find out things about certain people. He was in the Department of Foreign Affairs. On one occasion, when there was a change in administration, they called me into headquarters. The boss was a commissioner inspector with the last name Falcón, and I had to meet with him. He wasn't there when I arrived; I was greeted by Officer Kurevsky. We identified ourselves using a code, so he didn't know me as Jorge Polak or José Pérez, but just by that code. The guy picked up my file and he saw that I was reporting on the Jewish community, although it didn't say that I was undercover. "I see you're going to work with me," he said. But I couldn't, because his job was different. Later I found out that he was the DAIA contact within the force. He wasn't even supposed to know I existed.

When the commissioner inspector arrived, I told him: "Look, boss, that officer is part of the collective."

"Don't worry," he said, "you'll never come into the building again."

It was a very risky moment because Kurevsky must've warned the collective: "Watch out, the force has someone on us."

But they never found me out. To him, I was a code, a group of letters. I guess he wasn't able to figure out my real name or send them my photo. But he must've known that I was undercover, that's for sure.

One day, when the Meeting Center was still run above Precinct 46 in Retiro, Laura called me in. It seemed strange to me, because supposedly since I went undercover, I should never go into headquarters again. Her office was down near the cells in the basement, a terrifying place I referred to as the catacombs. She told me that the bosses had asked me to present my certificate of baptism to prove that I was Christian. I had it, of course, and I handed it in. I'd been baptized in the San José Basilica in Flores. But they still harbored doubts. They thought I was Jewish because they couldn't believe I'd been able to blend in so well within the collective.

THE KEYS TO AMIA

In addition to the machane, Jativá held a seminar on propaganda and counterpropaganda and a meeting of Latin American Zionist groups, hosted by FUSLA, the Zionist University Federation of Latin America, at 650 Uriburu, in a building that was directly behind the AMIA, the Argentine-Israelite Mutual Association. That meeting, which was held over a weekend, was attended by university groups from all the provinces, from Buenos Aires, and also from Chile, Uruguay, and Brazil. That weekend, every Jativá group had a job to do.

"Go to Uriburu early, take the key and start making coffee, setting out the cookies and pens and paper, and we'll get started at eight," Tamara told me.

I don't remember making a copy of the key but I must have, I generally made copies of everything I could. One of the delegations, I don't remember if from the provinces or from another country, had spent the night in that building. But, in spite of that, I walked the entire place, I drew detailed floorplans of the layout, access points. There was a back door by which you could access the auditorium of the AMIA, which was located on the next street over, Pasteur. Later, in a simulation, we used that back entrance. There was also a construction site, on the Uriburu side, two or three stories tall, by which you could access certain floors of the AMIA. I was very cautious, making sure there were no cameras. I went only a few paces in, not too far, because at that time I was still wary of the bitajon guys, believing they were highly trained, never imagining I could've walked right past them like fallen trees. I didn't take into consideration that I had elite preparation and they didn't. Because, the truth is, at the time the guys in charge of security were basically just boys who'd taken a little course, a few of them might've gone to Israel, or done a training with Gadna, which was a youth group, a kind of volunteer army where they received a little paramilitary preparation, generally done before age eighteen, but most of them just had some self-defense training. I later learned that the community did have something of a small intelligence agency that followed anti-Semitic organizations and certain right-wing extremist groups. But the security detail was mostly made up of students or young professionals. The ones I had to really look out for were the adults. Those were the ones who could sniff you out. It was a matter of experience, intuition.

Whatever I saw, read, or experienced, I communicated in the written reports that I turned into Red. That weekend, the FUSLA meeting included debates on different issues: assimilation, the Middle East, the situation in different communities in the provinces and abroad. Each group gave a presentation. In those forty-eight hours, I got to know them all: the leaders of each delegation and the members themselves. The Betar group, who were right-wing Likud supporters, the General Zionists, and Mapam, the Zionist Socialists.

All the groups defended the existence of Israel, but with major differences on many issues. For example, with respect to the Israeli-Palestine conflict, some were hawkish and some were pacifists. I absorbed everything like a sponge, I registered every name, every face, every position, I stretched my memory so that I could retain every tiny tidbit information. And at the same time, I had to come across as friendly, obliging, the perfect host.

The key to that building on Uriburu stayed in my possession until I returned it to Tamara of my own volition. It felt very symbolic to have the "key" to the AMIA, the Jewish community's most important institution, a major achievement in my career, which confirmed that I would be able to go as far as I wanted to. Tamara trusted me completely; I'd never given her any reason to doubt me, and she never had to ask me to return the key, because I gave it back before she had the chance. I'd already taken notes and reported everything I could anyway. But, most importantly, I'd turned in a hand-drawn floorplan showing a way to secretly access the AMIA through adjoining lots without anyone noticing.

This was something that would later cause me nightmares and regrets, a lump in my throat that I can still feel today, but at that time I was totally unaware of the damage I would cause. I'd encountered a weak spot in the AMIA security, and I demonstrated a way to sneak in at night, walk around, and do whatever you wanted without anyone knowing you were there. I could've never predicted that my superiors at the agency were jealously guarding that information and establishing a careful a plan to use it when necessary.

ROMANTIC ENTANGLEMENT

Meanwhile, I was burning the candle at both ends with Dafne and Tamara. Tamara already had the date set for her aliyah, she was going to Israel with her boyfriend at the end of that year, 1986, as she told anyone that would listen. For those guys and girls who had been in Tnuá, the Young Zionists Movement, their main objective in life was emigrating to Israel. If they hadn't done so yet it was because they'd decided to finish college first. For Tamara, as president of Jativá, it was impossible not to make aliyah, because the young people in those groups were expected to be Zionists in practice, not only in theory.

"We should start the paperwork and go too," Dafne started saying. I didn't know what to tell her, yes, no, nothing. I had to come up with some excuse for wanting to stay since I couldn't say I was going to go. Also, my secret relationship with Tamara was going so well that she wanted to leave her boyfriend and make aliyah with me, or for me to at least start the paperwork; promising she'd wait for me there.

Around that time there was a meeting of university students in Rosario. The agency didn't authorize the trip, so I made up an excuse and I stayed home. Tamara and Dafne both went with some other kids but a Mexican girl I liked had also stayed behind in Buenos Aires. She couldn't go because she had injured her leg. I called her with some excuse and invited her out to have a drink, to chat. An hour later I was seducing her. I didn't account for the fact that she was friends with the other two girls and would surely tell them. She didn't know I was seeing Tamara in secret but she told Dafne, and Tamara was there, and the three of them laid a trap for me. We all went out to a bar in San Telmo and the Mexican girl said: "I have to tell the group what happened." There was a guy there who knew what she was going to say and he tried to warn me, but I didn't pick up on his gestures. After the Mexican girl explained that I'd come on to her, Tamara stood up and she was so angry that I thought she was going to slap me across the face. That's how I ended up leaving the Jativá group.

I told Laura and she had to notify the boss, Commissioner Ramón Gutiez. I remember he was furious. I was forced to tell him what had happened, because I had to leave the group I'd infiltrated, and I couldn't do that without notifying them. "Let this be the last time you put your mission at risk for something like this," he warned me. But it was understandable, I was only twenty-five years old.

A LEADER IS BORN

During the period I was in Jativá, until October of 1986 when I had to leave because of that romantic entanglement, I'd experienced a meteoric rise within the Zionist sector of the community. Jativá was a Zionist university group, but there were also adult groups and groups for teens, like Young Israel, Hatzeirá. From its foundation, Zionism placed great importance on youth, who were, they believed, the ones who would preserve the culture and assure the future of the Jewish people. The goal of those teen Zionist groups was to have the kids make aliyah at age eighteen. The groups disbanded at that age because everyone was supposed to leave. So, for kids who weren't ready to travel, they created university groups.

I'd begun to understand that there were different lines of political thought within Argentine Zionism, a reflection of the Israeli political parties. Jativá was aligned with the General Zionists; HaTzionim HaKlaliym reflected the thinking of right-wing parties such as Likud, which created an alliance with Herut. Similarly, there was Meretz, which is the left-wing side of Zionism formed from the merger of the Mapam, Ratz, and Shinui parties.

After my romantic fiasco I decided to move to the university group that was even farther to the right: Tagar, which means "challenge" in Hebrew. I knew a guy who was a member, he was Tamara's cousin actually, she'd introduced us. His last name was Liberman, like her, a family from Río Negro. When I called him and explained the situation, instead of getting mad, he laughed. "Come join up with us, you won't have any problems, we have a lot of girls and they're all very upfront," he assured me.

Tamara was about to leave, to make aliyah, so she wouldn't even find out. I had imagined it would be hard to enter another group, because whether they were from the right or the left, all the girls talked to each other. I thought that the mess I'd made would be irreversible. But that wasn't the case. Between October and December there were no activities since the university school year had ended, so I wasn't going to be able to join a new group until January. Laura told me to spend those months doing an in-depth analysis of the Jewish press. It was a period of transition, but with the knowledge I'd obtained, combined with an analysis of the community media, I would be able to evaluate what the different sectors thought about various issues. I'd grown a lot, but, at the same time, it had made me more vulnerable.

At the start of 1987 I immediately started going to the Tagar meetings, which were held at Larrea and Córdoba, in a building that housed the offices of other Zionist groups. One of the speakers who came to talk to us there was a bigshot from DAIA (the Delegación de Asociaciones Israelitas Argentinas), the umbrella organization for the Argentine Jewish community. As a member of Tagar, I got even more insight into the internal debates. I also got my first chance to participate in an operation organized alongside the community security force.

"We're going to carry out an operation with the bitajon guys, do you want to come?"

"Yeah, of course. What are we going to do?" I asked. It didn't even occur to me to say no. I don't know what I'd imagined, but I felt a thrill of excitement. I was finally going to have a bit of action, put my skills to use.

The target was a group that answered to Suhail Akel, the Palestinian ambassador, who was scheduled to give a talk in an auditorium owned by some syndicate, a teacher's union I think, on the 700 block of Piedras. He was going to rant against Israel, over the Sabra and Shatila massacre, and we were going to graffiti the wall outside with messages like: "Palestine murderers," "Palestine liars." Because the truth was that Christian militants had killed the Palestinians in 1982 in those villages near Beirut, during the Lebanon War, but they blamed the Israelis because their troops hadn't stopped the attack. Us Tagar guys were going to do the spray painting, and the security team would be there for backup, if necessary.

There were around ten of us, men and women, and maybe ten or more from bitajon, who were going to come to our defense if there was any type of conflict. The graffiti was going to be sprayed on a huge wall right across from the theater, just as the talk was being given. And the guys from bitajon were posted with walkie-talkies a block ahead of us and a block behind us, on alert for any police presence nearby so that we could "work" in peace. The rest of us arrived in small groups from Peru and Avenida de Mayo, separately, with cans of spray paint in our bags and backpacks.

It went smoothly, we painted our messages on the walls across from the theater, made a huge mess, but no one saw us, not the police or any furious Palestinians. I was nervous, because any skirmish would've been my opportunity to show off my skills and win Tagar's trust forever. But I wasn't part of bitajon so I couldn't let my training show, I'd have to hide what I was capable of. Of course it was equally likely I could be detained by the police instead of winning a fight with the Palestinians, and that would've been a whole other problem. But I'd reported on the group's plans to Red, so the force was aware of what was going to happen. Suhail Akel's secretary was probably aware too because she was one of our assets. She had been undercover in the Islamic community for several years and she was Akel's right hand, his most trusted woman, who went everywhere with him.

The group carried out other actions, but they didn't ask me to participate. They once organized an operation against a group of Nazis who were passing out flyers from a table on José María Moreno and Rivadavia, in Caballito. They jumped out of a truck and pounded them to a pulp before they had time to react.

Despite all my preparation, there were circumstances that I couldn't anticipate. One time, in a meeting in which they were going to distribute funds from Israel, one of the leaders of the adult Zionists was there. He was very respected in the right wing of the community, and he'd brought along a girl, a law student, who worked with him. She asked me where I was from.

"From Entre Ríos," I answered.

"Oh, from which colony?" she asked. "Do you know so-and-so?"

When I said no, she answered: "How strange, because he's the only veterinarian in town and everyone knows him."

If she went on like that she was going to blow my cover but her boss saved me: "Leave the personal matters for later, we're here for other reasons."

I thought she was feeling me out. I had a solid foundation in Jewish culture and history, but personal connections were my weak spot. I couldn't admit that I knew anyone in the Jewish settlements of Entre Ríos because that person would know my family wasn't Jewish if they ever asked them about me. That's where my story collapsed, but it was too late to change it. I couldn't just invent a new backstory, a new past out of nowhere, it was too risky.

I could smell the girl's suspicion, and my mind played images of being locked in a room with someone asking: "Who are you? You're not who you say you are." I was constantly on alert. I couldn't get distracted, I couldn't go into any room without mapping an exit strategy, without knowing who I might run into. I had to be prepared for any situation. There's a permanent psychological pressure on a person doing espionage and undercover work. You become sensitive to every little thing, overanalytical, hypervigilant, extremely paranoid. That's why the role of the "handler" is so important. Their job is to constantly manage you, because your head could explode at any moment. No one can predict how you might react, there are a thousand different options. I lived on the edge, always adhering to best security practices, making sure I wasn't being followed. I couldn't let my guard down for a second. I went to two or three more of those Tagar meetings, but I knew I was going to have to look for a new group, this time not because of any romantic entanglement, but because I didn't know whether that girl, the law student, had alerted the people at Tagar, whether I'd run into her again. She could reappear at any moment and start rummaging around in my past. I needed to find another Zionist university group and I had to do it fast. I kicked myself for having no backup plan.

ALTERNATIVE

I discovered a group that was just getting started, called Breira, which means "alternative" in Hebrew, and which was run near the Once neighborhood. They were broader leftist Zionists who wanted to participate in community leadership and were affiliated with OSA, the Zionist Organization of Argentina. The 1987 elections were coming up and they needed campaign volunteers, so as soon as I joined they assigned me as a representative of Breira at a voting site in the Golda Meir School. There, of course, I had access to the voter registration list: names, last names, addresses. I needed to be a member of the Zionist Organization, so I asked Red for authorization and I joined as an independent. I remained a member until the year 2000, I probably still have my card lying around somewhere.

I made several attempts to get people to join the Breira group because there were only two or three of us and I needed to be a part of something larger, but for some reason no one was interested. I tried different angles, but nothing, and I couldn't waste any more time. I was still reporting to Laura on a daily basis, and I didn't want the quality of my work to suffer. So I decided to try my luck with another group at the Jewish Community Center, Tzavta, which means "united" in Hebrew. The student group was led by a guy named Daniel Grikman, I was told, at the community center on Junín Street. You could also pick up copies of *Aurora* magazine in Spanish there and even though I already had a subscription, I sometimes went to get more copies, so as to familiarize myself with the place and its employees.

I finished out the year doing a press analysis and going to Breira meetings, cross-checking information. At the end of 1987 I got up the nerve to approach the two secretaries at Tzavta, Clarita and Andrea, and express my intention to join the student group there in the new year. They informed me that the community center was about to move to a new location and that the university organization had temporarily disbanded. The new center would be on Perón Street, in the former Yelmo appliance factory. I would occasionally walk by and check on the progress of the remodel from the street. The move was planned for March. But one day Andrea and Clarita gave me some disheartening news: they would not be restarting the student group.

One of a spy's skills is the ability to identify a need and propose a solution. So I talked about what a shame it was that the group had disbanded, that someone should try to encourage the youth to join, blah, blah, blah. Then I offered to do it myself, in my own free time, if they could by any chance get me lists of students who'd been in the group before, so I could come into the center and call them and try to start a new group. That idea is what saved me. Andrea agreed, enthusiastically, and she gave me a roster of people who'd been through Hashomer Hatzair—the Youth Guard—and members of other university groups as well, who hadn't emigrated to Israel, with ages between twenty-five and thirty-five. I immediately started calling.

The initiative benefitted me, but also the community. I could continue gathering undercover intel while providing an opportunity to strengthen a sense of belonging among young people and help them stay connected. I still ask myself how they could've handed over all that personal information without question. Those women trusted me blindly. Clarita, for example, who was an older woman, had been a Socialist activist her entire life, she was fully transparent. Everyone I came across was good people; there might've been some murky dealings in the upper echelons of the establishment, but nothing that could pose a threat, by any means, to the security of the Argentine nation.

I had built true ties with these people, I'd begun to feel genuine concern for their safety, because beyond the fact that we're talking about a time before the attack on the embassy, I could tell that their defense apparatus was very weak, paper thin. If there was ever a conflict with true heavy-hitters, security would be practically nonexistent, as good as nothing. The worst thing they ever imagined was neo-Nazi violence, they couldn't even fathom a terrorist attack. That's why the structure was flimsy, there was no real expectation of conflict. They began to feel a bit more fearful, maybe, during the first Gulf War with the invasion of Kuwait, in 1990, because Argentina had entered the coalition and had become a target.

Mapam, the Israeli Socialist alliance, had its office within the Tzavta community center, as did Convergence, which was a coalition of Argentine Jewish organizations including Frai Shtime—which meant "free voice" in Yiddish—with roots in the Polish Jews' labor parties, Tnuá, a branch of

Hashomer Hatzair; later on there was Hamakom Shelí, which meant "my place," a school for kids with some kind of difficulty, and then Guili, offering a more secular Judiasm for mixed families and their kids who weren't accepted in other more orthodox spheres. And the *New Zion* newspaper also had its offices in Tzavta. This was a Socialist Zionist publication, whose very name was scandalous because the anti-Semites thought "New Zion? Why *new*? What are the Jews trying to take over now?" It's incredible how they can latch onto anything and find some way to rationalize it. All these organizations were in the same building, which was enormous. A three-story property, with two basement levels, about forty meters deep.

There were some youth groups forming within Convergence, but none of them were university organizations. I began to contact people, to invite them to meetings. "Hello, I'm calling from Tzavta, the idea is start up a university group . . ." I was able to interest so many people that we had to split the group in two, because, by late 1989, early 1990, there could be anywhere between a hundred to three hundred participants. It became one of the most recognized university groups in the Jewish community. When it came time to put a name to it, I had the idea to call it Ofakim Horizons.

I moved easily through Tzavta, I could go into all of the offices, and that's how I came across a folder with documents that seemed important, and I reported it to my superiors. It was a roster of all the members of the Zionist Organization of Argentina. They asked me what time of day the building was quietest, and I told them that it was from two to six in the afternoon, because the majority of meetings started at seven. They gave me precise instructions: I had to take the folder, leave the building, and walk diagonally across Plaza Almagro, which was just steps away. Halfway across the plaza I was going to cross paths with a person who would receive the documents and take them to be photocopied. There couldn't be any hesitation, I couldn't make any missteps. "We're going to have our people watching you. If we detect anyone leaving Tzavta, tailing you, we'll abort the mission," they assured me.

Afterwards, I had to go to a café on Corrientes Avenue, where I was going to meet a girl. I had the order to have a coffee with her and sit talking for an hour. Then I would retrace my steps, the folder would be handed back to me in the plaza, after having been photocopied, so that I could put it back in the exact same place I'd found it. That's exactly what I did and it worked perfectly.

I imagined that they must've photocopied the documents in an office above Precinct 9, which was fairly close. Because they wouldn't have had time to go all the way to the offices at Moreno and San José, or to Retiro, in an hour. There, above Precinct 9, was what we called Technical. It was the area of intelligence that assisted us when we had to make copies of keys, provided us with briefcases that held listening devices to pick up conversations from a distance, or cameras hidden in cigarette packs, which we were already using in 1986.

In Convergence, which was affiliated with Mapam, there was a guy named Andy Faur. Mapam had a youth department with two directors: Mauricio Tenembaum and Noé Davidovich, who tasked Andy with creating a group of youths that were committed to the community, secular, progressive, leftists: that became Convergence Youth. It started out with some eight to ten guys and girls. They invited me to join and I did, in spite of the fact that I was setting up Ofakim in parallel. The more connections I had, the better, I figured. That's where I met Eli, who had been recruited into the group by

Andy. She had been part of Hashomer Hatzair as a teenager, but she hadn't made aliyah.

As soon as I laid eyes on her, I wanted her above everyone else. Andy had started dating another girl in the group, daughter of a textile impresario who donated money to Mapam. The first chance I got, I asked Andy to find out if I had a chance with her.

HER

There was a demonstration outside the temple on Libertad Street, protesting the vandalism of a Jewish cemetery in France, decrying what seemed to be a resurgence of Nazism. There were speakers, among them Rubén Beraja, the future president of the DAIA, who had put out the call to members of the Jewish community as well as national leftist groups. We'd attended other protests against the right-wing military extremists; I remember marching with the Convergence signs. I had to go so I could report back on the event, but the truth was I was there because of Eli; if not I'd have gone for just a little while, the minimum to draw up a report for my bosses. I wanted to see her. By that point Andy had told me that she was single and that I had a shot, but that I should take it slow and not pressure her, because she was very special. She liked to walk, she was very athletic, so when the demonstration ended I walked her from Córdoba and Libertad to Lavalleja and Aguirre, in Villa Crespo, where she lived.

We chatted as we walked, finding things in common. I knew that I liked her a lot, but I never imagined any of what would happen to us in the future if I let myself fall for her. Because I'd had relationships with other girls, several, but I was always careful not to get too involved; I'd known from the outset that the relationships were going to end. For some reason, I could tell that with Eli I wasn't going to be able to control things. But what would happen when she found out that my reality wasn't what she knew it to be? Because I'd told the same story to almost everyone, that I was the son of a non-Jewish father and a Jewish mother, from the Jewish settlements of Entre Ríos, and that I'd reconnected with my roots.

The next Convergence activity was a dance, "Israeli Nights," held in the basement of Tzavta. There was Israeli music, the girls had made Yiddish food, European Jewish dishes: knishes, gefilte fish, varenyky. There was no Middle Eastern Israeli food, such as falafel, or hummus, because the girls had learned the recipes from their bubbes—grandmothers—who were all immigrants. Except the schlijim, no one in Tzavta had that kind of cultural heritage.

That night, I got up the nerve to ask Eli out and she said yes. We started dating. The first time we kissed I felt dizzy from it. That must've been March of 1990. By Rosh Hashanah I knew I was in love with her. So much so that I was anxious about the future. We had such a solid bond, much stronger than anything I'd felt before. She wasn't just another girl, she was my soulmate.

Eli was a Hebrew teacher. She always corrected me, but she did so in a very sweet way. She had that unique quality: she was soft but strong at the same time. When you saw her, so small, with her bright green eyes and her reddish blonde curls, you'd never imagine what she was capable of. She had incredible willpower. She seemed fragile, but she was a black belt in karate, trained at one of the hardest schools. She'd even traveled to Córdoba, where a Japanese master visited every four years to give the black belt exam. Seemingly so delicate, she could rip you to pieces. But she didn't like to stand out. She was like me in that way. She had strong opinions, convictions, but she kept a low profile. She dressed very simply, always in jeans or flowy dresses, in the rustic hippie style typical of the Hashomer Hatzair kids, like girls from a kibbutz.

Her grandparents were immigrants. They spoke Yiddish and I learned a lot of words talking to them. Eli was the first in the family who had studied Ivrit, modern Hebrew, the only one. Since she felt a calling to be a mora, a teacher, she read a lot about education. She corrected me sweetly but firmly. I had finished two levels and could follow a conversation, but I had a lot to learn. There came a time when I even thought in Ivrit. We said that when we had kids, we would speak Hebrew at home.

We had simple tastes: we liked taking the train out to Tigre to sit and drink mate by the river, going to the movies; she loved the theater. We went to art exhibitions, to walks around San Telmo. By then Ofakim occupied a large part of my time. On Fridays we would meet at 8:30 p.m. and then we'd all go out together. Eli would go to the Convergence meeting instead but she'd come out with us after. That year at Yom Kippur we fasted, because Eli observed the holiday. We went to a small Orthodox temple on Julián Alvarez, where the men and the women sat in different parts of the synagogue. She said that it didn't matter that we had to be separated, that it was important that there weren't too many people, that it be as intimate as possible. I remember that between the different times for prayer we went to Parque Centenario and sat on a bench looking at the lake, talking. It was a very spiritual moment, something that brought me closer to her, through religious faith.

Because of the Gulf War, the Jewish community felt a bit more exposed. Faced with the increased threat, I started looking more closely at Tzavta's security measures. The building was truly very vulnerable. I warned Eli to take precautions, we all had to be careful. She still didn't know who I really was, not yet.

In 1991, after a year together, we traveled to Entre Ríos to visit my family. I'd been to her house many times, I knew her grandparents on both sides. Her maternal grandparents were coincidentally both from the Entre Ríos area, where my family came from. That meant that my cover about being from the Jewish settlements was at risk of being blown. Her zayde had been born in the Jewish colonies and her bubbe had come over with her family from Russia and settled there as well. They were both from little towns between Monigotes and El Salvador, the whole area colonized by Jewish immigrants. Eli had never been to Entre Ríos but there were contradictions that could come up in conversation. This was the weak spot in my cover, which could lead someone to find me out. Another threat. I recognized that this was a failing on my part.

Eli's last name was Polish. Her zayde and bubbe on her father's side had met on the boat when they were both sent over in arranged marriages to other people. They fell hopelessly in love and decided that when they reached the port they were going to run away together and not even look for their spouses, who they'd never met in person. So they lived together as concubines, unable to legally marry because divorce didn't exist. Her zayde had a number tattooed on his arm: he'd been in a concentration camp. Eli's father, an only child, had no claim to the bicycle factory that had been expropriated from his grandfather in Poland because he had been born out of wedlock.

Her zayde on her mother's side had the last name Dubrovne. He was from Domínguez, where there are many mixed marriages. "I lived in Domínguez, my family had a furniture store, my sister took it over," he would tell me.

One of the sons of that sister was a pediatrician who had been my cousins' doctor. More overlap, more coincidences could emerge. At any moment it could be revealed that I was lying about my Jewish origins. Because my family lived in the area and everyone there knew that my mother wasn't Jewish.

But as cold and calculated as I had to be in my work, like a chess player, I could never be that way with Eli. "It's in God's hands now," I thought as we boarded the bus in Retiro. "If Eli says 'I can't go on like this,' my world will collapse," I thought. I stared at her the whole bus trip. I was tense but she was oblivious, excited to travel to a settlement of Jewish immigrants and meet her future in-laws. We were on two totally different trips.

When we arrived, my son was there visiting my parents. Eli had already met him; they got along well and were looking forward to spending more time together. My parents were country people, I had told them hardly anything. Only that I was on the force, in intelligence, but they didn't know what my mission was. I had told them that I was going to introduce my girlfriend to them, that she was Jewish, but that didn't matter to them. They knew many mixed Jewish and non-Jewish couples in the area, it was completely normal.

I'll never forget the scene: my son runs up, excited to say hello, to give me a hug. Then, my mom says to me: "Look at the pants he's wearing," it was a pair of gray shorts, "Take a good look, do you recognize them? They're the ones you wore for your first communion."

The air in the room turned to ice. Eli and I exchanged

glances. I could hardly breathe, I wanted the earth to open up and swallow me, I felt like the world was ending. Eli was so confused, she'd been fully convinced that my mother was Jewish. I imagine she must've felt a punch to the gut. She'd come there hoping to solidify our bond and it had blown up in a totally unexpected way. My mom, poor thing, didn't even notice. She must've imagined that Eli would think it was sweet, and me too. My son ran off to play.

That night Eli and I had a very long talk. Or rather, I spoke nonstop. I laid it all on the line. I had one chance and I had to get it right. It's hard to tell the truth when you've been trained to lie, to trick people, to play with their emotions. But I thought about what my mother had always said: "Honesty is the best policy, even if it hurts." I know that sounds ridiculous coming from me, but at that moment I swear that's what I thought.

I told Eli that I was in love with her, I explained how I'd infiltrated the Jewish community, but how I felt genuinely connected to and concerned for the collective. How I'd begun to feel genuinely Jewish, even though I hadn't been born into it. I explained that I worked for intelligence, that they'd ordered me to go undercover because my family came from the Jewish colonies and I had a lot of knowledge of Judaism, that the initial goal had been to prove whether the Andinia Plan was real, but that my mission had changed to reinforcing protection against possible attacks. It was the time of the Gulf War, and we saw on TV how they were bombing Israel, where she had family and a lot of friends who had made aliyah. She cried inconsolably, about everything. She cried for me and for her loved ones who could die over there. The two tragedies converged. She was very committed to me too, she said. I imagine that she must've been thinking, "What will I tell my parents, how can I keep this from them, what should I do?"

"It's your decision. I don't want to break up, but if you want it to end, the relationship ends here. I understand and I accept whatever you decide," I told her.

What else could I ask of her? I'd done something unforgiveable. There was nothing else to explain. She'd either accept me or reject me for good. Rationally, she should've broken up with me and turned me in, but there were other factors at play. There was love, and love doesn't always listen to reason.

We spent the week taking long walks down the dirt roads of the colony, through the countryside, talking, or sometimes in complete silence. I was bitter the whole time, convinced I was going to lose something so important, and it was all my fault. I had imagined myself starting a family with Eli, having kids, growing old together. It seems like a cliché, but it felt so important to me. I was desperate to know if she was going to leave me. But, at the end of the week, she told me she wanted to stay together. I felt like I had touched heaven. Not only because she had accepted me, but because that meant that her love for me was unconditional. Or at least I thought so at the time. And I still feel that way for her.

I think that my mother might've had something to do with Eli's decision. There was a part of the family, out there in the country, that was very Catholic. They went to mass every day and they didn't like that I was dating a Jewish girl. Added to that was the fact that I'd married before, "in a rush," and then divorced. I was the black sheep. My mom, however, was a free spirit with a strong personality. She would hop on horseback as a little girl and herd cattle. She drove, but my father didn't. She took Eli around everywhere in her little Fiat, to the general store in town, to visit her relatives. She was offended by her family's prejudices, their discrimination. She was a lot like a Yiddish momme, she wasn't content until we'd had seconds at every meal. But since she was overweight, she was happy when she learned that Eli was a vegetarian. "She's going to help me eat healthier," she said, and she laughed. Eli was charmed by her.

From the moment that Eli accepted me I had to reorganize my entire life, because our relationship implied that she was going to have to start taking certain precautions, like I did. She still lived with her parents and her brother. She was leaving her job as a coach at a recreation center to work as a mora at Beteinu, a Jewish community school in Belgrano for kids with psychological and physical disabilities who were not served by AMIA because they were children of mixed marriages. Most of them had serious economic problems and lived in the nearby shantytown. Some of the parents were alcoholics or had psychiatric issues. I remember one day on the train a little peddler boy gave her a hug and a kiss. I asked her how she knew him. "He's a student at Beteinu," she answered. That meant that there were Jewish kids who had to beg on the trains, and Eli was their teacher.

We kept up the story of my Jewish mother and the Entre Ríos settlements for her parents and there were no more problems. They always loved me and my parents loved Eli. Back in Buenos Aires, after Eli accepted me for who I truly was, I felt a renewed commitment to the community.

THE FEMALE AGENTS

I was truly concerned with the lack of safety at Tzavta, and I explained to Eli that, since I'd been able to get in so easily, someone else would be able to as well. And, sure enough, a strange woman showed up one day. I pointed her out to one of the guys in the group: "There's something off about that girl, we should keep an eye on her." That's the way people in intelligence like me operate, we never take action directly if we can avoid it. It's preferable to gather the information and let others act. Never get your hands dirty if you don't have to.

So the guy asked her out, and, obviously, she accepted eagerly. Nothing better for a spy than hooking up with one of the people you're supposed to spy on. But she took it one step further, she wanted to bring a female friend along on the date and she asked him to invite a friend from the group as well. Between the two guys, they laid a trap for the women. A few questions in, it was obvious that the girls were not part of the collective. I checked on them and it turned out they were from Naval Intelligence. They didn't show their faces at any more meetings, we'd blown their cover. But, if you ask me, the best way to infiltrate is using female agents. If I had to organize an undercover operation from scratch, I'd choose female assets. People aren't usually as suspicious of them, and if they're blonde with blue eyes, even less so.

Of course there are exceptions. I remember the huge scandal within the government in 2000, when it came to light that lawmaker Miguel Doy's wife, who was also his office manager, was one of ours. Her name is Mónica Amoroso, and I talk about her in the present tense because she's still on the payroll. I'm sure of that. She'd started out as a campaign volunteer and was married to Doy for two years. The guy swore up and down that he had no idea about his wife's double life, and I believe him. When he found out, he threw all her clothes out the window and filed criminal charges against her. The bosses were frantic, but nothing came of it. Fredi Storani, who was the minister of the interior at the time, denied the existence of an intelligence department within the Federal Police, even though a search turned up pay stubs with the code that Amoroso used.

In intelligence, female agents in the field have to do whatever their bosses order them to, with no limits, whether or not they have a boyfriend or husband. They're required to accept any situation, even if it implies sex. What happens stays between them and their superiors. But it's rare to see them go undercover; they tend to work more often in analysis, which presents less conflict in their personal lives. Laura was one of the exceptions, she was capable of anything, without hesitation, and Amoroso was apparently the same way. Those two women that we kicked out of Ofakim had the misfortune of going up against a well-trained agent like me.

A couple of suspicious guys showed up as well. One of them had been a Montonero, a left-wing guerrilla; Red confirmed for me that he'd been living exiled in Spain and had returned. The other was from the Humanist Party. I had tailed the Humanists before, when they asked me to do certain jobs, so I recognized him. Luckily he didn't recognize me. The party had an office in Almagro, on Mario Bravo or Salguero, I don't remember exactly. But that guy, a skinny dude, tall, didn't hide where he was coming from. He wanted to propose a joint action. It turned out he had a warrant out for his arrest for his participation in an attempted takeover. Those guys act all "peace and love" but there's more to it. I reported on the guy and I think they were already monitoring him. One of them stayed with us in Ofakim and the other joined Convergence. I wasn't too worried about them. The thing that kept me up at night were my concerns about a possible attack. The front of the Tzavta building was all glass, truly an easy target.

Then a sheliah, Loty Mehler, a representative for Mapam, asked Andy Faur and I if we wanted to join the Zionist Organization of Argentina. Since the last elections, the party had more seats open because the Organization included representatives from all the Israeli parties and the student movements, but the Zionists went from kids around eighteen or nineteen, to older adults around fifty or sixty, and there was no one in the middle. Andy and I, who were between twenty-five and twenty-eight, could breach that gap; we were just what they needed. The older guys called us "the young masters."

I informed my handler and they approved it, but they recommended I take extra safety measures. It was a great success for me professionally. Everything was easier now that I'd joined the Zionist Organization. From that moment in 1991, I pretty much stopped my work with Ofakim, which was already being led by a team I'd put in place that responded to me, and I concentrated on my activism in the Zionist Organization of Argentina, on one hand, and the protection of Tzavta on the other.

Why? Because my personal safety and the safety of the woman I loved, Eli, depended on it, along with the safety of my friends, the people I'd grown to care about. I was breaking every rule of intelligence. Meanwhile, something was breaking inside me. There was one incident that threw me into a panic: I came home to find that the apartment I rented had been robbed. My own home. Someone had violated my most protected, most inaccessible space. I always made sure I wasn't followed, I had confidential material in there, but, nevertheless, someone had managed to get in.

I got home at dawn to find an officer posted outside my apartment, because they'd taken the door off the hinges. It was a reinforced door, but they would've been able to pry open even a bulletproof door, because they'd used a pneumatic tool, the kind welders use. I lived on the second floor. They stole money, a legal firearm, my Federal Police badge, documents, my ID. I couldn't report everything at the station. I also had my intelligence agency credential, which was what allowed me to get into headquarters, not with my name but with my code. Also my health insurance card and a press credential, which I'd made myself under another name, something they'd shown us how to do at the Academy.

I'd called Eli, who borrowed her dad's car and came over with her brother. Red was already there with me so they met. Eli realized that she was my boss and Laura realized that Eli was my girlfriend. I felt completely helpless because we knew I wasn't simply robbed, there was more to it than that.

But work, in general, was going well: Ofakim continued to grow. I never revealed to my superiors the fact that I'd created the group myself because the assignment was to infiltrate an existing group. Andy Faur and I joined the Zionist Organization as subsecretaries for Mapam with Noé Davidovich writing us formal letters of nomination. The secretary general, "Fercho" Ercovich, who was a party member, introduced us to the president, Víctor Leiderfarb, as new members of the team. "Well, we're going to have new blood, look at Mapam, working its way up from the bottom," he said, partly in jest but partly serious, because we were the left-wing of Zionism.

Andy was a good guy. He was studying Social Sciences and his girlfriend, Haydée, was the daughter of a very wealthy but progressive businessman. There were several couples in our friend group. When Haydée graduated with an accounting degree they went to Israel together and Andy eventually became a sheliah envoy in Uruguay. Haydée's sister, who was also part of that friend group, married a guy I didn't like and they later divorced. They say he stole paintings donated by artists to raise funds after the AMIA attack, and that's how he began his career as a curator. This proves that not everyone in the community was perfect, but, truthfully, that kind of unsavory character was the exception.

As members of OSA, the largest Zionist organization in Argentina, we made regular visits to the Israeli embassy. Once, during a meeting to organize a demonstration, Andy introduced me as Eli's boyfriend to two guys from bitajon who worked at the embassy and who had been in Hashomer Hatzair at the same time as Eli. Entering the Israeli embassy for the first time didn't feel like that big of a deal to me. Because the true trial by fire was the day I'd been invited into the offices of Sojnut, the Jewish Agency for the land of Israel. To think that later on I'd be able to describe the eighth and ninth floor of that building with my eyes closed. Because the other floors couldn't be accessed from that elevator, I suppose they were part of the Natan Gesang school, which was next door. But those upper floors were all windows on one side and meeting rooms for the olim, people who were planning to emigrate, and the Sojnut offices. And I walked that hallway many times. But that first day I was allowed into the Sojnut bunker, I had to control my fears, my doubts, my body language, so that no one could read me. To such an extent that by the time I went to the embassy, I could behave naturally, unconcerned, totally convinced of my role and my identity. It would've taken someone very good, with better training than mine, to detect me. And I know that there wasn't anyone like that on their side.

In February of 1992 there was an international alert because the secretary general of Hezbollah, Abbas al-Musawi, had been killed along with his wife and five-year-old son. He was the cousin of the former prime Minister of iran, Hossein Mousavi, who had visited Argentina two years prior to sign the nuclear arms agreement that Carlos Menem later cancelled unilaterally, at the end of 1991, drawing ire from the Iranians who had supported him in his presidential campaign. Also around the same time that the nuclear deal was called off, Menem had become the first Argentine president to visit Israel, without being welcomed in Syria, as he'd hoped. Upon return from his trip, the AMIA administrative team paid homage to President Menem. Rubén Beraja had recently been elected as president of DAIA.

We knew that there could be a reprisal in the forty days following al-Musawi's assassination, because that's how those groups operate, and both the Syrians and the Iranians were angry with the Argentine government. The warning went out at an international level through the Israeli consulate. The information we received at the Zionist Organization was that there were plans for an attack against a US, English, or Jewish target.

When I told Laura, she said to me: "Yeah, we heard it too, but from somewhere else." That meant that the alert had also been sent to Protection of Constitutional Order, because at that time Laura and I answered to that division, which was headed by Commissioner Inspector De León. It might have been thanks to the Palestine ambassador Sukhail Akel's secretary, who, as I already mentioned, was one of ours. She was like me, an undercover Federal Intelligence agent.

At that time Eli was ganenet, a preschool teacher, at the school for children of embassy staff, housed within the IICAI, the Argentina-Israel Institute for Cultural Exchange, on Paraguay and Paraná. She was in charge of kita aleph, first grade, the littlest ones. Sometimes, when I went to meet her after work, I'd stop across the street and she'd let the security guards know that I was her boyfriend. The guys from bitajon at Sojnut and at the IICAI had better training than at the rest of the Jewish institutions. They were required be either Israeli citizens or Jewish Argentines, and had to have been through military service or, at least, taken a course in Israel.

Red had her eye on the IICAI; she'd told me that shipments sometimes moved, through the diplomatic post, between the embassy and Ezeiza Airport; large shipments that she suspected were weapons. She'd asked me to keep an eye out, because she was sure that some of the shipments ended up at the IICAI on Paraguay Street. In the schoolyard there, at night, the bitajon team held training sessions and, according to Laura, the neighbors had filed noise complaints.

In mid-March of 1992, three Israelis were going to come to Argentina on a nonofficial visit. They were three bigwigs: Uri Gordon, from the Department of Aliyah and Absorption at the World Zionist Organization; Victor Harel, from the consulate, dedicated to peace negotiations, and Matityahu Drobles, from the Department of Colonization and Settlements. They would arrive separately, through three different ports of entry and would participate in a closed meeting to be held on March 17th. The Zionist Organization of Argentina received the information and was invited to join. And I, as a member of the team, was included. I still have the invitation, signed by the executive director of OSA, and the schedule. First there would be a lunch with select members of the press, and then the closed meeting with the directors. The two events would be held at the Israeli embassy, on Arroyo and Suipacha. I'd reported the time and location of the meeting to Red.

LAST MINUTE CHANGE

At the last minute, the location for the second meeting was changed. We were told to go instead to a hotel on Suipacha Street. I was working at the Los Dos Chinos bakery at the time and that day I had to do the books. I'd let my bosses know that I needed to leave, but they asked me to finish up that task first. I was going to arrive to the area around the embassy at 3:30 in the afternoon. At three o'clock, or shortly before, I was closing the spreadsheets to leave the office when everything trembled like in an earthquake. Los Dos Chinos was at Brasil and Piedras, fairly far away, but we felt it anyway. On the radio, across all media outlets, I heard that there had been an explosion at the Israeli embassy.

I got there as quickly as I could. I could hardly breathe; I imagined the worst. I was tortured by the thought that Eli could've been there. As I got closer there was a suffocating cloud of dust, piles of rubble, people stained with blood, sobbing. Not only had the embassy building been destroyed, the Catholic school across the street had also been damaged by the blast and the glass in all the windows of the surrounding apartment buildings had shattered. Everywhere you looked there was twisted metal, wails of pain, people shouting for help; it was utter chaos. I found the Hashomer Hatzair guys, the bitajon members that Andy had introduced me to, stuffing classified material, everything that was written in Hebrew, into trash bags. I started to help them. In the midst of all that panic, I had to go back to Los Dos Chinos and finish out my shift. It took me a while to locate Eli. I called her parents' house. Of course, the community was in shock, so she'd left school. She knew that I was supposed to go to the embassy that day, but also that I was going to be late because I had to do the books first.

I went back the next day to help, after calling Red to inform her and ask for instructions. She didn't pull me out of the field, she just asked me to describe all the movements within the community. "Call us," she told me, "keep me updated at all times." I knew that people from Protection of Constitutional Order had been there right after the blast. At the time I assumed they must've been there trying to figure out how the attack had occurred. Laura later confirmed that they'd been there, because at that point I didn't know what they looked like, and they didn't know me either.

Two of Eli's friends from Hashomer Hatzair had been there during the explosion. A girl, an administrative employee, had died. Also, a guy from bitajon, who had just gone out to buy cigarettes. He'd just gotten back and right as he was about to go inside the building collapsed before his very eyes. He was saved, but he lost his hearing. He didn't see any van, which makes me doubt whether it ever existed.

I accompanied the director of OSA, Enrique "Tito" Szenkier to the morgue to identify the bodies of the victims. The following year, Tito committed suicide in Brazil. The attack shook me to the core. I had never experienced anything like that, so close to home. They'd instructed me on bombings, I'd read about them, but, up to that point, it was purely theoretical. There was my high school friend's father, who had survived the bombing at Federal Security in 1976, but it's another thing entirely to see it up close in person, to feel that your own life had been at risk. It was unbelievable. Because, let me try to explain, I could've easily been inside that building. I was supposed to be at the meeting with the three Israelis, which had changed location at the last minute.

I started to think obsessively about the fact that I'd reported on that meeting but I hadn't given Laura the information about the change in location. I was scared, terrified. Where had our guys been, the federal officers who were supposed to be guarding the place? Why had Protection of Constitutional Order done nothing, when they knew about the increased risk after Musawi's death? Was the federal officer in charge of security at the embassy injured or dead? No, he'd left before it happened. His replacement hadn't yet arrived. The patrol officer from Precinct 15 who was supposed to supervise the security detail had been called away on another crime. Maybe it was all a huge coincidence. But later it came to light that the other crime had never occurred.

The Israeli consul ordered the immediate evacuation of the three Israeli bigwigs, Harel, Droblas, and Gordon. "I want them out alive," was the message from Israeli minister of foreign affairs David Levy, who entered the country in secret. The men could've been the targets. There were twenty-nine dead and many more wounded in the embassy attack. I could've been there, as I said. Eli could've been there. The guys from Hashomer Hatzair could've died. I'd given my bosses information on the number of people who made up the embassy security team. I'd provided a description of the double entrance with cameras and all the places I'd been able to access inside the building, on the ground floor, because I had never been upstairs. I wanted to convince myself at all costs that I couldn't have contributed to the bombing in any way, because it wasn't enough information to carry out an attack like that. I don't know why I decided not to report the change of location for the meeting. It wasn't that I didn't have time. I didn't do it because something was starting to worry me. It came out of nowhere.

Laura asked me to write a report detailing everything that happened over the days following the bombing. Who I'd seen, what their reactions had been, what movements I'd witnessed. After the attack, my superiors only wanted to know where the investigation was pointing, what the community believed had happened, what the embassy suspected, what the Zionist Organization thought, what theories they were forming about who was responsible.

I, on the other hand, was more obsessed than ever with security at Tzavta. The community center was "my" institution and I had to make sure that nothing happened there, not within my circle. I felt that, since I was a professional, I had a responsibility. The community center administrators weren't overly concerned with tightening measures, if security was lacking across the Jewish institutions as a whole, they were even more lax there. I talked to a sheliah who understood the need and the risks. It was Eli who put me in touch with him. I had given her certain safety tips; I'd taught her how to take care of herself. At least, I told the envoy when I met with him, they had to be better about controlling who they let in. I offered myself as a volunteer to cover certain time slots, to guard the entrance. At that time there were no cement pilings, not even planters to keep a van from parking right out front with a bomb inside, those weren't installed until later.

Around that time we decided to get married. Eli was already

staying over fairly regularly at the apartment I'd rented on Scalabrini Ortiz between Velasco and Vera. I told my parents and they were very happy. We made an appointment at the Civil Registry on Uruguay Street, but they sent us to the branch at Córdoba and Bonpland. The ceremony was intimate, just family and a few friends. Our closest loved ones. Eli was working at the embassy school as well as at the Beteinu, so the morim, her fellow teachers from both places came, along with Andy and Haydée, other friends from Convergence. My parents traveled from Entre Ríos and Eli's parents were there. We weren't nervous about our families meeting, my mother could easily pass for a Yiddish momme, very lively, always joking. And Eli's parents weren't very religious so it was unlikely that anything related to Judaism would come up in conversation. My mother's sister and her husband were there too, my son, and Eli's brother. She looked so pretty that day in a little beige suit, with makeup on, with those big green eyes. I'd started dressing better too since I was no longer that hippie kid from Mapam, I was a civil servant for the Zionist Organization, so I had a nice suit.

There wasn't a party after, just a lunch in a restaurant on Scalabrini Ortiz and Castillo. There must've been about twelve or fifteen of us. There was no religious ceremony either, of course. But there was a honeymoon, in Chile, Viña del Mar. I was so happy I couldn't contain it, I couldn't have been more content. I had found the love of my life, and she loved me back. I was surrounded by my family and closest friends. I didn't tell anyone at work about my wedding, except Red, because I was supposed to ask for authorization through the agency administration and they'd never have granted it. She kept my secret for me.

I couldn't have ever imagined at that point that just a

few years later everything would fall apart and the only two contacts I'd maintain within the community would be two journalists: Miriam Lewin and Horacio Lutzky.

PART II

It was a very hot afternoon in February, and I was working in my office at the *New Zion* newspaper, in a building that had been an old appliance factory, on the 3600 block of Perón Street, steps from Plaza Almagro. The building had been purchased by a movement linked to the Israeli Socialist Party, which had secular, progressive, pacifist views. They wanted the State of Israel to live in harmony with its neighbors, Palestine in particular, and the group worked closely with various human rights movements in Argentina. I was revising some material for the March 2000 issue of the newspaper, which was going to be my last as director of the publication.

Jacobo Timerman had been one of the first directors of *New Zion* and several journalists that later continued their careers in national media worked there as well. Ernesto Tenenbaum and Gerardo Yomal had both been head editors there and many well-known writers and columnists would often send their articles to our modest community newspaper which had been founded in 1948, closed during the last military dictatorship, and reborn in the early years of the return to democracy. The theme for this issue, like so many others, was the continued lack of justice for the attacks on the Israeli embassy and the AMIA headquarters, with the complicity of Jewish community leaders. We'd run numerous articles denouncing the ineptitude of the investigations and the cover up of the "Syrian lead." The boldest title, on the front page, read: "COVER UP," with an image that represented "Justice," behind bars of nonsensical phrases. On page eight was an article entitled "The Police-run Mafia," written by Juan "el Pájaro" Salinas, a journalist who, like me, often wrote about the attacks.

I sat down at the computer to finish the editorial for page three. "Israeli Embassy: Eight Years of Impunity." I fleshed out the main idea, which I'd later fill in with more hard information:

> The attack on the embassy, just like the subsequent attack on the AMIA, was carried out in broad daylight, with the clear intention of assassinating and mutilating the greatest number of people possible. Indiscriminately. Or almost. Because in reality, in both of the two attacks, which led to over a hundred deaths including neighbors and passersby, the people who should have been most vulnerable: the officers in charge of security, went miraculously unscathed.

A CALL

As I was laying out the articles across the twenty-four pages of the newspaper, making notes on a large spreadsheet, the phone rang with an internal call. It was Eli, secretary for the offices housed in the building, and my former assistant at *New Zion*. I could hardly hear her. In a low, strange tone, she said: "Someone called me, and they want to talk to you about AMIA. It's a very delicate matter. And they asked me to ask you if you would listen to their story."

Over the years, I'd received several messages from strangers claiming to have "classified information." On a few occasions they'd had interesting things to say, but for the most part they were people with some degree of emotional or psychological dysfunction. I imagined this would be another similar case, a waste of time.

"Who is it? Do you know them?"

"It's my ex, Iosi. But I don't have anything to do with this, I have no idea what he's talking about, I don't have contact with him anymore. He just asked me to do him this favor and put him in touch with you, because he has something important to tell you, classified, that he doesn't want to talk about with anyone else. He's going to call back, and if you agree I'll put you in touch and you can take it from there."

I remembered Iosi from his time at Tzavta, the Jewish community center that housed the offices of *New Zion*, and I tried to rank him on an improvised scale of trustworthiness. I didn't know him that well: we'd had no more than occasional, fleeting interactions, but I'd seen him in the halls of Tzavta many times. I knew that he'd led a student or youth group that met in the building, Ofakim. He organized conferences and activities for what was basically a "singles" group for the collective, dressed up as political and cultural events.

Once, some ten years before that call, Iosi had invited me to give a talk on Nazi organizations in Argentina. I remember that he was very interested in the issue, especially in the Carapintadas and several anti-Semite and neo-Nazi cells that I was studying around that time. There was a group of girls and boys seated in a circle. Iosi introduced me as an expert and praised the newspaper. I ran into him on a few other occasions, at functions and seminars related to progressive Judaism in Latin America that I had to cover for *New Zion*.

STRANGE GUY

I'd never paid much attention to Iosi. But there was something strange about him that I couldn't quite put my finger on. It wasn't that his last name was "Pérez" with a "z," a Spanish last name wasn't something out of the ordinary in progressive, secular Judaism, which accepted mixed marriages. He was just somehow suspicious: a young man, who seemed street smart, a leader, super interested in the super boring community activism and a member of the Zionist Organization of Argentina, which I didn't know that well but which seemed uninteresting and antiquated. The average age for members of those Jewish institutions was over double Iosi's, who was the same age as me. Yes, I supposed that was it. Just that.

I also knew that Iosi and Eli had been married, but that the marriage had fallen apart quickly. After the divorce, he'd gone to live in the provinces and started a new life. She'd let it slip that the relationship had failed due to his infidelities. For years there'd been no news of Iosi. Until that phone call.

He wanted the meeting to take place at Tzavta in a room off on its own used as storage for chairs and other odds and ends, next to the building's kitchen. On the day we'd agreed to meet, Eli called me on the internal line to let me know that Iosi was waiting for me. He was around forty years old, average height and in good shape. Black hair, brown skin like a Sabra.

"Hello, Horace, how are you?" he greeted me, forcing a nervous smile.

"Good, you have me intrigued . . ."

Without losing any time, the tension evident on his face, he got straight to the point. "I'm not who you think I am."

He sat there looking at me. Everything froze.

"I don't understand what you mean. And I don't think anything about you, we hardly know each other."

He glanced—once again—at the closed door, took a deep breath and began to speak. "It might be hard to believe what I'm about to tell you: I'm not Jewish. I'm an intelligence agent for a government agency, and I was undercover in different Jewish organizations, gathering information for many years."

Just like that, without any warning, he dropped the bombshell. I took a few seconds, which felt like centuries, to process what I was hearing and to work out whether he was serious or this was some strange prank. As I sat in that state of bewilderment, he pulled out an internal intelligence document, with a recent date, something that not just anyone would have access to.

"This is to show you that what I'm telling you is true. I'll leave you a copy of it. I can't tell you any more for now. Not where I live, or how to find me. It's dangerous for you and for me. No one can know that we're in contact, not even your family. But if you agree, I'll reach out again and we can meet somewhere more discreet."

He seemed desperate and anxious. He was worried that someone was after him, and immediately I felt the same way. I remembered that line by Woody Allen: "Just because you're paranoid doesn't mean they're not out to get you."

Although the conversation was very brief, it was enough to convince me that what I'd just heard was true. He seemed sincere and there was nothing to make me think that he was a pathological liar. I knew about his former relationship with Eli and his participation in several Jewish organizations. As surprising as the story was, I believed it. I was scared but also curious, as a window into the shadowy world of spies opened before my eyes.

DOUBTS

When Iosi left that day, I looked, still shocked, at the piece of paper he'd left. It was an intelligence report, unsigned, drafted in the typical language of the services. It didn't contain any relevant information, just a routine report.

"What do I do with this?" I asked myself. And I also tried to decipher why he'd come to me, of all people. What if it was a trap? What would happen if I left the office and someone caught me with confidential report that I wasn't supposed to have? I had to go downtown to take care of something for work but I couldn't just leave that document lying around and I couldn't go walking down the street with a piece of paper that unwittingly linked me to the world of spies. After a few minutes pacing in circles around the empty office, I rushed to the bathroom. I took a lighter, burned the intelligence report, and flushed the smoldering ashes down the toilet.

That night I had trouble sleeping. I couldn't stop thinking about what Iosi had told me. I was somewhat frightened by the revelation, but I needed to know more. I felt the dizzying sensation of peering over the edge of an abyss. As an Argentine Jew who came of age in the terrifying times of the anti-Semitic military dictatorship, I knew that Nazi ideology had never been fully phased out of the security forces. When the attacks against the Israeli embassy and the AMIA occurred (1992 and 1994) I was just starting out as editor of the newspaper and we always made sure to point out the suspicious role that the Argentine security and intelligence services had played before and after the massacres.

This proof that the Argentine government was spying on, targeting its Jewish citizens, not just during the dictatorship but in modern-day democracy, was unsettling. Over the years, in my work as a journalist for niche publications, I'd felt watched, followed, without being able to prove it except on one occasion, years prior, after publishing a special issue of *New Zion* with an investigation into the powerful politician Jorge Antonio. One night, when I was arriving home, a Ford Falcon, the kind used by the military during the dictatorship, zoomed up and stopped right in front of my building, exactly where I was standing. There were three or four guys inside. They stared me down for a few seconds and then took off, screeching their tires. One or two days later, the employees at the garage where I kept my Renault 12 warned me about a strange visit from some supposed investigators who had tried, unsuccessfully, to examine my car.

What Iosi had said was confirmation that the government, or at least one of its institutions, viewed the Jewish community as a threat, a target to be monitored. This was my worst fear brought to life. Another strange episode had occurred some years prior. We'd organized a public debate at Tzavta, one of many. I don't remember the issue—probably an homage to the Warsaw Ghetto Uprising—but I do remember that the speakers included Alfredo Bravo, director of the Permanent Assembly for Human Rights, Graciela Fernández Meijide, and myself, as head editor of *New Zion*. Around that time I thought we were being watched and, on more than one occasion, I saw men posted on the corners near the office. That day, when I parked my car, I chose—naively—to leave it a few yards from the Precinct 9 station, thinking it unlikely that anyone would mess with it right there, as the event was going on. But when I came back out I saw that the trunk of the car had been broken into. Someone had stolen a briefcase full of papers, of no economic value, and nothing else. I went angrily into the station to report the theft—hoping that my briefcase might have been turned in—and, from the front desk, I heard the voice of someone reporting on the Tzvata event that I'd just participated in, describing the size of the crowd and a few other details I managed to catch before an officer came out.

I was now anxious again, mostly over that warning Iosi had given me: that I couldn't share his information with anyone, because that would mean pulling them into a circle of dark dangers, impossible to predict or measure. This, in a country where the intelligence services were barely controlled or even understood by political leaders. I imagined people following me and wiretaps and even some violent act that would silence Iosi's secret revelation. Telling my friends or family what had happened would mean bringing danger into their lives and mine. And, for now, I'd only heard the broad strokes of what Iosi had to say.

DROP BY DROP

Some fifteen or twenty days went by with no news. He had told me that he didn't live in Buenos Aires, that he was returning to a remote location that he couldn't reveal and that he'd be in touch. This time he called my cell phone. He cryptically asked if we could meet the following day and he gave me the name of a coffee shop that doesn't exist anymore, in the very busy area near Tribunales.

I arrived on time and he was already there, sitting at a poorly lit table off to the side. But his appearance had changed dramatically. He hadn't shaved in several days. His hair was no longer dark and curly, but dyed almost blond and gelled. He wore sunglasses and casual clothes, dark, with a kind of rocker style. I almost didn't recognize him but he immediately waved me over. He'd chosen, as he always would, a strategically located table, separate from the rest, in a corner, facing the entrance. Never with his back to the door. He was already having a coffee and there was a bag on the table under one of his hands. I ordered a coffee. I asked him how he was doing, and he began to share, very slowly, brief fragments of his story. He seemed very anxious, psychologically tormented by these stories that he'd kept inside for years, combined with his grief over the collapse of his marriage. He could hardly speak, stopping often to sigh, take a sip of coffee or water, glance at the entrance, and let out a sentence or two, whispering, insinuating more than he was actually saying, careful not to share too much information, and without ever providing concrete details. His mouth was dry and he was sweating in spite of the air conditioning. He told me that he wanted the truth to come to light, but that he couldn't trust anyone. He said once again that his life was in danger, that "the agency" considered him to be a traitor, he was a moving target. And that's why he needed me to help him. He wanted to share everything he knew, but he didn't trust the political or judicial authorities within Argentina, where he'd never be safe once he opened his mouth. The meeting was fairly short (as were most of our meetings); his nervousness limited the time we were able to spend together. He doled out, in drips and drops, a few more facts about his undercover work, mentioning events that I knew to have happend because of my work as a journalist and that he'd experienced in his double life as member of the Jewish community and spy. He insinuated that he had a lot more to reveal. And that what he had to say could implicate the government and the Federal police in the AMIA attack. But he said that he wasn't willing to testify in Argentina because they'd kill him. He wanted me to find "another option." To at least try. Bewildered, and without the faintest idea how I could possibly help, I promised that I'd come up with something and we agreed to be in touch, always at his initiative. All I could do was hope that he wouldn't break contact and disappear back into the shadows he'd stepped out of. I also hoped that he'd be able to relax enough in future meetings to share more of his story and to name his "agency," since, for the moment, he refused to tell me which intelligence organization he worked for. I didn't want to scare him away, so I tried not to pressure him with questions that might make him more nervous.

Meanwhile, my doubts only grew. How much more did Iosi know and how much was he willing to tell me? Where did he really want to go with all of this? Why was he doing it? What was he out for? And what if in reality he was actually "working" me?

There were other meetings, sporadically, in isolated cafés in the Constitución neighborhood. He would establish the location in a previous meeting, so that we could later refer to it in code. We always left separately: Iosi went out first. My paranoia increased exponentially after each meeting to the extent that I would go to extreme measures to ensure that I wasn't followed on the journey back home.

The chances of finding financial support for Iosi to testify outside the country—that was the only way he would agree to speak—seemed practically impossible. This was 2001 and President Fernando de la Rúa's government was breaking down. The people assigned to the case, such as Justice Juan José Galeano and prosecutors Eamon Mullen, José Barbaccia, and Alberto Nisman, inspired even less trust. We also couldn't expect assistance from Jewish community leadership, which still defended the preposterous official story of the bombing. DAIA president Rubén Beraja was accused of concealing information and of having suspicious business dealings with the Carlos Menem government as well as close ties to Carlos Corach, Menem's minister of the interior, the brains behind much of the dark dealings that swirled around the AMIA case. We didn't even consider going to embassies of other countries; their intelligence services had been clearly implicated in the coverup of the bombings to protect the Menem government. As for the Israeli embassy, photos of the ambassador, Itzhak Aviran, celebrating Menem's birthday at his home in Anillaco indicated that we were unlikely to receive assistance from him either.

There was no persuading Iosi to testify in Argentina: "The guys they send to protect me are the same ones that are going to throw me under the bus," Iosi said with conviction.

I believed him. And this was all before Jorge Julio López, protected witness to crimes of the dictatorship, had disappeared. The government was supposed to be ensuring his safety, but he left his home on September 18, 2006 and was never seen again. He was on his way to the trial in which the former Director of Investigations of the Buenos Aires Police, José Etchecolatz, was being tried for genocide.

I communicated my unease in therapy, without giving any details, only mentioning "unpublished classified material" related to the AMIA bombing. My analyst, who worked as a government consultant in treatment for disaster victims, offered to put me in touch with President de la Rúa himself. And he was surprised when I responded that I didn't trust the president.

I continued to meet sporadically with Iosi, more for psychological support than anything else. I had no solution to offer him. I slowly earned his trust and he started to tell me some of the stories from his "Jewish" life. But he was less forthcoming with information about his work in intelligence. His was always reticent and became visibly distressed when he spoke of the activities he'd participated in and the "things," as yet undefined, that he'd seen and heard. His situation seemed dire, which is why he felt an uncontrollable urge to share his secrets. But only—he insisted—with extreme security measures. Something that no one could guarantee.

TRIAL

Meanwhile, the start of the trial for the attack on the AMIA Argentine Israelite Mutual Association was finally drawing near. Back then—and until fairly recently—the AMIA was led by an alliance of central leftist and mainly secular organizations. I had known the secretary general, Noé Davidovich, for years because he worked with the Israeli Socialist party Mapam—later absorbed by Meretz—and he'd also been part of the editorial team of *New Zion*. Davidovich had been a community organizer and in his spacious apartment in the Belgrano neighborhood he displayed, among many valuable paintings and historical photographs, a picture of himself with Juan Domingo Perón and a framed letter from the general, from February 1972, addressed to him, in which Perón assured him that "the National Justicialist Movement is against all forms of discrimination."

The president of the AMIA at the time, Hugo Ostrower, was a member of a Jewish organization, HaAvoda. I'd had a conversation with him, a little over a year prior, when I went to the AMIA to alert him to the fact that President Menem had threatened to take action against *New Zion*, the *Rio Negro* newspaper, and a small group of media outlets who had published articles on the so-called "Syrian lead" in the AMIA case and its connection to Menem's inner circle. After speaking with him for a while, I was shocked to learn that the president of the AMIA had no knowledge of the things I was telling him and knew almost nothing about the AMIA case.

After debating the importance of the matter, I asked him: "So do you know who denounced Claudio Lifschitz for revealing classified information?" Here, I was alluding to the former pro-secretary to Justice Galeano, who had accused the judge in charge of the AMIA case of illicit dealings and tampering with evidence.

"No, who?"

"You. The AMIA denounced him."

Lifschitz had been an intelligence agent with the Federal Police and after becoming a lawyer he'd joined Galeano's investigation. Federal Police General Commissioner Jorge "Fino" Palacios had wanted Lifschitz on the case, supposedly to help balance out contributions from the SIDE, the state intelligence services, which had a growing influence on the way the investigation was going. Lifschitz worked on the case between 1995 and 1997. There were many internal conflicts between the Federal Police and SIDE, between sectors of the SIDE itself, and with the Buenos Aires Police. The investigation had been contaminated due to mutual rivalry, but also to cover up the illicit business dealings of government organizations. They all felt mutual distrust of each other, afraid that their mafia-like activities would be exposed.

In 2000, Lifschitz caused a public scandal when he denounced numerous instances of cover up and destruction of evidence committed by Galeano's office, citing names and details, in a book with the explosive title, *AMIA: Why the Investigation Was Designed to Fail*. The book included photocopies, images, and transcripts proving that a $400,000 bribe had been paid to Carlos Telleldín in exchange for a false testimony that altered the course of the investigation. Lifschitz described how the Menem government, along with the Federal Police Intelligence Service and Justice Department employees, created a false narrative to explain the attack. And something more disquieting still: he showed that the SIDE had infiltrated the Iranian terrorist cell suspected of participating in the bombing months before it occurred, and that after the attack they hid this fact and destroyed all evidence of their investigation, including more than three thousand hours of recordings of Iranian agents. Lifschtz alleged that the SIDE had full knowledge that the attack would take place, and for some reason they did nothing to stop it, then later tried to cover it up. He requested to testify before the committee auditing the investigations into the bombings at the Israeli embassy and the AMIA. But the members of that committee—with the sole exception of then-senator Cristina Fernández de Kirchner—chose to minimize his claims and defend Justice Galeano. Nevertheless, Lifschitz's revelations, right before the upcoming trial, offered some hope that we would finally be able to begin unraveling the tangled web of impunity surrounding the AMIA attack. Now that the mishandling of the investigation had been publicly exposed, we could now, perhaps, finally uncover the true culprits of the massacre.

The lawyers for the DAIA and AMIA, however, refused to base their case around the facts that Lifschtz had brought to light, instead aligning themselves with the SIDE in an attempt to impede Lifschtz from speaking publicly and accusing him of spreading false information. The DAIA and AMIA, along with the SIDE, went as far as to bring criminal charges against Lifschitz, for violation of state secrets. In addition, Lifschitz, for years after, received constant threats and an attempt on his life, as he was portrayed alternatively as an ally and an enemy of the SIDE. In the end, the former intelligence agent was charged with violation of state secrets. Things did not look good for the desperate Iosi.

Ostrower, the head of the AMIA, seemed more worried about the Jewish mutual association's financial situation and how he would pay his staff than about the trial over the bombing and Lifschitz's revelations. The heavy financial burden he'd inherited from the previous administration was made worse by the country's deepening economic crisis, with services suspended and salaries unpaid, creating difficult circumstances. He seemed overwhelmed and very reluctant to take on the forces of power that had granted impunity to those responsible for the attacks.

SPOKESPERSON

I felt strongly that the AMIA needed to have its own voice in the trial for the bombing, and so, in 2001, I petitioned the president and secretary of the Jewish mutual association, in an extensive letter, to allow me to serve as observer and spokesperson during the trial. I urged them to consider the association's historic responsibility to the Jewish community and suggested a dramatic change in the direction of their public discourse. They agreed, and I began to more fully understand how difficult it was to question the official investigation, contaminated from day one.

A month before the preliminary hearings, I was authorized to participate as an observer during the trial. My hope was to correct the misguided course that the DAIA had taken on everything related to the case, or to at least allow the AMIA to take their own unique stance, as agreed upon by the president and secretary. The AMIA, at that time, unlike the DAIA, was composed basically of volunteers dedicated to social work such as assistance to the disabled, the poor, sick, Jewish retirement homes, cemeteries, the Jewish school system, and cultural activities. The staff was made up of mostly older employees, people with a simple, honest vision of the world and scarce or nonexistent political experience. Good people formed in the tradition of Argentine solidarity and the Jewish collective spirit, who knew how to start up a soup kitchen, job board, school, temple, or theater. But who couldn't or didn't want to understand politics or high treason. They were weeks away from being on center stage in the trial that was set to begin. But they had not asked for this attention and had no experience in the spotlight. So I, along with several others, was trying to carve out a path different to the one marked by DAIA, which, through its president Rubén Beraja, was linked to the shadowy maneuvers of the Menem government.

I hadn't forgotten about Iosi, and I held out hope the trial might cause some shift in the case and pave the way for the testimonies that had not yet been heard. A short while before I joined as an observer, the court had decided that the DAIA and the AMIA would be lumped together as one plaintiff in the case and Active Memory, the organization of families of victims of the bombing would represent a second plaintiff. This meant that AMIA and DAIA would have to share the same legal representation. There was a fierce debate within the AMIA, but it was finally decided not to appeal the court's decision, because that would've delayed the start of the trial by many months. It was also decided that the representatives of AMIA, DAIA, and Active Memory would occupy the same space in the courtroom and take turns asking questions.

It quickly became clear to me that the legal team representing DAIA and AMIA did not differentiate between the two entities at all. And that the lawyers were sticking to the official story handed down by Judge Galeano, which left out many witnesses—like Iosi—whose testimonies contradicted the false version of the attack. Galeano's drawn-out investigation ultimately determined that the attack had been committed using a van with a bomb inside and placed the blame on Carlos Telleldín. This was the son of an anti-Semitic police officer of Arabic descent who had been chief of Intelligence in Córdoba during the dictatorship. Telleldín ran a car theft ring and had supposedly turned the van over to some Buenos Aires police officers who answered to the corrupt commissioner Juan José Ribelli. A fragment of a van engine with its serial number intact was found one night among the rubble of the AMIA. But the discovery was made under very strange circumstances with no witnesses around. Telleldín was the last registered owner of that engine, which had been received as part of a burned vehicle in a chop-shop linked to the Federal police. According to the accusation, Telleldín had rebuilt and conditioned the van to bear the weight of several kilos of explosives. They brought in a man who was supposed to testify to having seen the chunk of motor belonging to the van among the rubble, but he broke down during his testimony and admitted that he hadn't seen anything. So then they scrambled to come up with a new witness so that the evidence wouldn't be thrown out. They found an Israeli military man who had acted as first responder and he confirmed the discovery of the motor. Tellingly, well before the piece of engine had been uncovered, the head of Protection of Constitutional Order (POC), Inspector Commissioner Carlos Castañeda—one of Iosi's superiors who was later charged with cover-up and destruction of evidence—had already drafted a memo to his subordinates in which he instructed them to search for the remains of a white van. This was on the very day of the tragedy, July 18, 1994, at 13:40 hours. Castañeda's initial report showed incredible foresight, stating that an ammonia explosive had been used for the attack "probably located inside a van similar to a Renault Trafic." Less than four hours after the attack, Castañeda was already leading the investigation towards a Trafic (although the official version maintains that the investigation focused on the Trafic five days later, after the chunk of motor was found among the rubble). Castañeda is the one who set up the initial investigation and his report also describes the scene of the attack, going into great detail about what the entrance had previously looked like, what kind of door the building had before the collapse as he "recalled." His report revealed that he knew the building very well "from memory." Here is Castañeda's depiction of those dramatic moments after the bombing:

> I recalled the building that had been standing on that spot minutes prior. It was an older building, of some sixty years old, five or six stories in height and occupying two lots, some sixteen yards wide, with a façade of black granite or marble and a central door of bronze with glass and another in front of it which limited access to the building. (There could have been a staircase leading downward, which could indicate the existence of a basement level.) We will need to procure greater precision, but I reference what I recall from memory to sketch an initial image of the building that no longer exists in its previous form, with no reference points left standing in the collapse.

An impeccable description and another example of the level of detailed information that the Federal Police had about the Jewish mutual society headquarters before the attack occurred. Meanwhile, the SIDE State Intelligence had already tapped Telledelín's phone, almost as if they knew ahead of time that they'd find the piece of engine that would implicate him amongst the rubble. But Inspector Commissioner Castañeda later "lost" sixty-six cassettes and the corresponding transcripts of the conversations between Telledlín, SIDE employees, and other government officials. And he failed to look into Alberto Kanoore Edul, a Syrian suspect from Menem's inner circle who was close to Mohsen Rabbani, Cultural Attaché of the Iranian embassy, and to Carlos Telleldín. It was the SIDE itself that provided the $400,000 bribe to Telleldín so that he would falsely blame the Buenos Aires Police under Ribelli of taking the van from him. The president of DAIA, Rubén Beraja, was fully aware of the bribe. According to the official version, the Renault Trafic had been turned over to members of an unspecified terrorist group "from the Middle East" which, under orders from Iran, had placed the bomb in the vehicle and crashed it into the front of the AMIA. The non-verified story of a suicide bomber from a faraway country had already been used without much success as an explanation for the attack on the Israeli embassy two years prior, when they insisted that the discovery of a toe in a neighboring apartment proved that the suicide bomber was a man of certain anthropomorphic characteristics and "accustomed to walking barefoot, as was common in certain regions of the Middle East." The claims did not hold up in court.

What is certain is that any evidence that went against that official version was left out of the case. Numerous eyewitnesses were only called for the first time years later (upon petition of other parties) to give their statement. Among them, two bus drivers affected by the shockwaves from the blast who were able to prove that, based on the location of the buses at the time, the supposed Renault Trafic would've had to make a series of risky maneuvers to pass them on narrow streets to reach the AMIA at the time the blast occurred. Or a survivor from a shop across the street from the AMIA, who was sitting inside looking out the glass storefront. These and other eyewitnesses to the exact moment of the explosion never saw any van. The neighbor who was looking out over her balcony waiting for her housekeeper to arrive did not see the Renault Trafic, nor did the employee of a business on the 700 block of Pasteur who had double parked his car and had his eyes peeled for a transit infraction van. None of the survivors, in fact had seen any van at all, but some of them admitted to being pressured to say that they had seen one.

THE ELEVATOR OPERATOR

The AMIA building had been undergoing a remodel. I still have in my possession one of the last faxes that left those offices on Friday July 15th 1994, an invitation to the inauguration of a new auditorium and assembly hall, scheduled for August 14th with an homage to Shmerke Kaczerginski, the famed Jewish writer and cultural activist who survived the Holocaust and died in an accident in Argentina. The assembly hall was never inaugurated, but from the ruins of the unfinished auditorium came an essential witness to the moments leading up to the tragedy: Luisa Miednik.

The lawyers for AMIA and DAIA, along with Justice Galeano, paid no attention to Luisa, the AMIA elevator operator who stated that, five or six minutes before the blast, she saw two men outside the building unloading numerous bags of construction material from a flatbed truck and piling them up beside the entrance. She entered the building right before the construction dumpster was dropped off. Miednick described the scene in great detail the day following the attack, after being rescued from among the rubble. Her statement reads that "she observed a light-colored truck parked right in front of the building, in front of the door." And goes on to state that normally "no cars parked there, only the vehicles that dropped off construction material for the building's renovation. The parked vehicle had a large quantity of bags with a name on them that she could not recall. Standing over the bags was a man, with an approximate age of thirty-five to thirty-seven years old, with dark blond hair cut straight across the back of his neck, light-skinned with a Slavic or Polish appearance, with an approximate height of around six feet, thin, wearing a light-colored shirt, unbuttoned, and dark pants." Years later, a videotape surfaced showing a man with similar traits, who some journalists were able to identify as a heavyweight SIDE agent, walking away from the area near the disaster instants after the collapse; these images were never shown to Miednick. The elevator operator went on to state that: "The person standing over the bags was handing them down to someone," who she only remembered as "darker" with a short, stocky stature. She added that it seemed strange to her that "they were loading and unloading at that precise spot." She was asked if there was another person in the cab of the vehicle, to which she responded that there was another man, whose appearance she could not recall. She mentioned the unloading of a large quantity of bags which—she would say in another instance—"were not dirty like bags of cement," but instead "very clean," and all the same, stacked up to the right of the entrance forming a pile of considerable height.

Miednik then entered the building, greeted the receptionist and the three security guards and "went to punch her time card at 9:49, greeted the telephone operator, rushed to the locker where she kept her work clothes, and went to the auditorium bathroom to change. She was interrupted by two construction workers seeking access to other bathrooms that were also under construction, which made her angry. "Immediately thereafter she goes to pick up her coat, hears a thud, everything goes black, she feels a rush of wind, the doors of the bathroom are ripped off, the explosion throws her up into the air, she falls like a parachute, she hears the workers' shouts, she has difficulty breathing, telling the workers that they should leave, they all hold hands," until they were finally rescued. The explosion occurred at 9:53 a.m., the clock stopped at precisely that instant.

What is certain is that no one knows who sent all those bags to be piled up in the entryway moments before the detonation. The Francisco and José Mazzotta S.A. building supply company, which had been providing the materials for the renovation project, did have a delivery scheduled for that day, but they had not yet sent it out, according to statements from the employees and delivery drivers for that company.

MYSTERIOUS FLIGHT

Another detail that is not included in the official explanation of the bombing is a very unusual helicopter flight over the roof of the AMIA the night before the attack, witnessed by several neighbors. María Josefa Vicente was in the bedroom of apartment 3F at 594 Pasteur, on the corner of Tucumán, across the street in diagonal from the AMIA building at 633 Pasteur. The night of Sunday the 17th was cold and María was in bed waiting for her husband, who was smoking a cigarette on the balcony after having watched the World Cup Final. Suddenly there was a loud noise and her husband called out to her: "María, come here, come here, they're about to land a helicopter on the roof of the AMIA!" They both watched, surprised, as the helicopter hovered over the AMIA building, in the middle of the city. A spotlight—not very powerful— shone down onto the roof. Somewhere around twenty neighbors heard and or witnessed the dramatic flight in the early hours of July 18th. But no investigation into the helicopter was made for many years and by then the flight registry had vanished. No one claimed responsibility for the suspicious helicopter, which proves that it was doing something they couldn't admit to.

The official investigation also considered it irrelevant that a construction dumpster was deposited—minutes before the explosion—in front of the AMIA. The person who delivered it worked for Nassib Haddad, an explosives expert born in the small Lebanese village where Mohamed Hussein Fadlallah, a founding member of Hezbollah, preached. The inexplicable absence of several federal officers who were meant to be guarding the building at that time was not considered relevant either.

My first meeting with the lawyers assigned to the AMIA case took place in lead attorney Juan José Avila's office some three weeks before the start of the trial. The rest of his team was present. After the requisite greetings, when the meeting finally began, he got straight to the point: "We're not interested in the drama within the community. That has to be set aside. We're working with the DA's office and with DAIA as a single team, we all get along, we all share our findings and we're all pulling in the same direction. And we want things to work the same way in the press. Seamlessly. That's why we have Ariel Sujarchuk, our PR consultant, handling all our communication. We want to maintain this system, which is working very well."

I explained to him that it would not be possible to continue business as usual because I would be stepping up as spokesperson for the AMIA and, I added, to the lawyers' frustration, that I aimed to create some distance between AMIA and DAIA, whose administration was compromised by its relationship to the corrupt Menem government. I put an end to the meeting so that I could call the president of the AMIA and clear up the "misunderstanding." All further contact was put on hold until the issue could be resolved.

On Sunday morning, an urgent meeting was called to clear up the situation before the hearings began the following week. In the meeting room of the rebuilt AMIA headquarters at 633 Pasteur, I met with President Ostrower, Secretary Davidovich, two vice presidents, and Avila, the lead lawyer for AMIA. Toward the end of the meeting the treasurer joined as well. During the tense exchange, I insisted that we had to point out the irregularities in the case as well as the coverup of the "Syrian lead." Avila responded that that wasn't what he'd been hired to do. And that the people who knew the case very well—previous attorney for the case Luis Dobniewski and his assistant Miguel Bronfman—had checked the investigation point by point, and they'd never found anything related to the "Syrian lead."

The differences couldn't be resolved, but the AMIA secretary general explained that, as spokesperson and observer, I was a free agent who did not respond to their lawyers. That's how, in the few months I was able to attend the hearings and draft statements from the AMIA about the case, I sought to change the direction of the discourse whenever I had the chance. But my behavior caused obvious discomfort and I did not last long in that role.

During that time, Iosi kept a prudent distance, perhaps wary of my seat near that stage populated by investigators, police officers, lawyers versed in lies, and intelligence agents still aligned with the agency, unrepentant of their actions. The attorneys for the Jewish institutions were not interested in pointing out the cover up of the investigation or the suspicious actions of the Federal Police. Iosi was living proof, however hidden, that the intelligence services were spying on Jewish institutions before the AMIA attack occurred. At the same time, the very Federal agents who had behaved so suspiciously before and after the attack were preparing to testify in the huge courtroom reserved especially for the case, called "the AMIA room." I didn't know, because he hadn't revealed this to me yet, but Iosi was a federal agent, like the ones testifying.

The hearings officially began, with great public interest, drawing hundreds of journalists from all over the country and abroad. The recent, brutal attack on the Twin Towers in New York City had caused 2,800 deaths, and the two attacks in Argentina, on the Israeli embassy and AMIA, were associated with this event that had shaken the entire world.

THE FIRST HEARING

There I was, that first day, September 24, 2001, seated near the president of the AMIA and some family members of the victims, behind thick glass with a view of the entire courtroom. At the back was the wide platform for the three judges, Gerardo Larrambere, Miguel Pons, and Guillermo Gordo. More toward the center, a model of the AMIA headquarters and the neighboring buildings. The microphone for the witnesses. A large screen. Set out in an enormous semicircle were the desks occupied by the many lawyers for the different parties, seats for the plaintiffs, international observers, and the twenty accused persons, mostly Buenos Aires police, with their defense attorneys. Among them, the star defendant: the chop-shop owner Carlos Telleldín who was accused of having received a van and conditioned it to be used as a car bomb. This same man had also received a handsome bribe. Near the plaintiffs sat the four District Attorneys: Eamon Mullen, José Barbaccia, Miguel Angel Romero, and Alberto Nisman. The first two would go on, some years later, to move from prosecutor to prosecuted, charged with having accepted Telleldín's purchased statement. I would later ask Nisman to protect Iosi's life, never imagining at the time that the prosecutor's death would divide a nation and dominate the front pages of all the major newspapers around the world.

That first day of the trial was deemed "historical." A large part of the hearing was taken up by the reading of the extensive charges. The president of the AMIA fell asleep in his seat, a scene captured by a photographer for *Clarín*, which captioned the image: "A long day for the AMIA president." The article went on to say: "The first day of the trial had stretches so tedious that the president of AMIA, Hugo Ostrower, had trouble paying attention at times. It had been a long day for Ostrower, who had met with Claudio Grossman, representative of the Inter-American Commission for Human Rights at 8:30 that morning in the Presidente Hotel. Ostrower let the head of the IACHR know that the AMIA did not support the findings of the official investigation led by Justice Juan José Galeano." These were the AMIA's first public statements of dissent.

I had participated in that morning's meeting with the representative of the IACHR and had taken it upon myself to leak the information. Grossman had a very critical view of the AMIA investigation, reflected in a devastating report published by the IACHR at the end of the trial. It coincided with the court's ruling that false evidence had been taken as fact and that some ninety percent of the arguments presented were invalid. But, that first day, the excitement over the start of the long-awaited trial did not impede Ostrower from nodding off, something impossible to hide, surrounded as he was by so many reporters.

The sessions began after midday, and sometimes ended well past 10:00 p.m., with one or more recesses. The first few weeks saw a parade of survivors and eyewitnesses: dramatic testimonies that reconstructed the tragedy minute by minute. Mundane occurrences frozen in memory such as the last image of a co-worker or family member. Scenes immediately before and after the blast. The boom, the collapse, the darkness, the gust of wind, the suffocating cloud of smoke, the toxic chemical smell. The screams, the blood, the stampede, the desperate search for survivors. The rescue effort. People who saw something or someone. People who were miraculously spared, because they'd changed their plans. Those who died because they had the misfortune of having gone that very day at that very time to that very place. The neighbors, passersby, the fear, the terror. The emergency responders, the hospital waiting rooms, and the long lists of wounded. And the lists of the dead. Those who didn't appear on any list, and never turned up. Survivors reliving an intense, raw pain, because they could've seen something that might help understand how it happened.

Soon the members of Iosi's agency, the Federal Police who were supposed to have been guarding the AMIA, would appear in court. The suspicious actions of the uniformed officers on duty that day would be scrutinized by the three justices of the Federal Oral Tribunal No.3, the district attorneys, and numerous other lawyers. Just like when the attack on the Israeli embassy occurred, two years prior to the AMIA bombing, the federal officers tasked with protecting the institution had suddenly disappeared. Between the two events, more than a dozen officers in total were miraculously called away moments before the explosions.

For those of us critical of the investigation, it was clear that the Menem government wanted to keep the Federal Police free of all charges and place the blame instead on the corrupt Buenos Aires Police, which fell under the jurisdiction of Menem's political rival Eduardo Duhalde. Some of those Buenos Aires police commissioners were true mafia bosses.

THE FEDS

The feds were finally called to testify, this time not in the cozy confines of Galeano's chambers but before numerous interrogators asking them to explain an endless list of gross irregularities committed before and after the attack. In an unprecedented move, the representatives and lawyers for the DAIA, instead of dedicating their time to preparing questions for this suspicious police behavior, decided to hold an assembly in honor of the Federal Police for their "contribution" to solving the attacks. They presented a medal to Commissioner Jorge "Fino" Palacios—the specialist in counter-terrorist investigations who held back the evidence that implicated Menem's Syrian friends—and other superiors in the institution suspected of perpetrating the massive cover up. Among them—I did not yet know this—one of Iosi's former bosses. The homage was attended by Justice Galeano himself and the celebration culminated in a toast, led by the president of DAIA. The shocking ceremony took place a week before the date set for the tense police testimonies, in an obvious display of support. By that time, the lawyers for AMIA and DAIA would not even entertain talk of any possible responsibility on the part of the feds.

I had already seen signs of this attitude when, weeks before the start of the trial, I coordinated a round table discussion at Tzavta (the Jewish community center that Iosi had infiltrated). Lawyers for AMIA and DAIA participated as panelists. For a moment, I set aside my role as coordinator and asked what they thought of the accusation that federal agents had enabled the attack.

"Don't you think we should look into the role of certain

people, such as Coronel Carlos Franke, former head of the General Directorate of Military Industries?" I asked, adding: "Franke, around the time of the bombing, was known to be involved in arms and explosive trafficking to the Balkans, and was implicated in the bombing of the Río Tercero Military Factory. He also provided the only alibi for Nassib Haddad, owner of the construction dumpster dropped off in front of the AMIA minutes before the explosion."

It was then that one of the lawyers for DAIA, Marta Nercellas, answered angrily: "By no means will I accuse a public servant of my nation of being complicit in international terrorism. That would be shifting the focus away from where it needs to be. We can't let ourselves get distracted by things that will only be used to challenge the investigation and help the guilty parties avoid charges."

Nercellas had been a lawyer for the Syrian Alfredo Nallib Yabrán, who hired military repressors from the time of the dictatorship and was in charge of "security" in the area around the airport. There, shipments came and went freely under the supervision of Syrian customs agent Ibrahim Al Ibrahim, something else that should've been investigated.

On another occasion, Avila, the AMIA lawyer, told me that it was naïve to think that in an international attack the terrorists would bother to warn the local police. He was saying that we wouldn't get anywhere following that lead, that we didn't even need to consider possible police involvement.

I knew, as well, that the lawyers for AMIA and DAIA jealously defended Justice Galeano's official investigation and that they had left out of their arguments any and all evidence that could place that fictitious narrative in doubt.

GLITCH

Meanwhile, I continued to meet with Iosi. But it was clear that the lawyers for AMIA and DAIA, with their friendly relationships to several of the people accused of cover up, would not be interested in what the spy had to say. After the DAIA's event in honor of the Federal Police, Chief Rubén Santos said to the press: "The DAIA's gesture clears the Federal Police's good name." With that statement, he seemed to be recognizing the dirty laundry that the DAIA had washed clean.

That toast was one of Santos's last public appearances, since, a month later, in December 2001, he would order the savage repression of street protests against the country's extreme economic crisis, which resulted in over thirty dead across the country. After the DAIA's homage to the Federal Police, I published a brief message on the AMIA's website. I titled it "DAIA's Handover." I was expressing the dissatisfaction felt by many members of the community, including some AMIA employees who had survived the attack and continued to work there.

After that message was posted, the section of the website dedicated to the AMIA case suffered a "glitch" and when it went back online the title of my article had been changed. Now it was "DAIA's Homage." I sent a written complaint to my superiors, explaining that the new title implied AMIA's support of DAIA's homage to the Federal Police, the very police who had failed to protect them. The administration said they would look into who had changed the content, but, of course, nothing came of it.

What happened after that led to my resignation. Luis Dobniewski, former lawyer for the AMIA—who had resigned after being accused of purchasing a home for the widow of narco-kingpin Pablo Escobar—spoke to the president of AMIA and offered to organize an informal committee to help with the case, based on what he considered to be "weaknesses or failures in communication."

After some private conversations, the AMIA president decided to follow Dobniewski's advice and they set up a committee presided over informally by Dobniewski himself, who laid out an argument supporting Galeano's initial explanation of events. Prominent jurists were invited to give their opinions, such as León Arslanian, Raúl Zaffaroni, and Ricardo Gil Lavedra. Their very presence lent the initiative an outstanding political and judicial weight. Dobniewski, along with the AMIA lawyers, emphatically urged support of Justice Galeano's official version, insisting that, otherwise, the case would collapse. The rest of those in attendance agreed, with varying degrees of enthusiasm. Overwhelmed by the situation, I remained silent.

The newly organized AMIA support team got to work in late March of 2002. In April of that year I handed in my resignation as spokesperson due to irreconcilable differences with the direction the case had taken. A short while later I learned that the very day of the "glitch" in the AMIA website, on November 22, 2001, Ostrower, president of AMIA, had been appointed to a position in the Buenos Aires city government. The De la Rúa administration seemed to want to ensure that the cover-up continued, going as far as to offer the head of the AMIA a cushy position. Argentina was in the midst of an imminent economic collapse and the last thing De la Rúa wanted at the end of 2001 was to wage war with the outgoing Menem administration, whose help would be needed if the government had any hope of making it to the end of its four-year term. It was no time to begin poking into the irregularities in the AMIA investigation or to raise the ire of the Federal Police and Menem's inner circle.

GARRÉ, OUT THE WINDOW

The existence of a pact between the De la Rúa government and the Menem administration, as well as the executive branch's interference in the AMIA case, justified by a need to protect "state secrets" had been brought to light in late 2001 when Nilda Garré, head of the Special Investigations Unit for the AMIA case, was attacked as soon as she showed that she would take her new role seriously. She had been assigned to the position by De la Rúa himself and, in her first report, she requested further investigation into the statements made by Witness "C," a former member of the Iranian Intelligence Services. She also planned to look into several leads that had been abandoned, and she asked to audit the SIDE's internal files. I was present when she handed in a copy of her report to the directors of AMIA.

Garré's initial report, as well as strong public statements she had made, inspired hope for the first time in many years. Garré had done an interview with Diego Rosemberg for *Tres Puntos* magazine entitled "Menem Administration Cover-up." Among other things, she pointed out the protection afforded to certain Syrian suspects close to Menem.

And let's not even get into what the SIDE was like under Hugo Anzorreguy; very inefficient, with two rival internal groups tampering with evidence to hurt each other. As a result of that, for example, sixty-six recordings of wire taps on Iranian fundamentalists simply disappeared. The Federal Police had copies of those tapes but they disappeared too. [. . .] Agendas, rolls of film disappeared . . . It's too much of a coincidence: the entire government apparatus worked toward obscuring the investigation and ensuring impunity for certain people.

The talking heads that parroted the official explanation of the AMIA bombing, ever-present in the mainstream media, had never said a word about these matters. And in the seven years that had passed since the AMIA attack, no public servant had ever outright mentioned a cover-up in public.

Garré was turning out to be a real problem, an especially inopportune annoyance. Because former president Carlos Menem had been charged with trafficking weapons to Croatia and Ecuador, which presented points of contact with the bombings that were never investigated. To top it off, President De la Rúa was, at that very moment, negotiating a "governability pact" with Menem's party, which would allow Menem to leave house arrest in the country home of his friend Armando Gostanián and walk free. This would be decided by a ruling of the Supreme Court presided over by Menem's former business partner Julio Nazareno. So President De la Rúa was not at all pleased to hear that the woman he'd placed in charge of supervising the AMIA case was talking about "a Menem administration cover up" at that precise moment.

So, the minister of justice and the president's brother, Jorge de la Rúa, began by asking Garré to "tone it down." But that wasn't enough, they had to get rid of her entirely. How to fire her and who would do it were the two main challenges. Because although the De la Rúa government was willing to sacrifice her to make amends with Menem's party, it had to be done very carefully since all eyes were on the Jewish community.

And so a plan was hatched to charge Nilda Garré with "violation of state secrets." Everyone had a part to play, starting with the prosecutors of the AMIA case, Eamon Mullen, José Barbaccia, and Alberto Nisman, who presented a one-page letter in which, with notable mistakes and an overuse of conditionals, they accused Garré of the aforementioned crime. But that wasn't enough. Since it was such a delicate matter, the president of the DAIA had to publicly demand Garré's head on a platter to justify her removal to the public. This was the same man who led the homage to the Federal Police. It was exactly as Avila, the AMIA lawyer, had said to me: "We're all on the same team and we're all pulling in the same direction."

CHARGING GARRÉ

The prosecution team's brief message denouncing Garré said that "Dr. Nilda Garré made public statements regarding a classified witness on the televised program *Punto Doc/2* in the months of July/August of the present year." Here, they were referring to Witness "C" but the prosecutors were in such a hurry to present their charges that they didn't even ask to see the footage and they couldn't even clearly state the month in which the program had aired.

In reality, what was classified was the identity of the "witness of classified identity," just as the name indicates. But it was not prohibited to mention the existence of the witness. The *Punto Doc/2* episode was aired as "AMIA.doc – Why Didn't Menem Investigate?" and at no time in the interview does Garré reveal the identity of Witness "C." The identity of Witness "C" and parts of their testimony had been published in some national media outlets more than a month prior to that interview with Garré, before she had been appointed head of the Special Investigations Unit for the case. And the information was already common knowledge among many journalists. It could even be found online.

The reporter Rolando Graña, co-host of *Punto Doc/2*, said on air:

> A few months ago on this program we broadcast the testimony of someone whom the AMIA case has dubbed Witness "C." This person was third in command of the Iranian Intelligence Service and his testimony, after deserting his agency, directly implicated former president Carlos Menem in the cover-up or mishandling of the investigation into the AMIA attack. The Witness "C" testimony that we broadcast caused conflict between the AMIA investigators; for example, one of the things that Witness "C" said was that Menem was more anti-Semitic than the Iranians, and that Iran got what it wanted, politically, which was to not see any charges or evidence against them. Menem also didn't want the Justice Department to know about his connection to Iran. The prosecutors of the AMIA case have now requested to bring charges against the leader of the Special Investigations Unit, Nilda Garré, a Justice

Department employee, because they say that she leaked the Witness "C" testimony to us. Guys, you're barking up the wrong tree, Ms. Garré didn't tell us anything. You know we have reliable information on the AMIA case. Justice Galeano tried to sue us when we reported Lifschitz's testimony on the mishandling of the case and when we revealed the SIDE coverup. The truth is that Witness "C" makes you uncomfortable because this testimony demonstrates that you didn't want to investigate Menem's involvement in the AMIA attack, which you should've looked into. But don't try to place blame where it doesn't belong, please.

Immediately thereafter, the president of DAIA and his public relations team picked up any microphone they could get their hands on to demand Nilda Garré step down, with headlines such as: "DAIA Demands Nilda Garré's Resignation." It was the top story, with the president calling Garré's actions "shameful and frustrating." Faced with the DAIA's forceful demands, media outlets reported that President De la Rúa was deciding whether to fire Nilda Garré. Hours later, Minister Jorge de la Rúa requested her resignation, which she handed in on October 5, 2001. "Accused of Revealing State Secrets, Head of the AMIA Case Fired," read a *Clarín* headline the following day, with a subtitle to clarify: "DAIA called for her removal."

The momentary hopes I'd had of finding support for Iosi in Garré were immediately dashed. With Garré relieved of her duties, they could now "tone things down" and seal the deal between De la Rúa and Menem. Photos published on December 14, 2001 showed an exultant Menem alongside the disoriented sitting president. This was reflected in

Clarín: "Menem made no effort to hide his joy at being back inside the Casa Rosada after five months under house arrest, accused of leading an illicit ring of weapons trafficking. [. . .] Just like at his height of power, Menem walked into the Rosada at 9:22 a.m. surrounded by a large entourage [. . .] Alejandro Tfeli (Menem's doctor) and his private secretary, Ramón Hernández accompanied him on his visit to the Casa Rosada."

Several members of Menem's entourage that day had been the target of criminal investigations, and the president's personal doctor, Alejandro Tfeli, had signed over temporary usage of a vacant lot on Constitución Street, which ended up being used by Kanoore Edul, Syrian businessman and friend of Menem. A suspicious dumpster was delivered to that vacant lot the morning of July 18, 1994, dropped off by the mining company owned by the Lebanese explosives expert Nassib Haddad. This was the same company that also left a dumpster outside the entrance to the AMIA, minutes before the blast occurred.

The *Clarín* article from December 14 concludes by pointing out that Menem "pledges help in passing the 2002 budget through Congress before the end of the year." Menem also criticized the mounting effort to push De la Rúa out of office. But it wasn't enough. One week later, on December 19 and 20, the streets of Buenos Aires were ablaze with riots that would lead De la Rúa to flee the Casa Rosada.

COURT ON TRAIL

With society seemingly breaking down, the AMIA case no longer occupied the center of political concerns as Argentina saw five provisional presidents assume power over the course of ten days. Finally, still in the midst of a full-blown economic crisis, Eduardo Duhalde was named president. He gave the order to initiate a trial against the Supreme Court, accusing it—among other charges—of being Menem's puppets and of mishandling of the non-investigation into the attack on the Israeli embassy in March 1992.

The committee leading the charges was headed by Elisa Carrió and Nilda Garré, both legislators. Their consultants asked for my help, *ad honorem*, to analyze the report on the Israeli embassy bombing, and I accepted, drafting a section of the charges. Beyond the infuriating inaction of the Supreme Court during the first five years of the "investigation," there were once again flashing neon signs pointing to the involvement of the Federal Police, the very agency that had sent Iosi to spy on the Jewish community and the embassy itself.

Going over the files, it was immediately obvious that the attack on the diplomatic seat had occurred in an area cleared of all police presence. The federal officers assigned to guard the building had left early, their replacements had never shown up, and another officer was called away under some other pretext. These men were first asked to give statements a year and a half after the events took place, and the startling contradictions between their dry, formal answers had not warranted further questioning at the time. One of them, by the time his testimony was taken, had a new job in security for the Supreme Court itself. No one was interested in digging deeper into that line of investigation, not even the State of Israel, which never presented itself as a plaintiff or offered up any evidence at all.

Julio Nazareno, member of the Supreme Court, produced in his defense a letter of recognition from the Israeli embassy in appreciation of his efforts. It was clear that Israel did not want to share what it knew, in order to keep from implicating the Menem government, with which it had built a solid relationship. The Mossad Israeli Intelligence Service received orders to close the investigation, and not because the Mossad trusted the Argentine security forces. Shabtai Shavit, head of Mossad at the time of the attacks, said to journalist Jana Beris, in an interview published March 5, 2015 in the *La Nación* newspaper:

> President Carlos Menem was Syrian first and Argentine second. A large part of government work was carried out in Arabic. It's true that Menem came to visit Israel, he was very friendly and presented himself as a great ally to the country. But that was only for the media. [. . .] It's possible that elements within the police or security services aided, whether directly or indirectly, the people who planned and carried out the attacks.

If the top leader of the respected Israeli Intelligence service considered it likely that local police and other government officials in Argentina had helped carry out the attack, it's inexplicable that local investigators refused to look into the gross lack of police presence during the two attacks, and how not even the Israeli embassy nor AMIA ever demanded any investigation into it. The role that local security forces may have played in the bombings remains unexplored, protected as state secrets. Secrets that several states wish to keep quiet. They would prefer for people such as Iosi to remain in the shadows forever. Or worse.

ISRAEL'S ROLE

In his book *Mossad: A Secret* History, the investigative journalist Gordon Thomas makes reference to the Israeli intelligence agency's reaction to the bombing of the Israeli embassy in Argentina. A team was sent to Buenos Aires to inspect the evidence related to the attack and they turned in very critical reports to the head of the Mossad (the same guy who spoke to *La Nación* about it). They mentioned superficially cordial relationships with the Argentine investigators but alluded to their shocking ineptitude. They cited examples of important forensic evidence being removed before an adequate investigation could be completed, such as rubble from the destroyed embassy. Later he would say that a true investigation was not initiated until six years after the explosion, something I verified in the trial against the Supreme Court in 2002. Thomas also states that the Mossad team discovered close ties between Menem and members of terrorist groups within the Syrian community of Argentina.

Weeks after the 1992 attack, the then-ambassador to Israel in Argentina, Itzhak Shefi, began to cast doubt on the explanations that pointed unilaterally to Iran and unidentified terrorists who had disappeared into thin air. Shefi informed Tel Aviv that—unlike what was publicly reported—on the day of the explosion, the two security guards who were normally posted outside the embassy were absent. One of them had been previously employed for six years at the Syrian embassy. In the documentary *Third on the Way* by the journalist Shlomo Slutzky, an irritated Shefi points out the ridiculousness of the justification for the total absence of police presence. It had been said that the guards were escorting him that day, when, in reality, this was not the only police detail to disappear from its assigned post at the diplomatic headquarters immediately before the attack. An Officer Ojeda left his post outside the Israeli embassy at 2:15 p.m. on March 17, 1992 without waiting for his replacement to arrive, as he should have, according to protocol. His relief, an Officer Chiocchio did not show up at 2:00 as he was scheduled to, and had not yet arrived forty-seven minutes later when the explosion occurred. The officers of the Precinct 15 mobile unit, Soto, Acha, and Laciar all failed to fulfill their duties that day as well. They had the obligation to cover any lapse in personnel, but instead they all quickly left the embassy. The crime they claimed to have been called away to help with was a real event, but it had occurred at another time that day.

The Mossad team, Gordon Thomas writes, discovered that First Lady Zulema Menem hailed from the small village of Yabrud, in Syria. Monzer Al Kassar, a figure well-known to the Mossad as a veteran trafficker of weapons and drugs whose friends included Oliver North and Abu Nidal, dubbed "the grand master of global terrorism," was also from this same village.

Thomas writes that, in Buenos Aires, Ambassador Shefi had shown himself to be disdainful of President Menem for clinging to the crazy notion that a neo-Nazi group had carried out the attack. He also accused Argentine investigators of dragging their feet. He believed that Iran was behind the bombing but that Syria was implicated as well, and he tacitly insinuated that President Menem should answer some questions. Menem raised a complaint with prime minister of Israel Shimon Peres and Shefi was then called back home, replaced by Itzhak Aviran, who, according to Thomas, was a cautious career diplomat known for not rocking the boat. Aviran immediately set about trying to calm the fears of the Jewish community in Argentina and pacify Menem and his advisors.

Thomas also states that, two years later, when the attack on the AMIA occurred, the Mossad group that had been dissolved after closing the case of the bombing of the Israeli embassy was sent back to Buenos Aires to sift through the rubble with dogs trained for these types of circumstances. Just like before, the Mossad came and went without turning up any useful evidence. In private, members of the team expressed their doubts that anyone would ever be specifically accused of either attack due to the obstructions caused by the ineptitude of the local officers. When, a short while later, there was a change in leadership at the Mossad and the new chief, Danny Yatom, took over, superior officers asked for the two cases to be reopened. But the pragmatic political powers responded that Syria was not their priority target at the time, that position was occupied by Saddam Hussein. And that reopening an investigation which could very well unearth unpleasant connections between the Argentine president and the land of his forefathers was no longer a viable option. During the years that followed, Menem had continued to play the role of honest mediator between Syria and Israel and it was important that he continue to do so. Yatom was informed that the files for both attacks would remain closed, Thomas says. And they did.

Back to mid-2002, amidst the political chaos of the time, Duhalde ordered a halt to the case against the Supreme Court (which would be reopened later, for other reasons, by Néstor Kirchner), but those of us who had read the reports had seen our worst assumptions proven: a flat-out refusal to investigate any evidence that implicated the government or the Federal Police.

It was an inopportune moment to try to bring Iosi's secrets to light, but we continued to meet. In one of those meetings he announced his intention to contact a Channel 13 journalist who was very committed to human rights causes. She was a member of *Telenoche Investiga*, the most prestigious investigative journalism program on TV at the time: Miriam Lewin. I did not know her personally, but I respected and admired her work. The thought of Iosi sharing his story with her lessened to some degree the heavy burden of responsibility that I felt. I also held out hope that Miriam could perhaps open more doors for him than I had been able to. I fully supported the spy's decision.

PART III

I'm Miriam Lewin, journalist. I don't have any other title although I have passed myself off as other persons, for work, in order to unmask criminals, expose corruption. And, of course, I used other identities as an activist during the dictatorship, in that time of so much secrecy. But I'm not sure why Iosi chose me, out of so many people, to share his story.

Sitting at a Formica table in a coffee shop with dirty windows, I met Iosi for the first time. It had not been easy to get to that point. I had been very busy, in the final stretch of what would probably be the most difficult investigation of my career: working meticulously to expose a priest with an impeccable public image who was also a child abuser.

For weeks my email inbox had received insistent messages from an anonymous person who claimed to have information that could solve the AMIA attack. "Of course you do," I thought when I read the first message. Another crazy person looking for notoriety. A pathological liar like so many others who'd contacted me repeatedly for years. After several attempts to put off the meeting with the mysterious author of the emails, one afternoon, I broke down and agreed.

Before leaving work, I went into my boss's office and shut the door. "I'm going to meet with someone I don't know. They claim to have information about the AMIA attack."

He smiled.

"Yeah, I know. Another lunatic. But I have nothing to lose by meeting with him for a little while. We're going to the coffee shop at Humberto Primo and Salta. If I'm not back in two hours, send somebody to look for me."

"Do you want me to send someone with you, to sit at another table and keep an eye out, just in case?" he asked.

"No, I don't think that's necessary," I answered, although I wasn't so sure.

This was August of 2002. Kids huffing glue, cardboard collectors, dilapidated boarding houses crowded with families that would soon run out of money to pay for a room, drifters with lost looks in their eyes: the three blocks I had to walk through Constitución to get to the meeting looked like the trailer for a movie about the December 2001 economic collapse. I walked quickly, gripping my cell phone and purse.

My eyes took a few seconds to adjust to the dimness of the coffee shop. At the end of a narrow room, facing the door but with the light behind him, was a young man with a thin frame. I gradually made out his face. He had dark, wavy hair. The table he had chosen was for four people. On the chair beside him was a backpack, facing the door. I immediately feared that he might be filming me with a hidden camera, something my own team did for the majority of our investigations, allowing us to get evidence that would be otherwise impossible to obtain. "I won't let the hunter become the prey.

I'm not going to open my mouth more than absolutely necessary," I thought to myself.

The stranger said something I didn't catch and it took me a second to realize he was speaking in Hebrew.

"I don't understand," I said.

"But aren't you Jewish?"

"Yes, but I don't speak Hebrew. My grandmothers spoke Yiddish, and I understand a little, the basics."

He seemed annoyed. If I had understood him, the entire conversation would probably have taken place in Hebrew, which the stranger seemed to speak perfectly. But no. In Spanish, in a low voice—so low that I had to strain my ears to hear him—he began to tell me an absolutely incredible story.

A SURPRISING STORY

Iosi told me that he was an intelligence agent for the Federal Police. It was not the first time I'd sat down with an agent for journalistic purposes, but I felt a shiver run down my spine.

He continued speaking. For many years, he said, he had been undercover in the Jewish community. At first he'd just been following orders, but over time he became one of them, a youth organizer, a full-fledged member of the collective.

"Why did they assign you there? What was the reason behind it?"

"They wanted to keep an eye on them, they suspected a conspiracy."

It sounded ridiculous, antiquated. "And did you . . . believe it?"

"Yes, at first I did. Later on I started to realize that what I was looking for didn't exist. But it was too late by that point," his monotonous voice became shaky, he was trembling. "I can't sleep," he said. "I'm so anxious. I can't stop thinking. I expected it to get easier over time, but I'm tortured by guilt. It's getting worse."

"Why?" I asked.

"Because I think that, without knowing it, I might have contributed to the attacks."

I stared at him for a second then glanced to the suspicious backpack. When I looked back at him, I realized he was crying.

At a table in the back, a regular was sipping a gin. The coffee I'd ordered from the waiter as I walked in, to keep him away, was growing cold. I was disconcerted, uncomfortable. I didn't feel any sympathy for this man confessing before me. I didn't understand why he'd chosen me.

"I know who you are," he said. And I didn't know whether to take it as a threat, coming from him, even though he seemed so vulnerable. "There aren't many people I can talk to about this. I looked into you. I think you're honest, that I can trust you."

I remembered back to the morning of July 18th, eight years prior, the day of the AMIA attack. I was leaving my home when I received a message with instructions from the producer of the TV news show where I worked as a reporter. He told me to go as quickly as I could to 600 Pasteur, where an explosion had been reported. Two years prior, preparing to start my first job as a journalist, I was trying on a skirt in a shop on Santa Fe around July 9th when everything shook like there'd been an earthquake. The windows rattled. The shop assistant and I both rushed to the door. Two girls in private school uniforms were running past on the sidewalk, hugging each other, bloody, bathed in tears. The Israeli embassy had been blown up, a few blocks away. I reported my first story in front of the police barricades as dead bodies were removed.

The day of the AMIA attack, the taxi couldn't make it to Pasteur; the street was blocked. I got out and ran without anyone trying to stop me and I stood in front of the scene of the disaster. I had been there several times, most recently to file the paperwork for the burial of a family member in La Tablada Cemetery. The building was now reduced to a mountain of rubble with a few people climbing it, shouting. Others called for silence, in order to hear the calls for help that could come from beneath the mound of concrete. I was paralyzed, holding my breath. I inhaled the dust floating on the air. The ground was covered in broken glass, twisted metal.

Around me, broken, mutilated bodies were being hauled away. There weren't enough ambulances for everyone. In any case, there was nothing left to be done for some of them. I found it impossible to tear my eyes from the pile of bricks, thinking about the people buried beneath all that horror, suffocating. Again, again, was the word that repeated over and over in my mind.

My camera crew arrived and we somehow managed to report the story. It was a long day, endless. I spent the next night on the terrace of a building across the street, with a group of colleagues, trying to capture images of the relentless rescue effort.

In front of me, now, reduced to ruins, was someone who could be key to determining who had truly been responsible for all that death and destruction.

REGRETS

"After what happened at the embassy I started to have doubts," Iosi said in that first meeting. "But after the AMIA I couldn't take it anymore. I started thinking about the fact that so many of my friends and colleagues could have been there, the people I'd met in all that time. Even the girl I was in love with, a Jewish girl, my wife."

He was too upset to speak. It didn't make sense to try to press him. He was struggling with his emotions but he was clearly unable to control them.

"I tried talking to other people, even my wife's brother, who was a journalist. But no one will help me, they've all turned their backs on me. They won't listen to me, and I can't do it on my own anymore."

It was a desperate plea. But sincere.

"Did you consider making a statement, reporting what you know?"

"Yes, of course, but here, in Argentina? To who? I can't testify here, they don't want to know the truth. It's a circus."

I couldn't argue with that.

"Also, if I talk here, they'll kill me," he whispered.

"Who, the terrorists?"

"No, the feds. They'll crush me."

My mind began to race. What if they'd followed him here? What if they found out he'd met with a reporter from an investigative news program? That he'd revealed the scandalous secrets of those in power? There was no reason to drag out that meeting any longer. It was clear that he wasn't going to tell me anything more. Maybe he didn't want to, maybe he was gauging my reaction. But most likely he couldn't go on without breaking down. It wasn't worth it to go on sitting there, putting him at risk, putting myself at risk.

We established a method for future meetings. We would speak, but never give all the details at once. If we communicated the day and time, the place would have been agreed upon previously, or the other way around. Going forward, Iosi always initiated contact. It wasn't until much later that I had any way of contacting him. His calls were always a surprise, sometimes weekly, sometimes more spaced out.

LOCKBOX

We met many times. In the conference room of a downtown hotel, in a hotel room in the Belgrano neighborhood, at gas stations, in countless cafés. The locations almost never repeated.

After several interviews in which, after an hour of conversation, I managed to pry some details from him, I realized that the spy was like a lockbox that I didn't have the key to open. He could be guarding something very valuable inside or it could just be a bunch of worthless newspaper clippings. These meetings could all be a monumental waste of time, but I wouldn't know unless I arranged the conditions that he demanded before opening up.

How could I know that what he was telling me was true? How could I verify that he'd really been a member of the Jewish institutions, the Zionist youth groups that he claimed to have infiltrated? Had he truly fallen in love with a young Hebrew teacher and married her without his bosses finding out? It sounded improbable. When he talked about that relationship he always got choked up. And was it true, as he told me, that there was backlash when he stopped being the model intelligence agent, when he could no longer achieve the most impossible tasks, when he began to hold back information about the "targets" he'd grown fond of?

"I realized that everything they'd told me about the community was a lie. I met good people, our connections were sincere. I found no evidence of what the bosses had filled my head with. There were no conspiracies, no threats, nothing. Just the opposite. I thought my head would explode. When I fell in love with Eli there was no turning back. They became my world, not the other, previous one," he told me.

NAZI HUNTER

I had to find a way to create the conditions under which Iosi could share his story. His real name was José Alberto Pérez, he told me, and he'd presented himself to the community as a product of a mixed marriage who was looking to connect with his Jewish roots. The first thing I thought was to put him in touch with some Jewish organization that had ties beyond Argentina, some prestigious, influential institution sensitive to anti-Semitism, interested in solving the AMIA case.

The Simon Wiesenthal Center, I thought, met the criteria. Its founder had survived two concentration camps and had dedicated his life to the persecution of Nazi criminals the world over. I had no doubt that the local delegation of the Center would be interested in Iosi's story. I knew the director, Sergio

Widder, who I'd been in contact with through my work and who had gone to the same high school as me. Sergio had spoken publicly about neo-Nazi activity in groups with ties to leaders of the military coup. The Center sent out communications on every occurrence that they considered a threat to the Jewish community in Argentina, from robberies to the destruction of tombstones or any other anti-Semitic aggression. Of course, the organization was among those calling for justice for the attacks. I called him and asked him to meet with me.

I went to his office and, after listening to me in silence, Sergio seemed upset. He turned pale and his huge eyes went even wider. I was requesting financial support to get Iosi out of the country so he could make a statement. It seemed logical to me that the center led by the greatest Nazi hunter in all of history, with delegations in America and Europe, was in a unique position to offer such support. But that's not what happened. Sergio made it clear that they did not have the resources, that what I was telling him sounded serious, but that he recommended I contact one of the lawyers for Active Memory, the organization of victims and family of the AMIA attack, whose members were more combative when it came to demanding truth and justice from the government. That was all the help he could offer.

THE COMBATIVE LAWYER

Active Memory was a non-profit organization set up to bring to justice those responsible for the AMIA attack. Every Monday, without fail, they held a public event outside the courthouse on Plaza Lavalle. They started out by blowing a shofar, which made a dull, deafening roar. After that, there was always a guest speaker. Journalists, intellectuals, and artists lent their voices to the demand for a continued commitment to justice for the AMIA bombing.

Iosi might be the link that could help them achieve their goal. They'd surely want to meet him, talk to him, help him obtain the conditions under which he could share his information. Or maybe not. Maybe, and not without reason, they'd be distrusting of him. They might consider him a murderer, an enemy, a terrorist trained to lie to them. They might think he was offering information solely to distance himself from the other criminals who, like him, had aided the attack, in order to obtain immunity for himself. Was Iosi truly remorseful? I still didn't know. In truth, I couldn't even be sure he wasn't lying to me . . .

Pablo Jacoby, the person I chose to contact, was a lawyer for Active Memory and represented the organization in the public trial for the AMIA attacks. He was also a lawyer for some newspapers and other publications, among them *Página/12*, in matters dealing with freedom of expression. He and I had been in touch for years and I knew that he was quick, efficient, and he could recognize an opportunity when he saw one. Also—and this was the most important thing—he was the lead lawyer for the plaintiffs outside the DAIA–AMIA monolith, whose legal team was upholding Justice Galeano's ruling. Jacoby and his partner, Alberto Zuppi, had publicly stated that they weren't afraid their case would fail in court. And I was offering them a contact that could bring them closer to the truth.

Jacoby was in the process of moving to his own offices, bigger and more modern, in front of Plaza San Martín. He listened to everything I had to say about the strange informant. He thought for a moment. He crossed his legs and drummed his fingers on the desk. "But how can you be sure that he knows something that will really lead to solving the attacks?"

"I can't be sure, but I believe he knows a lot more than he's saying. What he's told me is just the tip of the iceberg. If we meet his conditions, this could pave the way to identifying a local connection, Pablo. He knows every officer who wasn't at their post, what duty each of them had. He reported floorplans and schedules to Federal Intelligence; he told them what degree of protection each building had. But he was also undercover for years in the Jewish collective by orders from above. That means that the state was spying on us. This was after the end of the dictatorship, under democratic rule. There are Nazi sympathizers running the institutions that are supposed to protect us, and this proves it. It has to be exposed."

Jacoby shrugged his shoulders. "It doesn't seem that important to me. Seriously. It happens in every country."

I sat there in bewildered silence. The meeting had ended. Jacoby was already standing up to show me to the door. "Do me a favor, convince him to testify in the trial."

"What about his safety concerns?"

"That's why we offer immunity for informants . . . but we can't promise him anything."

But testifying in Argentina, the way things were at the moment, was not an option for Iosi. We didn't even know whether he might be arrested if he confessed to having provided information that was used by the terrorists' local partners. In the next meeting, I'd have to tell him that I'd failed in my second attempt to secure support for him. We were back at square one.

I didn't know where to turn. The meetings with Iosi

occurred in random places, with him establishing the frequency and the necessary security measures. He changed his appearance. Sometimes, he turned up with his head almost shaved bald. Other times, with a beard, wearing glasses, with longer sideburns than usual, with a moustache, with his hair dyed. He always carried a briefcase or a backpack containing documents that proved he'd been part of different organizations within the community, while, in parallel, he was receiving a salary from the Federal Police. Reports, invitations, letters. He almost always talked about Eli, his ex-wife, and his desire to see her again. He would get his hopes up with the most minimal gesture, such as a brief online chat that he initiated and she found any excuse to end.

HORACIO, CONFIRMATION

Iosi shared his information in small doses and only sporadically answered my questions. I still had deep doubts. I had no way of confirming anything he'd said. The documents he showed me could have been falsified. The credentials, reports, pay stubs. He had the resources to do it. I didn't understand what his motive could've been, but that didn't mean that it wasn't all a perverse lie. Until one day he said he wanted me to meet someone. It was a person he had chosen to speak to, like me, because he trusted him. That's how I met Horacio Lutzky.

Horacio was able to verify that what Iosi had told me was true. I was more trusting after that, and, at the same time, more committed to helping Iosi. I no longer had reservations, I could be certain that, at the very least, Iosi had accessed intimate parts of the Jewish community; this part of his story, at least, was not made up.

In that first meeting with Horacio, when Iosi got up to go to the bathroom and left us alone for a few minutes, we shared similar contradictory feelings, the same sense of initial disbelief and subsequent helplessness. Horacio and I began to evaluate, together, what the next steps should be. We hoped it would not be another misstep.

THE FIRST LADY

The political landscape had changed dramatically in a short period. In May of 2003, Néstor Kirchner, former governor of the Santa Cruz province, had been elected president. His wife Cristina Fernández was a bold senator who had been part of the committee that audited the investigation into the attacks and had challenged Justice Galeano's actions in the AMIA case on more than one occasion.

Horacio proposed a simple plan. We had to request a meeting with Nilda Garré. Horacio knew her and was confident in her commitment to justice, and, in addition, she had a direct line to the First Lady. No one better than Nilda Garré to hear Iosi's story.

We met with her and explained everything. Before we could even ask to be put in touch with Cristina, she'd already offered to do it. We called the First Lady's office to request an audience and it was immediately granted. After walking the mosaic-tiled hallways of the Senate, Horacio and I waited for Cristina Kirchner in her wood-paneled office. We were exultant. We couldn't possibly get any higher in the pyramid of political power and we believed that we'd reached the end of our small odyssey. If Néstor Kirchner had authorized SIDE agents to testify in courts almost immediately after assuming the presidency, his wife was going to have the power to get what we needed, what Iosi needed, what the AMIA case needed to uncover the local connection, perhaps even the perpetrators of the attack themselves.

She didn't keep us waiting long and we told her the whole story, without leaving anything out. Just like Garré, she was angered by the news of the infiltration and felt especially moved by the love story between the spy and a Jewish girl.

"Incredible," she said over and over. "Like something out of a movie."

Cristina was fully aware of the risk this man was facing. She offered to protect him, even, she said, to place him under her custody. "I have a guy from the feds who made a very serious accusation. An excellent guy. And as long as he's with me no one is going to touch him." She asked us for a few days to make some calls. We left, walking on air.

Horacio went on his own to the second meeting, because a last-minute story kept me at the station. "He can testify here, and we'll protect him," Cristina said. "He can talk to Prosecutor Nisman. We've given Nisman everything he needs to work on the case, so he can go all in." It was real, the government had finally made the decision to spare no resources, whether human or financial, to solve the attacks. Iosi heard the First Lady's response, but he refused to testify in Argentina, much less before Nisman, who he did not trust at all. So we returned to hear Cristina's counter offer. Her proposition was totally unexpected: "Go and see Jamie Stiuso. That man knows more about the AMIA case than anyone."

STISUO, THE LEGENDARY SPY

We left the First Lady's office confused. Jaime Stiuso had a terrible reputation. He was the director of counterintelligence for the SIDE, the state intelligence service, a shadowy figure, and word had it that he'd weathered every government since 1972 because he had dirt on politicians, government employees, and journalists. This was how he had built his power, how he maintained it. Iosi had told us in passing that Stiuso was also enemy number one of the Federal Intelligence, although he also mentioned historical connections between the two institutions.

We were standing in the plaza outside Congress trying to work out the First Lady's reasoning, when Horacio's phone rang. It was Stiuso himself. He was calling on the recommendation of Mrs. Kirchner, he said. Not fifteen minutes had gone by since we'd left her office. Stiuso wanted to see us as soon as possible, at the SIDE headquarters. Horacio insisted on a few conditions. He explained that, as journalists, it was risky for us to visit the SIDE offices and so we couldn't leave any record of our names when we entered. I think Stiuso laughed.

We were faced with a conundrum. We couldn't refuse to go. On the one hand, we'd been put in touch with him by the First Lady, who had given us more than enough proof of her commitment to solving the AMIA case. Who knew, maybe this was the first step she needed us to take for some reason, so that later, she would be able to save Iosi once and for all and enable him to testify safely. On the other hand, we couldn't go to the meeting without notifying our guy, without asking him how far we could trust Stiuso and what information we needed to hide. Or more like, what we wouldn't be able to hide, because Stiuso already knew it.

We met with Iosi at a pizza place on Rivadavia and Larrea, in Once. We sat at a table in the middle of the room, far from the windows. All of a sudden three men barged loudly into the restaurant, as if they deliberately wanted to draw attention to themselves. They looked like caricatures of intelligence agents, wearing sunglasses, jackets. One of them took a seat and the other two sat down at another table. They spoke loudly, making forced comments about a soccer match playing on TV, waving their arms around like windmills and openly staring at us.

Iosi gave us instructions: "Stand up like you're going to the bathroom," he said to Horacio. "Go to the cash register to pay (it was hidden behind a column) and when you get back, we'll get up and leave quickly."

Horacio didn't argue. When he reappeared, we left as fast as we could. On Larrea, farther down the block, was a bar, long, dark, and narrow. We rushed inside and sat down at the back, where a rodent was startled by our arrival. A few seconds later, we saw the caricatures outside, disoriented, looking for us. They walked right by. We'd lost them. Had it been a warning from Stiuso? Was the men's extreme clumsiness, like the Three Stooges, deliberate? What was the message?

That episode made Horacio and I feel even more uneasy about our visit to the SIDE headquarters. We rang the buzzer, the door opened for us, and we announced ourselves at the front desk. The space was dimly lit. As agreed, they did not record our names. It was a naïve precaution. I was paranoid that we were going to be filmed, which I warned Horacio.

Stiuso was waiting for us in an office on a top floor, wallpapered and with dim lighting like the rest of the rooms. He was a man of around fifty, with a startling resemblance to a famous actor from the seventies, Rodolfo Bebán. All over the desk and even on the floor, were piles of papers. Through a half-open door that led to another office, we could see more stacks of file folders.

"We have copies of the entire case," he said.

I don't think he said too much. We didn't either. We told him we were in preliminary talks with a member of a security agency, without specifying which one, who claimed to have valuable information on the attack, but that there was nothing concrete yet. That we would get in touch if anything credible turned up. Stiuso surely had all the information that we didn't want to share and more —he wouldn't have called us in if he didn't—but he showed nothing. We stood up, said goodbye, and walked back down the street, deserted at that time of day, mulling over what had been one of the most bizarre situations we'd experienced in our lives. Suddenly, Horacio stopped dead and patted his chest with his hand.

"I have to go pick up my daughter from a birthday party and I can't find the piece of paper with the address. I think I left it in Stiuso's office!"

I tried to calm him . . . there was nothing to worry about.

"No, nothing to worry about," Horacio said. "I don't know where my daughter is and I left the address with the most sinister figure in Argentina, who we just tried to lie to like he was some preschooler. I have nothing to worry about."

We started laughing hysterically. We agreed to give ourselves some time to process everything. We'd tried to find a solution through respected members of the Jewish community. Then, we'd tried the political route, seeking out people committed to solving the AMIA case. But that had only led us to another dead end.

A FOREIGN DOCUMENTARY

Out of the blue, one of us had an idea that seemed to be the perfect solution. In order to avoid the prejudices that Argentine readers and listeners might have about Iosi, we had to bypass the local media. Solving the case of the AMIA attack could be of interest to an international audience. The story of an undercover spy infiltrating a Jewish community that had been the target of not one but two attacks, blending in perfectly and betrayed by his own emotions. It was exceptional raw material for a documentary, even for a fictionalized version of events in a feature length film. Maybe we could get some producer interested in the idea. The key was to break free of the local media cycle and also obtain funds for Iosi to settle in some remote foreign city, safe from any possible revenge. We didn't need much money, just enough to support him someplace where the cost of living wasn't too high for six months or so until he got a job or maybe started up some modest business. We met with Iosi and proposed the idea. He agreed, and even gave us ideas to pitch.

"I'm Eli Cohen in reverse," he said, referring to the Israeli spy who, from Argentina, had infiltrated the top levels of Syrian power in the seventies.

"Let's hope your story has a happier ending," Horacio said, since Cohen had been discovered, tried, and hung in Damascus.

We decided to pitch the idea to a production company I'd been working with since I'd left Channel 13, almost three years prior. I'd always thought that Iosi and his incredible story would make a good investigation for my former show, which had run my most important journalistic investigations, but it had been impossible, the timing wasn't right.

Now I would try my current employers, a smaller production company who'd had some success in Argentina but—of more interest to us—also abroad, in markets that rarely consumed content from Argentina. One of the bosses was a Jewish man, very intelligent, informed, and skilled in business. We met with him at his office, in an ultramodern building in Belgrano. We summarized our proposal, and he was very enthusiastic about the possibilities the idea presented. We had no less than a fantastic story on our hands, he said, a goldmine for someone who knew how to handle it correctly, but the project also had prestige: it could, quite possibly, finally provide the missing needed link to solve the bombings.

We agreed to meet again to round out the negotiations. Many days went by . . . too many. Just when we couldn't bear the wait any longer, we received an e-mail with a contract that was impossible to sign. It seemed like it had been drafted in such a way that we'd be forced to reject it, so that they wouldn't have to be the ones to pull the plug on the project. One of the main obstacles was that Iosi would only begin to receive payment once the company had recovered everything it had invested, down to the last cent. That meant that he wouldn't be able to get out of harm's way until well after the film was released. And if it turned out to be a flop, after having exposed himself, revealing the most intimate details of his life, cutting off his only source of economic support, his Federal Police salary, he wouldn't see a single peso.

CHILDHOOD FRIENDS

In spite of this new disappointment, our meetings continued. Iosi had told me that he reported to his bosses about his meetings with me because I was a recognizable figure and he had to get out in front of any hint of suspicion. It would be dangerous for them to find out that he was meeting with a journalist. So he made up a story about us being childhood friends from a country club I went to with my family called Comunicaciones. His concern seemed valid even if the story didn't sound entirely believable. All I could do was trust him to find a way to keep from further weakening his already vulnerable position within the force.

Iosi was assigned to a city in the provinces, but neither Horacio nor I knew which. I tried to avoid revealing my movements to Iosi. But in autumn of 2005 I was invited to Paraná, in the Entre Ríos province, to participate in the launch of *Fernanda's Flowers*, a book about the mysterious case of Fernanda Aguirre, a missing girl who's supposed kidnapper had died by suicide in a prison cell. The author was an old friend, Daniel Enz, and I agreed to participate in the book launch, which was publicized in several local media outlets. That was how Iosi learned that I was going to travel to Entre Ríos and how I learned that he lived and worked in the capital of that province.

In a meeting around that time, Iosi told me that the archives of the Federal Police headquarters in Paraná, Entre Ríos, contained files with information on forced disappearances during the dictatorship. He mentioned the case of a Jewish boy who had been kidnapped and was transported in the trunk of a Ford Falcon. The boy somehow managed to open the trunk, jump out, and take off running, stark naked, through the streets. They gunned him down. A sergeant of Iosi's current team openly bragged about having participated in illegal repression. "The other times," was a euphemism Iosi often used to refer to the years of government repression and especially when he talked about that sergeant in Paraná, who was nostalgic for the military dictatorship. The man had a swastika screensaver on his computer. Iosi wanted me to get a federal judge to order a raid of the Paraná office and obtain evidence that could uncover the persons responsible for the disappearances in that province. The laws that had provided immunity to the perpetrators of certain crimes during the dictatorship had recently been declared unconstitutional and the trials against the military repressors, halted in the eighties, were expected to resume. The time was right but it wasn't that easy. A judge would have to issue the search warrant but how could I make the accusation sound credible if I couldn't explain where the information had come from? As I was working to make contact with human rights organizations in Entre Ríos to ask for their help, Iosi called me, beside himself.

"They're having a barbeque."

By order of their superiors, they had burned all compromising documents. The Nazi-loving sergeant had presided over the ceremony. Iosi hadn't been able to do anything to stop it, and neither had I.

"I'm going to your event," Iosi told me. "Ruso" Enz's book launch was going to take place in an old railway station that had been converted into a cultural center. But, busy preparing, I forgot about Iosi completely. I arrived in Paraná and, after checking into my hotel, one of Ruso's colleagues in the human rights movement came to pick me up. She took me on a drive around the riverfront and we were passing Parque

Urquiza when my phone rang. I wasn't able to answer in time, but I saw that it was a local number. Thinking it was Ruso, I called back immediately. "You have reached the offices of the Federal Police of Argentina," said an automated message.

I hung up. "Why are the Federal Police calling me?" I said to the young woman. I swear that I never thought of Iosi. And even if I had remembered him, I would've never imagined that he'd call me from his office.

The girl went pale. "Let me see," she said.

She pulled the car over, called the number and asked to speak with an official. She made a huge scene, saying how dare they call and try to intimidate a journalist. She threatened to report them, to file a request for information with the legislature, explaining that I was visiting for the launch of a book about a suspiciously unresolved case . . . Suddenly, I had a revelation. The person who had called me was my spy "friend." I didn't know how to get out of the mess I'd inadvertently made. I had to think up an excuse . . . quickly.

"Oh! I know who called me! I have a childhood friend who moved to Paraná and works as a civil servant for the police department. I mentioned a while ago that I was going to come visit, but I didn't tell him when. He must've seen it announced in the paper, right?" I then apologized profusely.

I'm not sure the girl bought the story, but I was able to diffuse the situation.

That night, Iosi was the audience in the cultural center until the end of the book launch, when Rep, the cartoonist, unveiled a mural dedicated to Fernanda, which brought down the house. No one ever suspected Iosi was an intelligence officer. He was just another face in the crowd. I don't know if he was there because he wanted to see me and say a quick hello, or to hear the other presenters, all investigative journalists, so that he could later add it to a detailed report for his bosses. Maybe both.

Beyond these anecdotes, we'd failed again, there would be no movie or documentary to make the case public abroad and thus allow Iosi to testify safely. We were back to square one of the game that was feeling impossible to win.

PART IV

After the wedding, Eli and I set out on a journey that was very important to both of us: my process of conversion to Judaism. I was all in. I already felt fully Jewish and I adored Eli. I wanted to spend my life with her, to raise our children in the Jewish faith. We'd been shaken by the bombing of the Israeli embassy and we were convinced we wanted to make aliyah, to go to Israel. We talked about my conversion at length and decided to visit the Varela temple, in my childhood neighborhood. They were conservative but non-Orthodox and they accepted conversion. I'd played baseball at the DOAM club with the rabbi's brother. We went in, asked to speak with him, and I told him everything. Well, I didn't say that I'd been sent undercover to spy on the Jewish community, but I did tell him that I was a federal intelligence agent. He was a young guy. I must've been thirty-three at the time and he would've been no older than thirty-five. He was very open minded, he helped us out a lot.

Eli and I went to several talks at the temple for mixed couples and then I had to start a course at the Latin American

Rabbinical Seminary, in Belgrano, on José Hernandez Street. But the secretary there knew me from Convergence Youth and she was shocked to see me taking conversion classes. I explained that I didn't have my parents' ketubah, their religious wedding certificate, so I had no way to prove that I was Jewish and since I wanted to marry Eli, I had to convert. Fortunately, the girl didn't seem at all suspicious.

During the conversion course I had to hide my prior knowledge, because I knew a lot more than any of the other students. They explained to us the difference between the Torah and the Talmud, they talked about the Jewish diaspora, about the creation of the State of Israel. Eli taught the kids who were preparing for their Bat and Bar Mitzvahs, so I had learned a lot from her as well. I knew enough to get an A in Jewish history, customs, and religion, but I had to "play dumb." The course lasted an entire year, but for me, none of it was new.

We hadn't told anyone at Tzavta that I was in the conversion course. But somehow, Mauricio Tenembaum, father of journalist Ernesto Tenembaum, found out and he came up to congratulate me at a Convergence meeting. We got to talking about the need for non-religious marriage ceremonies (Eli and I, who had married at the courthouse, could be a case study in that sense) and about Bar and Bat Mitzvahs for children of mixed marriages.

I don't know when it shifted for me, when I realized that I was truly a part of that community they'd sent me to spy on. Was Eli the reason for the change? Yes, but also Andy and his girlfriend, the kids from Ofakim, Convergence, the secretaries at Tzavta, Clarita and Andrea, Davidovich and the people at Mapam, the guys from Hashomer Hatzair. The fact that I worried something might happen to them, that I felt they were so vulnerable, was proof that I couldn't continue to do the job I'd be sent to do. I hated spying on them. These were my people. There was no room for betrayal.

For the men in the course, conversion culminated in the bris, circumcision. Eli had never thought it strange that I wasn't circumcised because that was common among sons of a non-Jewish mother or father. We met with two moalim, specialists in religious circumcision. We chose one who was young and offered more affordable rates, because the procedure was not cheap and we had to pay for it ourselves. Then things came up and we ended up postponing it. But it wasn't because I lacked conviction.

WATCHED

I began to feel observed within the agency. There were growing suspicions that I was a Mossad spy, a double agent. To top it off, one day, the *Public Informer*, a rag read mostly by members and former members of the intelligence services, published one of my reports. Down to the letter. All that was missing was my name, Jorge Polak. It could've spelled the end for me. It was a report on a meeting at the embassy that I'd had for Sojnut. Because, after the bombing, the embassy functioned there in part and also in the building on Paraguay Street at the 1500 block, where the Hebrew Institute was also located, two places considered Israeli territory, diplomatic headquarters. I'd reported that they were going to reinforce security measures. The article was exactly what I'd written, word for word.

I called Red, furious. I don't know if it was a reprisal, designed to make me want to leave out of distrust. Later I found out that there was someone at headquarters who was selling reports. That leak put a price on my head. Anyone who had been at that meeting with me could've asked themselves where that information had come from and deduce that I'd leaked it.

Red told me that she would take care of it, but she was very cold, I have to say. She felt I should be taken out of the field because of the leak, or, at the very least, that I shouldn't turn in any more written reports. It was a palliative measure, the damage had already been done. "We can no longer guarantee your safety," she said. Neither one of us knew where my reports ended up. Also, as I said, the agency was convinced that I was a spy planted by the Israeli intelligence services because they couldn't believe how far I'd gotten. It could be revenge of the worst kind.

"Ask to be taken out of the field and then you can return in six months," Laura said. That wouldn't really solve anything, but at least it would get me out of the line of fire. I'd have a one-year period in which to reenter the field. I made my request to Commissioner Carlos Castañeda, head of Protection of Constitutional Order and his second in command, Nicuesa, the deputy commissioner. I claimed I had a family emergency, that I had to move to Entre Ríos for an issue related to my parents. But neither of them wanted me to quit for good. "Take as long as you need," they said, "but don't leave the agency."

I, on the other hand, did want to quit. It would be such a relief not to have to lie anymore. Eli also wanted me to leave. We had, for a brief moment, the hope of being able to live a normal life. With my job at Los Dos Chinos and her teaching salary we could get by, without any luxuries. But the truth was that my sabbatical was only a temporary measure until Red could figure out how my report had been leaked. My own colleagues had betrayed me. This proved that someone couldn't care less about risking me. Undercover agents have to be the most protected people within the force. And evidently I had co-workers who were wholly unmoved even by the thought of my death.

I went back to work after a few months, but I shouldn't have returned. Of course I'd continued my life in the meantime, what had become my real life with Eli, Tzavta. There was a kid named Juan, who had started working at the community center and he wasn't part of the collective but he was a good guy. Together, we built concrete piles on the sidewalk outside as a defensive measure. He was always at my side. I trained him little by little in security measures, and he responded well, he was a quick learner.

In late 1993 or early 1994 it was decided that the offices for Sojnut and the Zionist Organization of Argentina would move to the AMIA building. And the embassy school on Ayacucho Street, called the Argentina-Israel Institute for Cultural Exchange would be closed.

This move implied that security would have to be tightened at AMIA because Sojnut was considered foreign territory, like the Israeli embassy. The decision was discussed with the presidents of DAIA and AMIA, and, once they agreed, they began to design the remodel with an architect. I don't remember what month this was, but during one meeting they showed us the plans for the renovation, what the new offices at AMIA would look like, where the office for the Zionist Organization would be, and they told us that the entire floor was going to be guarded by Sojnut. After that meeting, I went to the office of the Secretary General Itzik Horn. On his desk were two copies of the blueprints for the AMIA building. It showed the entrance on Pasteur, the stairwell, where security would be posted, and the OSA office on the first floor facing the street. I took one.

It was important information. I passed it on to Laura as quickly as I could since I couldn't hold on to that incriminating material. I also told her that once the Sojunt offices, in their capacity as part of the Israeli government, were moved to the AMIA building, at the end of 1994, security would become much tighter. I was clear on that, because security at Sojunt was much stricter than at the AMIA up to that point since so many people were in and out all the time for the job board or to file paperwork for a burial at one of the Jewish cemeteries.

I don't know why I gave Laura that information, if, by that point, I was already suspicious of the agency's role in the first attack and I felt like an outsider in that world of betrayal, where no one was what they claimed to be. In some way, those of us in intelligence often have a lot of denial, a refusal to accept the reality we're a part of. It's complicated and contradictory. It's hard to get out and you might do things that make it hard to look yourself in the mirror afterward. But I handed over the AMIA floorplans to the Federal Police Intelligence Department a few weeks before the bombing in July 1994. I did that.

In the next OSA meeting it was mentioned in passing that one of the blueprints had mysteriously disappeared. Around that time we received notice through the embassy of a new security warning, because Israel had sequestered the head of Hezbollah intelligence, Moustafa Dirani, and killed part of his family. Just days after that, Israel killed, also, dozens of combatants, and another Hezbollah leader, Mahmud Said Mortada. In a sermon, sheik Fadlallah vowed revenge and used the previous bombing in Argentina as an example. Years later it came out that sheik Fadlallah, the spiritual leader of Hezbollah, had met around that time with Mohsen Rabbani, the Iranian diplomat posted in Argentina who was from the same village as Nassib Haddad, the owner of the mining company that left the dumpster at the entrance to the AMIA minutes before the explosion.

The Zionist Organization had been informed that Carlos the Jackal, the Venezuelan terrorist, had been called to Damascus to organize a reprisal in Argentina, where security was very weak. I passed that information on to my handler, Laura, and my other direct boss within the agency. The notification also reached the Argentine government, something that Carlos Menem later denied, but that those of us who were there knew to be true.

WARNING SIGNS

In June 1994 several warning signs appeared. The annual Latin American Union of Progressive Judaism conference was held in Montevideo. I went along with some other members of Mapam. I saw Horacio Lutzky, the editor of *New Zion*, who I knew from Tzavta and who was covering the event for the newspaper. The conference was held in the Columbia Hotel and lasted three days. The first day was in reality a separate meeting for Socialist Zionism, the so-called Mapam World Alliance, where issues such as the relationship between Israel and the diaspora and the peace process were debated. There were presentations from Chilean, Brazilian, and Mexican delegations. The focus of the debate was the need to increase support for the left and for pacifist sectors in the Middle East and Latin America. The next two days were broadly attended by other groups and by Uruguayan political parties. Two legislators from the Uruguayan Frente Amplio party participated, along with Alejandro Rofman, an Argentine Socialist economist. The secretary general of the Mapam Party in Israel, a Uruguayan man named Víctor Blit, gave a talk on the Middle East and the need to support attempts at peace.

One night I had to return to Buenos Aires by plane, file a report, and return to Montevideo before anyone noticed my absence. My superiors wanted to know immediately what was happening and what was being talked about in that meeting of "leftists and Zionists." Such rush was not the norm.

Around that same time, some anti-Semitic graffiti appeared in Once. A group connected to the right-wing Carapintada military leader Aldo Rico was blamed for it and arrests were made. Months later I found out through the *New Zion* newspaper that those Carapintada vandals were connected with the Iranian embassy. But the most worrying thing was, one night, when Eli was at Tzavta, a strange man entered with a briefcase and sat down in the waiting area. The community center was a busy place, with a soccer field at the back which was rented out to other institutions, and it wasn't unusual to see someone with a bag. What was strange was that he sat down in the waiting area. The man then got up and left but he didn't take his briefcase with him. I opened the door and saw him running down Perón toward Mario Bravo. He hopped in a car and it took off. When I got back, I said to Eli: "That guy left a briefcase and ran off. We have to evacuate, I'll go get everyone downstairs, you go upstairs."

Eli let a secretary know and they called the police. We all evacuated. The last people we notified were the directors at DAIA. It had been impossible to let them know in the middle of the crisis. They initiated protocol, the fire fighters arrived along with the police anti-explosive brigade. They blew up the briefcase. In my professional opinion that was a mistake because if there had been explosives in there and they put a detonator on it there wouldn't have been anyone left alive. The glass front was instead shattered to bits. The briefcase contained anti-Semitic pamphlets. I couldn't go into the station to give a statement, so I made up an excuse and Lito Jantzis, the sheliah for Mapam, went inside Precinct 9 to do it. Lito was the right person to make a statement since, as sheliah, an envoy from Israel, it was his duty to inform the embassy of everything that had happened.

I believe that it was a rehearsal, that the guy was there trying something out. They didn't choose that location by chance and the Federal Police had all the information about the movements in and out of the community center, all the security devices, because Tzavta was the place where I spent the most time and I had obviously reported on it to them.

That raised suspicions for me at the time, and even more so later on, with what happened. After that, I became more strategic. I began to think twice about what information I reported. Going over what had happened at the embassy two years prior and now this, I reached the conclusion that they were using me. I knew that, at any moment, I could become cannon fodder and be shot into the air thanks to the very information I'd handed up to them. And Eli and everyone else would be shot out of the cannon right along with me.

I never again reported on real locations or identities. And after July 18, 1994, the day of the AMIA attack, I began to question everything to the core.

JULY 18TH

That day, Eli had to go to Vaad Hajinuj, the equivalent of a teacher's conference held by the institution that manages the Jewish school system. At that time, the World Zionist Organization sill funded an international program of free Hebrew instruction. The funds arrived through the Zionist Organization of Argentina, and I brought Eli on as mora, since she was an excellent teacher. Later on, she would end up running the program.

Eli was supposed to stop by the AMIA to pick up some educational material. The week prior we'd met there with the executive director of the Zionist Organization of Argentina, Itzik Horn, to check on the renovations of our new offices, because the OSA was going to move into the AMIA building on the 600 block of Pasteur. But that weekend I'd traveled to Entre Ríos, because my son was there on vacation and I went to spend a few days with him and my parents. By that time I was no longer notifying the agency of my movements, not even when I left the province.

I was in Basavilbaso, my parent's small town, and I saw on the Crónica TV news: "Explosion at AMIA." I didn't know if Eli was there. I panicked, my head was a whirlwind. I don't even know how I managed to dial the numbers over and over until I located her at home. She had been delayed and hadn't left yet.

"The whole apartment shook," she said, crying.

"Don't worry, I'll get a ticket and come straight home," I told her.

I called the office and my bosses ordered me to stay out of town, not to return for a few days, to lay low and wait for them to find out what had happened. But I went back that same night. When I got to the apartment Eli and I hugged and cried. She had found out some of the names of the victims. They still hadn't identified everyone, there were some people unaccounted for, their loved ones going from hospital to hospital.

Around noon the next day I went to Pasteur. It was hard to leave Eli in that state, but I had to go. I called Itzik Horn, who told me where they were gathering: the Sojnut building, at Perón and Larrea, and Rambam, which was the Jewish teacher's college, across the street from the Lasalle School, which ended up being used as the AMIA headquarters until the offices could be rebuilt. Bitajon volunteers also began working out of the Max Nordau School, at 150 Ayacucho. I went to sign up because they were starting to recruit people to sift through the rubble. On the 19th of July, at night, I was there, shoulder to shoulder with the other rescue workers. The Jewish community had mobilized, people were everywhere. There were guys from the civil defense squad and active members of the Israeli military had arrived. At first it was total chaos, but then they began to evacuate survivors by Uriburu street, parallel to Pasteur. That effort was led by DAIA and Horn was one of the coordinators. He'd been miraculously saved, because he was supposed to be in a meeting at the AMIA that day but the subway had been delayed. They interviewed him for the Télam news agency, I remember, they called him head of the "Zionist Commandos," who were coordinating "the FBI, SIDE, and Mossad rescue efforts." Utterly ridiculous.

I volunteered with the bitajon team. We identified ourselves with yellow helmets and white Rambam T-shirts with an image of a menorah. I went several times with some of the other guys, for different reasons, to Precinct 5, where we were talked to a deputy commissioner with the last name Retrive, who I later crossed paths with at the Entre Ríos branch of the Federal Police.

People came to help, they brought us food, thermoses of tea and coffee. But it turned out that some of the drinks were laced with insecticide. Some of the guys got sick. So, from that point onward, it was decided that only members of the Jewish religious congregations would provide food and drink, and everything had to be kosher. We also learned there had been looting. Between Tuesday and Thursday we streamlined the efforts until all volunteers who weren't part of the Jewish community and bitajon were eliminated, and controls at the barricades became stricter.

The morning of the bombing, on July 18, the main leaders of the Jewish community in Argentina had been on the radio, participating in the inauguration of a news service for the World Zionist Organization. Ambassador Itzhak Aviran was there, along with Rubén Beraja from DAIA, Alberto Krupnicoff from AMIA and Oscar Hansman from OSA. And joining in from Israel were an Israeli general and several members of the World Zionist Organization. They had just gone on the air when the attack occurred.

We stood on the top of the enormous mountain of ruins and removed buckets of rubble, sometimes uncovering human body parts and corpses. We worked from seven in the morning to six in the evening on Thursday, removing huge chunks of concrete, two stories high, to free the corpse of a girl who had been crushed to death. She had probably been on a top floor when the explosion occurred. For a long time I dreamed about her hands, with her painted fingernails. I never found out her name. The guys who were working with me got sick to their stomachs. I felt nauseous too. I went back to the apartment. Eli hadn't moved. She couldn't stop crying. Her green eyes were bloodshot and swollen. I didn't know what to do to help calm her.

On Friday of that week there was a rally at Tzavta so massive that people overflowed out onto the sidewalk. Horacio Lutzky was one of the speakers. I helped to organize the security effort, something essential. I rounded up some guys from bitajon to serve as guards. Also, at the last minute, Dov Puder, from the Mapam Israeli Socialist party and director of the World Zionist Organization, was added to the list of speakers, which increased the risk. Everyone was very emotional, with an unending flow of people crowding into the main hall of Tzavta. It was difficult to control. A lot of people were upset and sad, but there were also some who seemed euphoric.

Just before the event was set to begin, a pile of newspapers was delivered. It was a special issue of *New Zion*, fresh off the presses, and they were all gone in a matter of minutes. I was surprised that the first thing I saw after the front page was "An Open Letter to President Carlos Saúl Menem," a full page, written by Lutzky, where he called out the nation's security forces and Menem's inner circle, blaming them for what had happened and for spreading misinformation. Afterward I learned that several paragraphs of the letter were published in *The New York Times*, something unheard of for a small news outlet like *New Zion*.

Dov Puder called for solidarity with Israel and blamed Iran for the terrorist attack. Lutzky responded that he respected Puder's point of view, but that, as an Argentine citizen, the local criminal investigation was his priority. That's when I realized that there were two very different perspectives on what had happened. And this conflict would reemerge with Rubén Beraja and the other directors of DAIA, who prioritized the international issue, ignoring anything that could reflect badly on Menem.

This conflict waged on, as I confirmed on the first anniversary of the attack, when Tzavta received a copy of a journal published out of California, *J Weekly*. In it, Lutzky was quoted saying that proving whether Iran was or wasn't behind the attack wasn't the priority and that "what truly matters is finding the local connection, those who provided intelligence, safe houses, and support for the terrorists," and that the rest would follow. He emphasized that we had to continue focusing on Fascist sectors within the security forces, linked to the last military dictatorship. "Fascists don't investigate other Fascists," he said. But, in the same article, Beraja, head of DAIA, on the other hand, "energetically rejected insinuations that local police and security forces were involved in the attack." I remember the quote exactly because I was so bewildered by it.

After the bombing, I began to walk around armed everywhere I went. I had reached the conclusion that there was no way to guarantee the community's safety without weapons. If the Argentine government wasn't going to take care of us, we had to do it ourselves. And I'm speaking as a Jew. I applied all the knowledge I'd acquired through my training. And I would soon add on more training with the Israelis.

My favorite weapon was always the .22, a good "service" weapon which, depending on the kind of ammunition used, can kill a person in the middle of a crowd without it being heard. This is achieved by lowering the amount of gunpowder in the bullets so that they are subsonic and it's easy to mask the sound, just slamming a door is enough. The intelligence services never use larger weapons because they'd be too noticeable, we prefer smaller guns that can be carried in a pocket.

The weapon of choice for the Israeli Intelligence Service is the Beretta .22, which is very small. Mine was always the Bersa .22. At one time, there was a clandestine gun shop in an apartment on Avenida del Libertardor, where they sold weapons to the bitajon staff. They were sent over from Israel, I think by diplomatic post. There was also a gun shop called Red Rider and another that was owned by the Chabad-Lubavitch Hassidic Jews, on Córdoba and Billinghurst. The Chabad guys knew what they were doing. In fact, their chief of security, who they called Negro, walked around with a Magnum .357. In the time leading up to the inauguration of the new AMIA building on Pasteur, in 1999, the concern was what would happen if a member of the bitajon staff was forced to use a weapon that they didn't have a license for. Of course, DAIA would provide them with lawyers. But Negro, the chief of the Chabad group's bitajon, said not to worry, that if anything happened they could get them out of the country in forty-eight hours.

Tzavta's security had always been weak and it needed to be reinforced urgently, it couldn't be put off any longer. Juan, the employee I'd been training, helped me put my plan into action. We bought cement and ordered armored doors. We had planters built around the concrete barricades. It was one of the first institutions to have built-in security measures. We then constructed a concrete wall with a special component that was mixed into the cement, which made it much more resistant, and that had been brought over from Israel by the shlijim, the envoys. I didn't mind the work: Tzavta was my home and I had to protect it.

Among the dead was one of Eli's classmates from morim school, Silvana Alguea de Rodríguez. She had a baby only a few months old, born in Israel. She and her husband had made aliyah and had returned to Argentina out of fear over the war in the Middle East. I also knew at least two guys from bitajon on the list of victims. A while later, Samuel, Eli's zayde, died and they buried him in the Berazategui Israeli cemetery. I was there, wearing a kippah, listening to the Kaddish, the prayer for the dead, when I realized that two graves down was one of those bitajon guys. They say they had to bury an empty coffin because they never found his remains.

Around that time, one of Eli's former Hebrew students, who was a member of bitajon, offered me a job at the Martín Buber School, on the new security team that had been set up to deal with the new reality. So I started as part of the school's bitajon staff. There were fifteen of us working in shifts. Some of us were volunteers, others had been to Israel and had some military training. The chief was named Marcelo Chámez and he was a physical education teacher. No one asked me where I'd obtained my knowledge, there was a tacit agreement among the people at bitajon: that wasn't talked about. I wanted to be involved without revealing how much I knew. I had to be cautious, only make suggestions, offer guidance. It was my obligation to contribute as much as I could, that's how I felt, but I had to be careful.

They assigned me first to the high school, where our hours varied. I started out working the night shift, which started after the preschool let out, when the three-year-olds left. The Martín Buber School and the Tarbut were the first schools to set up security teams, a suggestion passed down from Israel. On Charcas Street, at the high school, they built a double entrance, which looked like glass. We knew that it was really bulletproof polycarbonate that could resist a FAL rifle assault. We had a metal detector, like in airports. There was nothing like it anywhere, we didn't even have that in the intelligence services. Although, in reality, the metal detectors were never plugged in. It was a very Argentine thing, a detail that would be almost comical if it weren't so tragic.

To guarantee that the kids could be evacuated during a possible attack, we thinned out a wall in the gym to such an extent that it could be broken through with a few blows of a hammer. The wall was shared with Nilda Garré's home next door, and she came over to complain that she had leaks. I always imagined the expression on her face if we had to break through that wall and send a crowd of kids rushing through her personal library. I never told her, even much later when I ended up working for her. But we felt that the kids' safety was more important than a few ruined books.

I didn't tell my bosses that I had become involved with bitajon. They knew that I was part of the Zionist Organization of Argentina but that was it. I kept going back to Red's answers from when we spoke right after the explosion at the Israeli embassy: "Don't worry, nothing happened to anyone from the agency." And, when I'd asked how that could be possible, she responded that they'd gone off somewhere else, to the bathroom, blah, blah, blah. It was very hard to believe. The agents who were supposed to be posted at the embassy entrance had all left. Someone had let them know not to stay there. Now, at AMIA, the exact same thing had happened. The agents who were supposed to be at the entrance had all left. Someone had warned them not to stay there. The same, exactly the same.

I knew full well from my anti-terrorist training that, in order to carry out an attack, you needed to know the access points, what kind of the security system the target had, the names of the guards. This was the exact information I'd provided to my superiors. And I knew that there was a leak at headquarters, someone was selling information. To whom and why, I didn't know. But there was an agent who had sold my report to *The Public Informer*. I'm sure they're still there today, doing the same thing. Also, among my co-workers and bosses, there were people who hated Jews. I'd seen that firsthand, the undercover mission they'd assigned me was proof of that.

I began to hear talk of a van. I'd been there, at Pasteur, with the Israeli rescue team, walking all around the area near the explosion, and they hadn't turned up any evidence of a car bomb. And in the training courses I'd taken they'd taught me that when the explanation for an attack isn't found within forty-eight hours, everything that turns up after that has been planted.

Meanwhile, Eli was unable to get over the trauma. She had constant fits of sobbing, she thought about her friend, the baby left motherless. She was in shock. We needed each other, we helped each other the best we could. There was no one else in the world who knew me better than her. I started to share my doubts about the agency, about my deep unease, not over living my day to day life in the Jewish community, but because I'd become one of them. I didn't think about Jorge Polak, my spy name, nor about José Alberto Pérez. I was one hundred percent Iosi. And, nevertheless, I'd provided my bosses with floorplans showing how to get into the AMIA headquarters via Uriburu, via Pasteur, and another entrance, on Tucumán.

"I reported things I shouldn't have reported," I confessed of Eli. "I'm tortured by it because I feel like the agency had a hand in this."

"I don't feel safe here, anything could happen to us. Let's leave," she said.

One of the things that plagued me was that I'd told them

there was no nighttime security on Uriburu, and that the first and second door could be easily opened with any Trabex key, and then you'd reach the auditorium, which communicated with the back of the AMIA. For anyone experienced with breaking and entering it would be no trouble at all. Through that entrance, you could also access the new building that was being constructed, which couldn't be seen from the street. The Uriburu building had doors that were metal and glass, the kind with little windows that open with a latch. It was the headquarters of FUSLA, the Latin American Student Zionist Federation, and there was a little temple in the basement used on certain religious dates, including Yom Kippur or Day of Forgiveness. There were also offices where they gave the exams to people who wanted to go to Israel to study. Also, through a terrace there, you could get to the three-story building under construction and access the windows at the back of AMIA. In fact, the rescue effort had been carried out from that little unfinished skeleton of a building, just cement columns and a roof. We had to climb up there with our buckets and go in through a window to the third floor of the AMIA. But someone had made a hole in the wall on the second floor and we went in that way too. The wall was thick, you'd need a sledge hammer to make that hole. I'm convinced, in spite of what they say, that the hole was already there from before the attack, made not to rescue people but as a way to bring things in. I'd put my hands in the fire for it. The night before the bombing there were Federal helicopters circling the AMIA building, shining spotlights on it, as seen by several witnesses.

I drew a floorplan to explain the layout (see images section at end of book) with the bathrooms, auditorium, terrace, the three buildings. The three-story one, the old one, the one that was five or six stories, and the one that was destroyed in the bombing. We went in through that hole in the wall and we pulled out rubble. Because it was all rubble. The old building was still standing, but there was total darkness, everything was broken, the tables, everything. It was a catacomb. I describe it as a catacomb, it felt like we were entering Dante's inferno. It was something out of another world, with absolute silence . . . the smells. I couldn't get that smell out of my nasal passages for a month after. I saved the face mask and other things I used those days, and I'm going to keep them until the day I die.

KABAT

DAIA's Department of Institutional Security, which was headed by Gustavo Dorf, recognized the need for a kabatim course to train a local branch of Israeli security in Argentina. Generally the training is given only in Israel for those who have been through the army and it lasts two and a half years, but the urgency of the situation led to the decision that an intensive course would be given in Buenos Aires. Volunteers and members of bitajon could sign up, but it was highly selective: only fifteen candidates would be accepted and participants would be paid a stipend so that they could dedicate themselves to the training full time. Arieh Geva, a retired general from Israel, came to give the course. The recruitment happened over two weekends at the Hacoaj Club on Estado Israel Street and Gascón, with physical and psychological evaluations. They didn't accept a single woman, the training was too demanding, but I think that in later iterations women were included. Each person was assigned a number and an evaluator. It was two very intense days of physical activity. Then came the interviews. There were tests, they had us draw pictures. They asked us our reasons for wanting to participate and what we felt we were capable of. It was funny to me because they asked if I could ever use a gun. And of course I answered that yes, if it was necessary, as a last resort. Other questions were identical to the ones they'd asked me when I entered the Police Intelligence. I passed all the tests with no problems. The course began in January 1995, and I was one of the fifteen selected out of 2,500 people who had applied.

We would be an elite force. Those of us who completed the course were going to be designated by DAIA as heads of security for the community's institutions, even at the embassy. We would be anointed to defend and safeguard the lives of the Jews in Argentina. Of course, I had to ask permission from Chámez, by boss at the Buber school, because the course was full time and I would have to miss work. He refused and so I had to quit. I didn't care, because becoming a kabat was much more important to me. Also, it would give me the chance to openly display my skills, since, up to that point, I'd always had to play dumb.

Eli was happy and proud, but she knew that being a kabat put me in increased danger. Red was aware that I wanted to do the training course and she did not approve. She said it would call too much attention to me, that it wasn't compatible with my undercover work. We went back and forth and I finally told her I was doing it after the course was already well underway. But I never revealed the locations of the training. When we went to Burzaco, I told her we were going to the Hacoaj Club in Tigre, when we went to Hacoaj, I reported that we were going to Tristán Suárez, to CISSAB.

I couldn't stop making reports, but I spaced them out,

they were no longer daily. I had to be careful, because I didn't know if they had another person within the community who they could use to crosscheck the information I gave them. I was playing Russian roulette and I had to proceed with great caution, always leaving room to explain any information they found to be incorrect. I trusted my intuition, but I was walking a tightrope.

The course was given partly in Spanish, partly in English, and partly in Hebrew. It started out with an intensive month from seven in the morning to seven at night. After those first thirty days, General Geva was going to return to Israel, and the local trainers would take over. The first classes were held in the Hertzliah school, at Juan B. Justo and Nicasio Oroño. We even did some simulations in the street, at the Tel Aviv School. One time, I don't know how, they even let us use the Gran Rex theatre to simulate a Yom Ha'atzmaut celebration. The huge theatre was full and the fifteen of us were divided into three groups. One team was responsible for setting up the security system, and the other two acted as either terrorists or participants. At a predetermined moment, someone would stand up with a grenade or try to enter with a weapon, or was found with a suspicious package. They evaluated our reactions and then we rotated so that every team had the chance to play each part.

I don't think that the Argentine government knew about all this, or even that General Geva was there. I remember that, one day, one of the groups was simulating an attack on a school on Azcuénaga Street and someone inside noticed something off and alerted the police. They surrounded them, they wanted to arrest everyone. The guys said they were tourists, but they had to own up in the end. We were in another group and they notified us by walkie talkie to go back to Hertzliah.

When there was some conflict, Gustavo Dorf, from the

Department of Institutional Security would show up, along with Jorge Brotsztein, who was the executive director of DAIA at the time, and Alfredo Neuburger, an advisor. They had also been at the opening ceremony for the course and they communicated the message that Rubén Beraja, president of DAIA, sent us his congratulations and was sorry that he couldn't make it.

Geva didn't want us to call each other by our last names. To everyone there, I was Iosi. But since they knew my last name was Pérez, my classmates started to call me "Gaita" or "Gallego." Weapons training was carried out in the Israeli Home for the Elderly in Burzaco, which has a huge campus, but we never used live ammunition, always blanks. In the period in which we were still with Geva, we practiced loading and unloading our weapons and simulated attacks. Shooting practice happened later, halfway through the year, in a shooting range that belonged to a man from the community, on Lavalle and San Martín. It was called Red Rider and it also functioned as a gun shop. The guy who taught us was a retired federal officer who worked for the owner, which I found amusing. The Red Cross also gave us a course at Rambam in first aid for disasters and attacks, and the fire department trained us at the Sholem Aleijem School in rescue efforts and evacuation.

The course lasted for all of 1995, but before the general left, they had us all turn in a field report of a Jewish institution. This was an evaluation of the surrounding five block radius: buildings, the presence of medical professionals who could be called upon, hospitals, local police stations, political parties that might be sympathetic to the community or, on the contrary, might have anti-Semitic tendencies, personalities from the political, cultural or social sphere who lived or worked in the area, access points and escape routes in the case of an attack. Our reports had to be very detailed, more in depth than anything they'd ever asked me to do in intelligence. They also asked us to explain, in the case that we were terrorists, how we'd attempt an attack against the institution. And what measures we'd suggest implementing to improve defense.

The Israeli general had very clear ideas with respect to the AMIA attack and its possible culprits. He said that the methodology could have been foreign, but that the execution of it had been in local hands, not Hezbollah's. He based his theory in the fact that many Nazis had taken refuge in Argentina after the Second World War, meaning that there was an affinity between the Nazi ideology and the country's military and security forces and that explosives could be easily obtained in Argentina. He maintained that the three main points to analyze when investigating an attack were motivation, financing, and the means to carry it out, and that the motivation and means were present in Argentina: the financing alone may have come from abroad.

And he even went as far as to say: "If the motivation, the financing, and the means exist here, there's no need to look for an answer abroad. If you're walking through the jungle and you see elephant tracks and elephant droppings, it's not necessary to find the elephant to know it was there." With this, he wanted us to understand that Hezbollah needn't have been present.

There were certain lessons that I still remember; I kept my notes. For example, they told us that the first phase of an attack is intelligence, which is fundamental. You have to find out what security measures are in place, the entrances to the targeted location. One way, the easiest way according to Geva, is to establish links with security personnel. If they're men, they might send women to seduce them. If it's women, they try to seduce them too. When it's not possible to connect with security staff, they try to gather intelligence through cleaning services, and if not, as a last resort, through anyone who works there. They first try to get information secretly, and if that's not possible, they attempt to purchase it.

With our field reports in hand, Geva called us in for our evaluations. At the end of the year they ranked us from first to last. I ended up in tenth place. But the general had noticed something unusual in me and before leaving he made an observation: "Iosi, I don't know why you limit yourself, you could be a very good kabat."

He could see, obviously, that I was capable of more; I was making an effort to seem like I was less adept. For example, I pretended to be unskilled in the use of weapons and when I turned in my field report, which others typed up on a computer, with photos, I just wrote mine by hand, on purpose.

SAFEGUARDING AMIA

After completing the security training course I applied to work security at AMIA. I got a good recommendation and they accepted me: I joined the bitajon group there. I was on the night shift and at around eight or nine the La Royal cleaning company came in. They were part of the Orgamer Group, which was owned by Alfredo Yabrán, a powerful businessman known for hiring illegal repressors from the time of the dictatorship, especially from the Naval Mechanical School, one of the largest clandestine torture centers. He controlled key sectors, for example, the movements in and out of the airport. Red later told me this, because at the time I didn't know it. But, while I worked at AMIA, we found one of the La Royal employees going through drawers in the DAIA office. We kicked him out, the chief of bitajon was notified, and we asked for the company to be dismissed. But La Royal had been cleaning AMIA since before the bombing, in the old building on Pasteur, and it continued to lend its services even after that incident. I later learned that the lawyer for DAIA was also a lawyer for some Yabrán companies, what a coincidence.

Until recently, there was a photo hanging at AMIA that I took at a dinner, of the whole bitajon team. We went out together often, there was a real sense of comradery. After the meal, they brought us a bottle of Turkish anise liquor, and we got a little tipsy. Obviously, I volunteered to take the photograph because I didn't want to appear in the picture. Everyone got a copy. Three of the guys in the photo died very young, of heart troubles. One of them was the director of security at the temple on Iberá Street, another one worked at the Emanuel Temple.

I only served as kabat at AMIA for a few months and after that the Department of Institutional Security hired me to set up security for Hertzliah, the school that had served as our base for the training course. It was an elementary school in the La Paternal neighborhood. I chose a girl and a guy to be on my team. We worked in shifts from six in the morning and into the night whenever there was some activity such as a parents' meeting. On the weekends the school served as a temple, so we had to be there too. I prepared a very detailed report for the school's board of directors.

I also organized a bitajon training in Tzavta, with authorization from the Department of Institutional Security. I set up the course and trained the students myself. As a kabat, I no longer had to hide my weapon, and in fact I used it to train the younger guys. I didn't have to ask DAIA to provide a gun to teach the students how to load, unload, shoot. I used my own. Geva had said to us: "You can't set up a security system for the community if you aren't armed, otherwise you'll just be doormen." It was a lesson I'd already learned.

My relationship with Eli was good, but she sometimes complained about my absences. Not my physical lack of presence so much as the times I seemed to be lost in another world. She would talk to me but I wasn't listening. My thoughts kept me up at night, my mind raced at top speed.

ZIONIST LEADER

In parallel, I continued going to meetings of the Zionist Organization. There were about fifteen of us in general but every once in a while there were as many as twenty-five. Every meeting opened with a summary of the conflict in the Middle East and the political situation in Israel, because the groups that made up the OSA were representatives of the different Israeli political parties. I represented Mapam, and the meetings were often debates over the decisions made by whatever government was in power.

The Zionist Organization of Argentina was the nexus between Israeli politics and the Jewish community in Argentina. One of their main objectives was to foster the Argentine Jews' commitment to Israel. By that point they already had representatives in the cities of other provinces such as Córdoba and Paraná.

I remember one story from the period right after the attack on the embassy. The OSA had met in the Sojnut offices on the eighth floor the building on Perón and Larrea. Jorge Kirszenbaum, who went on to become president of DAIA, was there. He had joined OSA as a representative for the Convergence Party, and he was secretary general, but he didn't attend meetings very often. In fact, he once took me aside and said: "Listen, I'm not going to be able to come every time. So you pay attention in every meeting so you can fill me in, I'm going to ask you to call me and tell me what happened."

I did this as a favor to him, I would call him after the meetings. One day, one of the few meetings Kirszenbaum attended, there was a bomb threat and they evacuated the Natan Gesang School, which occupied the rest of the building, except the eighth floor. They had us stay there, and the security team told us to get in front of the window at the back of the building. We couldn't use the elevator or go anywhere. The only way out was to jump. There was a car parked across the street that could've been loaded with explosives. I saw the terror on everyone's faces, especially Kirzsenbaum, who looked like he was about to cry. After a little while they let us out. The anti-explosive squad had arrived and surrounded the car. About half an hour had gone by, thirty endless minutes. The Israeli embassy bombing had just happened and we were terrified. I imagine Kirzsenbaum had been thinking what bad luck he'd had, deciding to go to a meeting that day of all days.

I participated in the OSA elections again, the first time had been as a representative for the short-lived Breirá university group. I also served as the nexus with the youth organizations, especially when the funds came in from the World Zionist Organization to guarantee the free instruction of Hebrew as a tool for community building, because the kids were very enthusiastic. That's when Eli came on as a Hebrew instructor, because that was her area of expertise.

I had always been a member of the OSA and eventually they made me sub-secretary. The secretary who took the minutes stopped attending meetings and so they said to me: "Albertito, you're young and I bet you have pretty handwriting." And so I started to take the minutes. Alberto is my middle name and that's what they called me, affectionately. But sometimes I received correspondence with my Hebrew name, Yosef Perez. Apparently José Pérez seemed too goy to some people so they translated it. If you were to check, you'd see that all the minutes of the Zionist Organization meetings for two or three years were all signed by me.

The first OSA president that I had the chance to meet was Víctor Leiderfarb, who ended up making aliyah. After the attack on the Israeli embassy, Oscar Hansman took office. I stuck to him like a stamp because I was convinced he was in serious danger, he was clearly a target. Rubén Beraja had bodyguards, as president of DAIA, and Crupnicoff did too, as head of AMIA, but not the president of OSA. So, of my own volition, I always followed him when he had a public activity. By that time I was already carrying my gun. I even entered the Sojnut building armed and they didn't search me. I never had any problems walking around with my gun because everyone associated me with bitajon. No one ever thought to be suspicious of me, because they saw me, for example, as part of the security team at the massive community events, making sure there were no problems.

There's one event in particular I remember. It was held in Rosario on the Israeli independence day, Yom Ha'atzmaut. I traveled there by car with three other guys, among them Beny Zugman, the accountant for OSA who later served as treasurer for AMIA, also a man named Cohen, from the Sephardi community, and another guy. We were the advance team. As soon as we arrived, one of us had to contact the AMIA, another one of us had to notify OSA. I was in charge of contact with the guys from bitajon. Our presence was absolutely necessary because the event was going to be massive: it was held in the Newell's Old Boys stadium, in Independence Park. There was police presence all along the highway to guard the buses that left from Buenos Aires. There were two teams who had to keep an eye on the meeting points for the anti-Semitic and Arabic groups in the city. We didn't share all our information with the Federal Police or the Provincial Police, there were some things we kept secret. We talked about following groups that might want to attack the community or organize some protest against the Jewish people who'd traveled to the city. What we shared or not, in general, was decided on by DAIA, which communicated with the chief of police or the minister of the interior.

There was also a two-day OSA conference in La Plata attended by delegations from the provinces: on that occasion they stayed at the campgrounds owned by a Jewish institution and we had to guarantee everyone's safety. And then, in 1997, there was an event in Paraná, but I didn't attend that one. My participation in the Zionist Organization of Argentina gave me a broader panorama of the community and I based my reports to Red on what was discussed in those meetings. The debates often centered on the Israel-Palestine conflict, whether or not to negotiate, if Palestine should be recognized as a state or not, if we could ever live together in harmony. I truly wanted peace. But I worked in security, that's how I spent my time. I went to meetings, gave talks at organizations, schools, and clubs; I tried to make people aware of the danger, the vulnerability of different locations. I never reported on those meetings of the kabatim staff to the agency. Never.

The fact that I had become secretary for the Zionist Organization of Argentina was enough of a success for my bosses, an accomplishment beyond anything they'd imagined. Nevertheless, around the time of the kabatim course, when I reported the lists of names, they asked me what the people's real names were real and I responded that I didn't know, that for obvious reasons we only used nicknames. For example, they asked me to find out Mati's real name and I told them I didn't know.

SUSPICION AND EXILE

Around that time I began to get the feeling that my bosses, not Red in particular, but her superiors, were receiving information from another source. It wasn't just paranoia, they asked specific questions several times or interrogated me more than once about something I'd reported. They did this through Red or through a commissioner who met with me occasionally. What they asked most insistently was for information about the progress of the AMIA investigation or which way the suspicions within the Jewish community were leaning, what leads they were following.

On a few occasions I was asked to meet with Commissioner Amartino, who was the had of intelligence at the time. They called him "Tigre." I was told to wait in a pastry shop and his driver pulled up and took me to Belgrano Avenue past Paseo Colón, across from Customs. Amartino was waiting for me there in another car, with another driver, who got out. I got in and Amartino drove in circles around Costanera Sur. Much later I learned that Mariano Amadeo Amartino, which was his full name, was accused of participating in kidnappings and tortures during the military dictatorship, in La Pampa. He requested retirement at the end of 1996 and was granted it. He died before they could try him. Another of the holdovers from the other times. I wasn't surprised: there were many like him.

They rarely asked me specific questions, more often they just wanted to confirm receipt of something I'd turned in or verify certain information a second time, but they stopped asking for details on anyone. In retrospect, I can only conclude that they were receiving detailed information from someone else. That's why I'm convinced that around that time, I don't know if it started in 1996 or 1997, they began to suspect that I wasn't providing as much intelligence as I could. I began to fear that they would kill me. That they would discover I'd been lying to them and it would confirm, in their minds, their theories that I was a double agent, working for the Israelis.

I asked Eli to help me translate a letter into Hebrew to send to a contact she had at the Israeli embassy, to then send on to Tel Aviv. I didn't know the person but she was going to put me in touch. It was supposedly someone from Israeli intelligence. In the letter I very vaguely explained who I was, what I'd been through, what I'd done. I thought of it as a way to protect myself. I don't know if they ever read it, I don't think so. Maybe it was a mistake to use Eli's contact and maybe she never even gave it to anyone, out of fear, to protect me.

Then, in one of the trips I made to Entre Ríos to visit my parents, I decided to record a video. I got ahold of a camcorder and locked myself in my room. I sat on the bed and started to tell my story, in more or less twenty, twenty-five minutes. At the end, I filmed my credentials, all the documents that proved what I was saying: the certificates of services rendered signed by different police commissioners, my license to carry a firearm, my passes, internal receipts, and the proof of enrollment in the Federal Police pension plan, from the first years of my service up to that moment. And to close out the video, I stated that if anything were to happen to me, to look to my superiors at the Federal Police, Commissioner General Pelacchi, the Chief of Superintendency of the Interior, Commissioner General Ramírez, and others. They would be the ones responsible for my death, my murderers.

I didn't rat Red out, I was loyal to her. I had a certain respect for her, still do. I think that as a handler she trusted and believed in me. She knew that I had excelled at my work, that in a short time my knowledge went well beyond hers, which came only from books, readings on the Jewish community and the conflict in the Middle East that she'd had to undertake in order to supervise me. But I had first-hand knowledge that I'd picked up on the ground. And there was no comparison. I never doubted Laura. She was very Catholic, an Opus Dei sympathizer even. But I don't think she stopped trusting me. At one point, before my report was leaked, she said to me: "I have so much information from your reports that you could take a year off," because she didn't report everything as soon as I gave it to her, she doled it out. The suspicions came from higher up. She once told me that they questioned her, that they asked her for certain things, and she argued that I couldn't provide that information. I would listen to her but I never felt that she was pressuring me, she never asked me for anything.

But the bosses evidently thought something smelled fishy,

because one day Laura told me: "I'm not going to be meeting with you anymore."

"Oh, and who's going to handle me now?" I asked.

"Commissioner Baigorria wants to talk to you," was all she would say.

I felt like I'd been punched in the gut. They were ripping me out of the universe I'd built behind their backs.

Baigorria was the head boss of Security. "Look, the superiors have decided that from now on no one's going to be undercover," he informed me.

I didn't know if it was true or not, but it was an order. The head of the Federal Police, General Commissioner Adrián Pelacchi, was leaving. He had replaced Brigadier Antonietti as secretary of security, and he was leaving his post to Baltasar García. This was September of 1997.

"Choose someplace in the province, wherever you want, but you have to leave Buenos Aires," he said.

They would've sent me anywhere I wanted. To Salta, to Córdoba, or Mar del Plata, but I chose Paraná. It was the lesser evil, because it wasn't that far and I could also live near my parents. But I had Eli to think about. They didn't know that I was married, on paper it only showed that I'd divorced the mother of my son. Because I'd married Eli in March of 1993, and I'd taken leave after the publication of my report in *The Public Informer* in May of that year. I'd returned to work in December, although my official reentry was in 1994. That's when they registered my details again, but I didn't state that I was married, I continued to hide it.

The best terms I was able negotiate was that they wouldn't force me to leave Buenos Aires from one day to the next. I couldn't tell them that I was involved up to my ears in bitajon, the Jewish community security force! I hadn't even told Laura, to whom I'd only reported the course. My argument was that I was the secretary of OSA and I couldn't just disappear, it would be too odd and it could work against us in a very dangerous way. They gave me enough time to think up a good excuse, and the one I ultimately provided is what allowed me to come and go from the community whenever I pleased, without obstacles.

The initial idea was for Eli to move with me. There were active Jewish communities in Santa Fe and Paraná and two Jewish schools, where she might be able to work as mora. I couldn't even imagine living apart from her. But at the last minute Eli decided that she wasn't coming with me. She didn't want to. It was like a bucket of cold water being dumped on me. So I arranged to spend twenty days there and twenty in Buenos Aires. A divided life. Now I realize that distance was the beginning of our break up.

The truth was that I didn't live in Paraná. I'd told my superiors that people might recognize me within the community there. Mostly the guys from bitajon, because people from all over the country would come to Buenos Aires for trainings and so those guys had met me. There were also plenty of people who had come to Mapam meetings at Tzavta. So living in the capital of the province wasn't ideal. Instead I would stay with my parents, out in the country, over a hundred miles away.

In fact, one day, shortly after taking the bus at the Paraná station, I ran into two guys from security in Buenos Aires. Someone had vandalized graves in the Jewish cemeteries in a few towns and they had been sent to find out if they were anti-Semitic attacks or simply grave robberies. When they asked me what I was doing there, I provided an evasive answer, giving the impression that I'd been assigned to some important, classified mission. We arranged to meet again and

I had to travel back to Paraná the next day just to have a coffee with them, so that they wouldn't suspect anything.

THE ENTRE RÍOS OFFICE

I worked nights at the Federal Police headquarters in Paraná, Entre Ríos, in the Intelligence Department. We'd agreed I would work the night shift so that no one would see me. I clocked in at 11:00 p.m. and got off at 7:00 a.m. Then I would take a bus out to the country. I got home, had some mate with my mom and dad, ate lunch, and went to bed. I got up at four o'clock in the afternoon and had a shower. By six in the evening I was on the bus headed back to Paraná. I did 180 miles there and 180 miles back every day, Monday to Friday. I slept a bit on the bus and also at work, in the stretches where nothing happened, generally after 1:00 a.m. Before going into the office, I would call Eli. We never talked from the phones at headquarters, because we didn't know if they were bugged. Someone could be listening to us.

The first two hours I spent doing a press analysis. Not the Jewish community press, but general newspapers and magazines. I wasn't in contact with the Jewish community at all anymore, supposedly, but I did have contact with the intelligence community, which was very active. Once a month we'd all get together for dinner; we all knew each other. One of the agencies would host and invite the rest: the Entre Ríos Police Intelligence Department, Air Force Intelligence, Army Intelligence, Border Patrol, Coast Guard, and SIDE.

Shortly after arriving to Paraná, in 1998, the boss, Commissioner Rogelio Mallebrera, called me in to his office. All they'd told him about me was that they were sending someone from intelligence who shouldn't have any contact with the rest of the staff. No one could know my identity. They recommended I be exposed as little as possible. I told him a little bit about myself and we had a conversation, he was the one who put me on the night shift. When the conversation ended, very politely, he asked: "But, where were you, kid?"

"In the Jewish community."

I got the feeling that my response had impacted him. Then, when I left the office, as soon as I closed the door, I heard a loud crash. He'd had a heart attack. He had been the one to discover Alejandro Monjo, the owner of the chop-shop that had supposedly provided the part of the van that they say smashed into the front of the AMIA building. Monjo was linked to Telleldín, but also to the Iranian diplomat Mohsen Rabbani and to the federal and provincial police. When they searched his chop-shop, they uncovered a Federal Police keychain, which later disappeared, just like the recordings and so many other things. Because of this, my new boss, Mallebrera, had been taken out of circulation and sent far away, like me. After his heart attack he spent some time at the Churruca Hospital, getting treatment for his condition, and he didn't return to Paraná. Later on, he became a Commissioner Inspector, head of Internal Affairs, the department that managed political relations within the force. I ran into him once and asked him to bring me back to Buenos Aires, but he didn't. In 2003, when Gustavo Béliz became minister of justice and human rights under Néstor Kirchner, he accused Internal Affairs of illegally gathering intelligence on political and social organizations.

SIDE GIGS

The guy who came on after Mallebrera was named Castelli. He was very direct with me, right from the start. "There's an order for you not to return to Buenos Aires," he told me.

I had a good relationship with him, because I did some work for him on the side, of a personal nature. He assigned me to follow his wife. She was much younger than him and Castelli was convinced that she had a lover. They were from Tandil and had a daughter together. The woman was studying to be a veterinarian, and when he got promoted to the main delegation in Paraná, she refused to move, saying she had to finish her coursework and would follow him halfway through the year. He thought it smelled fishy. He paid for all my travel expenses, of course. I would take a plane from Santa Fe to Buenos Aires, and go to Tandil by bus. In the end, it was true, she was cheating on him with a guy in one of her classes. I was able to provide photos that proved it. After that we became friendlier. And thanks to that side gig, when I returned from Tandil, he let me stay a week in Buenos Aires with Eli. He gave me freedom, at a time when I was trying to save our relationship.

It wasn't the first time that I'd been asked to do something like that. It was common for the higher ups to send us to investigate things that had nothing to do with official matters. Back when I worked at the Meeting Center, above Precinct 46, before going undercover, they'd asked me if I wanted some extra work. They used us to guard the shipping containers that left from the port. We had no idea what was inside. It could've been weapons, drugs, anything. We would drive up to Puerto Nuevo in a Ford Falcon and no one ever stopped us or asked any questions. If we crossed paths with the Coast Guard, they would salute us. We would use the back doors to the warehouses and they'd pay us a hundred pesos, I remember, which at the time was a load of money, because we're talking about 1986 here. I did that extra work a few times.

In intelligence, since there's nothing written down, they can use us to do anything; the agents have no idea who they're working for. They can set up a tail without any problem, they just say, "Go follow so-and-so, it's an agency issue," when in reality you might be working for the narcos. They teach you to lie, supposedly as a matter of "national security." But in reality you're the one being fooled; I discovered many times that I'd been the peon sent on "top-secret" missions that ended up being personal matters with no relevance to the interests of the nation and its citizens.

PART V

I was friends with Gabriel Levinas, who had been head editor of *El Porteño*, a very important journal in the post-dictatorship period. I knew him by name, obviously, but I later contacted him and asked him for help on two stories. The first was an investigation into the director of the Museum of Fine Arts, Jorge Glusberg, an architect with a long career in the art world who had been accused by painters of charging them for expositions and receiving commissions from the printing press where he required the artists to print extremely expensive catalogues. Levinas was an art dealer and he got several artists, reticent at first, to agree to publicly denounce Glusberg, who, after the overwhelming evidence was published, had to resign and was prosecuted.

The other investigation I asked Gabriel to help with was the disastrous state of the Israeli Ezrah Hospital, an institution that had been a model within the Jewish community and had fallen into the hands of unscrupulous administrators. There had been several deaths from septicemia caused by lack of hygiene and resources, mostly in elderly patients who received government subsidized healthcare. The patients' family members were beside themselves and doctors were quitting left and right. Several of them refused to operate there due to the risk. "My dad invested money in that hospital, they're pocketing it," Levinas said, referring to the directors at the time.

The story got a lot of traction within the Jewish community and led to changes in the hospital administration. After those two articles Gabriel and I saw each other often. He invited me as a guest on the radio program that he hosted and I would fill in for him whenever he had to travel. I met his family and visited his home regularly. We were connected not only by our recent work history, but by a similar sense of humor, and we planned to co-author a series of comedic Jewish anecdotes, which he knew dozens of and told better than anyone. He had a sharp wit and I spent several Jewish holidays in his apartment, where the food was divine.

Levinas was working on an in-depth investigation into the AMIA attack. He was one of the few journalists, who, like Lutzky, did not hesitate to point out the holes in the official explanation of the attack that blamed the Buenos Aires Police. He deeply disbelieved that there had ever been any white van, although he allowed that some pieces of the vehicle could have been planted as false clues. Gabriel had contacts in the influential American Jewish Committee (AJC), and although now, in hindsight, it seems naïve, at the time Horacio and I believed that this powerful organization, with so many resources, could provide the support that Iosi needed. That meant we had to tell Levinas about the spy. As a journalist and a Jewish man, he immediately understood the importance of this possible witness and agreed to put us in touch with the AJC. But first, of course, he wanted to meet Iosi.

He agreed. "If you two trust him, I do too," Iosi said.

We all got together several times, mostly at Gabriel's house in the Once neighborhood. Gabriel interrogated Iosi at length, but he didn't get any more out of him than Horacio and I had. Just like us, he got the impression that only when Iosi's conditions were met would he share what he knew. Horacio and I already had plenty of documents proving that Iosi had been able to rise to great heights within the Jewish community with barely any obstacles blocking his ascent. There were pay stubs, invitations to events, the minutes of meetings. Levinas said, bitterly, that Iosi could've been named head of DAIA, the Delegation of Argentine Israelite Associations. We also had proof that Iosi worked for the Federal Police, despite all the security measures they made him take to hide his role.

Dina Siegel, the director for Latin America of the AJC was planning a visit to Buenos Aires and Gabriel and I took the opportunity to request a meeting. Dina, who is from Mexico, was in charge of all matters related to Latin America for the Committee. She was around forty-five years old when we met her, her hair was dark and curly and she was energetic. She met us for breakfast at the posh Hotel Alvear, at a table set with fine china and silver, a huge spread of everything from croissants to smoked salmon. She listened to us intently and promised to take care of the matter. With her was a thin, dark-haired young man—who we later learned was a lawyer—also Latino, who would be our contact going forward.

The next meeting we had was at Gabriel's apartment. Horacio, the young AJC envoy, and myself were there along with two Jewish businessmen of considerable wealth, friends of our host. They would supposedly finance the spy's exit from the country, if, and only if, the AJC was in agreement.

Like we were giving a presentation, we explained the importance of Iosi's testimony. One of them, as if playing devil's advocate, questioned all of our arguments. The AJC contact took feverish notes.

In reality the amount we were asking the businessmen to provide to set Iosi up abroad wasn't that much. Just enough to support him for a few months until he could secure other income: some twenty-five thousand dollars between the two of them. It wasn't the money that made them hesitant, but the fear of being criticized by the community if they participated in something that didn't have approval from "higher up."

Just like on other occasions, everything seemed to be on track. "Seemed" is the operative word. Levinas believed, like us, that Iosi was at risk. That's why, to protect him, he proposed—and we agreed—that we should record a video telling his whole story. Iosi, in fact, had already done this himself not long before. Gabriel somehow managed to schedule the filming for a day when Horacio and I couldn't be there, but he assured us that he'd made two copies. If and only if something happened to Iosi, the recording would be made public. We talked about storing the video in a safe, and even sending it to be kept somewhere abroad. At that time, no precaution seemed too extreme. Horacio and I never suspected any ulterior motives on Gabriel's part, although I have to admit that Horacio was bothered because he felt that Gabriel wasn't being careful enough. I would've liked to have been present for the recording and to have helped draft the questions. At our next meeting, Horacio had a confidentiality agreement that he'd written up for the three of us to sign, but Gabriel managed to put off reading it and never ended up signing. I wasn't especially worried about it, because I considered Gabriel to be fully trustworthy. He was like family to me.

ATTEMPT IN WASHINGTON

In February of 2006 I went back to work at Channel 13 on the same investigative journalism team that I'd left three years prior. My first assignment was a trip to Washington D.C. to cover the Inter-American Commission for Human Rights and film the records that the members of the Commission had made in September 1979, when the military dictatorship allowed them to visit Argentina. The families of disappeared persons had lined up down Avenida de Mayo to greet the team from Washington, decrying the government-sponsored kidnappings. The images and interviews were going to form part of a documentary that we were preparing for the thirtieth anniversary of the military coup. The person I would interview at the IACHR was Executive Secretary Santiago Cantón, an Argentine man.

It was a unique opportunity to plead Iosi's case at the highest international level. The American Jewish Committee had not followed up on our last meeting and the Inter-American Human Rights Commission had shown past interest in the AMIA case. President Néstor Kirchner, along with the Center for Legal and Social Studies, and the Active Memory organization, had made a promise to the IAHRC that they would bring those responsible to justice. I would arrive in Washington just before the interview, I was there for work, but no one could stop me from having a separate conversation with Cantón. We had several friends in common since I had been exiled in the United States in the eighties and had prepared my first testimony about my kidnapping in Argentina there, in 1982, with help from human rights lawyers that he knew. If Iosi were to testify in international court with the support of the IAHRC, he would be untouchable, with the most solid protection possible. Horacio was in agreement. We prepared our arguments and after getting Iosi's enthusiastic permission, I traveled to D.C. with the Channel 13 team.

We arrived on an unusually warm fall day. The IAHRC offices were large and bright and Cantón showed us to a room where we'd be able to film the contents of some books that looked like old accounting ledgers. It was a hand-written list of names of disappeared persons, the circumstances under which they disappeared, and the identity of the person providing the information. On the long list, unexpectedly, was the name of our sound engineer's sister, and he had to leave the room to cry in the hallway. Neither the cameraman nor I had known about his sister's forced disappearance. We stopped recording for a few minutes. Moved by the situation, I left the room as well. That's when I ran into Cantón and I told him what had happened. As the conversation went on, I took the opportunity to tell him about Iosi.

He leaned against the wall of the hallway, listening with great interest. He told me that he believed Iosi's testimony could be very valuable and he proposed taking Iosi's statement in a third country. It sounded reasonable and we agreed to remain in touch via e-mail and to schedule a meeting when he traveled to Buenos Aires.

This new possibility gave Iosi some hope, but around that time he began to have other concerns. His mother had gotten sick and the prognosis was grim. Iosi had to spend a lot of time with her, in Entre Ríos, out in the country. Over the following months, and until her death, he spent his time taking her to doctor's appointments, getting tests run, having her admitted to the hospital, and also providing emotional support for his father.

It was right around this time that Cantón arrived in Buenos Aires and asked me to set up a meeting with the spy. We met in a café in the Belgrano neighborhood. Cantón suggested that he could summon Iosi to make his testimony before the Commission abroad, in some undisclosed location where Iosi would be safe to start a new life. Iosi agreed, but he said that he couldn't abandon his mother at that moment. Cantón understood and agreed that, given the circumstances, the testimony could be postponed until Iosi was ready.

Iosi's mother died not long thereafter and we sent word to Cantón that our man was now prepared to testify. Several months went by before I received an e-mail from one of Cantón's assistants inviting Iosi to travel to Guatemala, where he would be called for a meeting with the Commission. The date set was July 16. It was strange, because July 16 was just two days before the anniversary of the AMIA attack. And it had become almost a tradition—no matter what government was in power—for a new witness to appear almost magically right before each new anniversary, almost like some sort of peace offering to the families, evidence that the case was still being investigated. Generally, the information would explode in the media like fireworks for a few days, but then fade out without resulting in any major advance in the case.

We were hesitant. Why, after waiting so long, would the meeting be held forty-eight hours before the anniversary of the bombing, just when politicians, community leaders, and the organizations of victims' families would be gathering in an act of commemoration and the demands for justice would be at a fever pitch? Was it all a coincidence? Something smelled fishy.

By that time Justice Galeano's investigation had been fully discredited and there was pressure to come up with new evidence, something more credible than the Buenos Aires Police involvement. We trusted Cantón, but we wouldn't put our hands in the fire for him. Maybe he wanted to move home to Argentina with a government posting and was doing someone a favor that they'd later return.

So we decided to wait. We knew we might be missing an important opportunity, but some sixth sense told us that we were being used for political ends. We decided to cool off contact, convinced that any misstep on our part would cancel out all possibilities of making a real impact with the information Iosi was willing provide. If he felt manipulated, he would clam up for good.

That year on July 18 the demands for justice were levied at the government officials in attendance. President Néstor Kirchner was on a state visit to Paraguay—from where he sent his continued support—and Cristina was home sick in Río Gallegos. The speakers called for the attacks on the AMIA and the Israeli embassy to be classified as crimes against humanity in order to assure that the cases remained open. The Israeli Ambassador was there along with a delegation from the World Jewish Congress. They all demanded that Argentina break ties with Iran. Among the five thousand people in attendance waving photos of the victims, not far from the stage, was Iosi, just like every year.

The undercover spy was an endless source of surprise. One afternoon I entered the café where we'd agreed to meet (he always arrived early) to find him filling out a worksheet.

"I'm studying Russian," he said. "And I think you know my teacher."

He was taking lessons from Vladimir, who had been my Russian teacher for many years. From then on, the spy would call me "padruga," which means "friend" in Russian.

We never knew, until much later, that Iosi's handler had been a woman. A high-level agent who lived and still lives the life of a middle-class woman in a middle-class neighborhood of Buenos Aires. A woman who had two faces, handling dozens of undercover agents with an iron fist. Iosi had an unshakable loyalty to her, and still does.

Iosi had become aware that he could not put off his request to leave the Federal Police any longer. He'd filed a complaint with the force, because they didn't recognize injuries he'd received that produced a constant buzzing in his ears along with serious sleep disruptions. Meanwhile, they moved him constantly from office to office, assigning him routine desk work. When he arrived to each new posting, he had to figure out how to protect himself. He was desperate to find refuge in some superior officer, who he'd revealed part of his story to, and in whom he almost obsessively tried to find positive qualities, with a naivety that surprised us, trying to convince Horacio and I of their benevolence and honesty against all evidence to the contrary.

I met those dark guardian angels of his on two occasions. The first of them was a commissioner named Miguel Colella, who looked almost like a caricature of a spy: signet ring, black-framed glasses, dark shirt and light-colored tie. Iosi introduced me to him at a pizzeria in Boedo, under the pretext that he might make a good source. The man trained dogs on the side and he did not want to be a source but he asked if I had any contacts in the government because he wanted to set up a company that provided canine security. The last meeting we had was in the basement level of a traditional pastry shop in Constitución, Los Dos Chinos, where a well-known politician stared intently at the bizarre and suspicious meeting taking place at our table. Colella must've sensed that his time in the force was coming to an end and was seeking out new business opportunities. A while later, in 2007, he founded Homeland Brokers Security, a company dedicated to data security, hostage resolution, and negotiations involving extortive kidnappings, narcotrafficking, and money laundering. His business partner, curiously, was Martín Lanatta, who was later sentenced to life in prison for the kidnapping and murder of three businessmen, a crime related to the trafficking of ephedrine.

The second of the officers Iosi had pinned his hopes to was a man named Daniel and it was thanks to him that Iosi began working for the minister of security, Nilda Garré. She had been defense minister, ruling with skill and a firm hand, and, when Cristina Kirchner became president, she put Garré in charge as the newly-created ministry of security, meaning that the Federal Police, then, answered to her. Iosi told me in a meeting that Garré was going to need a guide to lead her through the force, to tell her who was who, because if not, "they'll steamroll her," he assured me. He was willing to be her guide. No one better than him, he maintained.

"These guys won't let their arms be twisted. I have a lot to tell her. You don't know what it's like in there. They'll smile and wish her well and if she falls for it it'll be a disaster. I trust her, I like her. I think with her there's a chance things might change once and for all. And also, she could help me. She already knows my story so there's no need to tell her anything. You've already told her."

He asked me to put him in contact with Minister Garré and he added that he wanted his co-worker, Daniel to be involved as well. I wasn't prepared to recommend Daniel but I was just starting to think about how to contact Garré through a member of her team when Daniel got there first. He was in a shopping mall in Cariló when he saw, through a storefront, the minister with a young woman, surely her daughter, picking out a ring. He waited patiently and approached her when she left the shop. They traded cards and agreed to speak once they'd both returned to Buenos Aires.

In the meantime Horacio and I set up a meeting with Minister Garré to let her know that the federal officer sent undercover in the Jewish community was now offering to be her guide within the force that saw her as an enemy. We were summoned to the Ministry, a mansion on Gelly y Obes Street. Immediately prior we'd met with Iosi and he'd brought along Daniel, who was especially anxious to go with us to the meeting. We managed to convince him that it was better for Horacio and I to go alone and that they stay behind in the café. As we waited to meet with Garré, I saw the contact I'd used to set up the meeting, a prosecutor. She seemed exhausted, but content to be working in that serpent's lair.

The minister's office was huge and her desk was full of Peronist knickknacks, photos, figurines, and fresh flowers. She apologized profusely for making us wait and offered us coffee. She rejected all calls so she could give us her full attention. She seemed relaxed. We laid out the situation, explaining Iosi and Daniel's offer to be her guides, making it clear that we couldn't vouch for Daniel because we didn't know him well enough.

NEW ROLE

Nilda was warm as always, understanding, and grateful. She told us that she was honored to have her office in that building, because there, she said with a complicit smile, Evita and Perón met in secret when their relationship was not yet public.

Several hours had gone by at that point and Iosi had to leave, but Daniel was waiting for us, nervously. We told him the results very broadly and we left. Garré made good on her word and brought the two men onto her team. Daniel and Iosi became, then, inside men for the minister of security. The spy's life had changed. After long years on the fringes, he finally had stability in his work, even if his new position made him enemies within the force. This was because the kind of assignments that Minister Garré tasked him with were often related to internal affairs, which is to say, the investigation into corruption within the Federal Police. "If they didn't like me before, they hate me now," Iosi said.

Everything he did was legal, by order of the Justice Department. The team he was part of tailed targets only with a judge's order, as stipulated in the Intelligence Law. They generally worked cases that couldn't be trusted to the Federal Police because it involved one of their own.

"She has a target on her back, you have no idea how much we need to protect her." He spoke of Nilda, as he called her, with great respect, almost reverence. He described her gestures and expressions in detail, doing impressions of her saying certain phrases, mimicking her postures and her way of describing scenes. It was obvious he felt at home. He had access to her office and communicated with her via e-mail; she responded immediately.

One time, in private, he told her that he wanted to take his story public. "It's the wrong time," was her response, and he didn't ask for any further explanation. Iosi was not a politician and he trusted that she had her reasons. The rest of the feds may have hated Garre's guards but there was also dissent within the ranks of the minister's team. One day Nilda received a message revealing supposed misconduct by Daniel, stating that he lived an illicit lifestyle that included racehorses, a lover. It didn't seem very credible at first glance, but it's possible that a more in-depth investigation turned up further evidence because in the end Daniel was excluded from the golden circle. Iosi, however, stayed on. Even though he harbored doubts about the veracity of the accusations against Daniel, he supported his boss's decision.

Horacio and I were getting impatient, chomping at the bit to speed up Iosi's testimony, something we let him know every time we met with him. We believed that the circumstances couldn't be better for Iosi to step into the light.

As for Gabriel Levinas, he hadn't had contact with the spy for years. The last time he'd reached out to Iosi had been to ask him for a favor: one night Gabriel's teenage son was nowhere to be found and he beseeched Iosi for help. His bosses set up an urgent search and the boy turned up safe and sound. Gabriel would randomly ask after Iosi when we saw each other. On one occasion, he told me he didn't think the spy would ever talk and that since so much time had gone by we had the right to publish the story, including the documents that Iosi had given us and the video Gabriel had in his possession.

I responded that I strongly disagreed, insisting that information should only be published with the source's consent, which was not the case. I told him that even if a reporter had impeccable evidence, all facts checked, but at the last minute the source, out of fear or whatever reason, wanted to back out, their wishes had to be respected. All we could do was try create the correct conditions for Iosi to testify. That, for me, was an indisputable law, the code of ethics I had always worked under. Gabriel didn't seem fully in agreement. He tried to persuade me a few more times, but my answer was always the same.

UNDERCOVER REPORTER

I told Horacio about Gabriel's suggestion and it made him very uncomfortable. But I trusted Levinas not to do anything without my permission. It was true that a long time had gone by, but I was convinced that Iosi was going to end up leaving the force and testifying very soon. Also, a recent episode had given me proof of what Iosi was made of. He had offered a list of intelligence agents on the force, and one name stood out to me: Américo Balbuena.

"He's undercover in the Rodolfo Walsh Agency. Do you know anyone there?"

Yes, I did. The agency was dedicated to reporting on social conflicts: recuperated factories, student protests, occupations of schools. One of its members had worked alongside me on a team to help set up a co-op for young people recently released from prison, to help them get work and keep from getting sent back to jail. This was in the Ejército de los Andes housing project, nicknamed Fort Apache, where many kids fell into the trap of crime. We exchanged numbers at the end of the project and he gave me a book that the Rodolfo Walsh Agency had published with the results of their social work in prisons.

"Can you get in touch with the agency?" Iosi asked. "You can't mention me, obviously."

"Yes, of course. But I can't believe what you're telling me. This Agent Balbuena, why is he undercover? Is he police?" the questions fell out of my mouth in random order. I was furious.

"He's undercover, yes. Pretending to be one of them."

"Like you were before?"

"Yes . . . but it's illegal now. Just take a look at the Rodolfo Walsh Agency webpage," he added. "You'll see he's written a ton of articles for them."

I didn't ask why he was sharing this information with me. All I thought about was everyone who was at risk, the unknowing members of the Walsh Agency. But before moving forward, before meeting with them, I had to verify that the photocopied page I had folded up in my purse was valid. I called a member of Nilda Garré's team who had been present when I visited her as minister of defense to request the flight logs for the Marine death flights, which I'd used for a story I was working on.

We met in a café in Congreso. She made a phone call and verified that the intelligence agent Américo Balbuena reported to the Federal Police. She told me that she was going to talk to Minister Garré and that they would remove the agent and go public with it. I told her that I had to warn the reporters at Walsh immediately. She agreed.

Two of the journalists from the Walsh Agency came to meet me at another café, a few blocks from the first. Oscar Castelnuovo was the reporter I'd worked with in Fort Apache but I had never met the other one, Rodolfo Grinberg. I took the sheet of paper out of my purse and placed it on the table, still folded.

"Do you guys know Américo Balbuena?"

"Yes, of course, he's one of our co-workers at the Agency."

"He's an undercover federal agent."

"That's impossible."

I unfolded the page with the Department of Criminal Intelligence Letterhead. It clearly showed Balbuena's name, rank, and other information.

Rodolfo seemed the most shocked. He shook his head and said: "I can't believe it."

He'd known Américo Balbuena since elementary school. They'd lost touch during the dictatorship, which was logical, but they met up again at journalism school and then, again, in December of 2001. He was the one who had invited the undercover spy to join the agency. The work was unpaid, done out of passion for journalism and activism. Everyone opened their doors to the respected agency and there had been no space the spy had not been able to access. He always had the time, no matter the hour or distance, he was always willing to put up his own money to buy batteries for tape recorders, gas for the car. His excuse was that he managed the books for his family's lumber company. Américo visited Rodolfo's house often; his wife adored him and they'd had countless barbeques together.

"My wife is going to die," he said.

Oscar was less surprised.

"I thought there was something strange about him," he said. "Something that didn't quite fit. He once put a FAMUS event on the agency's online agenda." Here, he was referring to the group of family members of the military repressors. "Another day he came up behind me and he stuck his finger into my back, like it was a gun. That joke's not funny for leftist activists like us, you just don't do that, you know. That's more typical of the police, isn't it? I didn't like it."

He asked me for a copy of the list. I didn't give it to him, but I told him that I'd talked to people in the ministry and they'd confirmed that Balbuena worked for the police and that they'd soon be taking the matter public and removing him from the force.

I was mistaken. The ministry took longer than acceptable and it was the Walsh Agency who exposed the spy among them in a press conference. They called it an attack on all popular organizations. Balbuena had joined Walsh in 2002, during the Duhalde government, and had been an intelligence agent since the dictatorship. The joint statement from the social organizations that participated in the press conference said: "We denounce the repeated repression and attempts to break us by any means necessary, such as Project X."

Project X was a Border Patrol espionage program set up to infiltrate leftist and human rights organizations. It had been approved by one of Nilda Garré's predecessors, Aníbal Fernández, but the blame was being placed on Garré, who had to remove nineteen commanders. The Intelligence Department was implicated as well and this new issue with Balbuena being illegally undercover for the Federal Police would further tarnish her reputation. As soon as the matter was made public, Balbuena was pulled out of the field and the head of the Federal Police, Román Di Santo, was ordered to make sure that no other agents of the Federal Police Information Gathering Department were violating the Intelligence Act, which considered it a crime to spy on social organizations.

DISPLACEMENT

Twenty days later, Garré was removed from her post as minister of security. Had Iosi been the unwitting cause of the internal affairs disaster? It was uncertain. With Nilda gone, Iosi's position within the ministry was in jeopardy. The team he'd formed part of would surely be disbanded. From her new post as Organization of American States Ambassador, Garré, grateful for Iosi's loyalty, asked that those still left at the agency help him find a new posting. A few months went by. And when the situation became untenable and Iosi had to appear before his bosses, alarm bells once again started to ring. Horacio and I tried to convince Iosi that he was in more danger than ever and that he should leave the agency and the country as soon as possible.

We got back in touch with some film producers, and we met to try and come up with an effective solution. Iosi came back with ideas that were not only difficult to achieve but also dangerous. For example, traveling to Israel to reveal everything there, in the office of some progressive politician who could send him to live out his life in peace on a kibbutz. Horacio and I didn't think he'd be safe in Israel since we'd reached the conclusion that, in this instance, Israel wouldn't want the public to know that their security structure had been breached so easily. And that was the best case scenario. Also, we assumed that the pact between Argentina and Israel to deflect the blame away from government security forces would still be in effect.

"You need to watch the movie *Munich* again," I said, and Iosi laughed. In that film, Steven Spielberg tells the story of an Israeli intelligence agent sent to eliminate the Palestinians supposedly responsible for the attack on eleven athletes in the Munich airport in 1972. He then has to escape the hitmen sent by his superiors in Mossad. "You'll be digging up potatoes on the kibbutz and a Palestinian is going to come up and shoot you. But it won't be a Palestinian," I warned him.

NO TIME TO LOSE

Meanwhile, Levinas was at it again. "I'm going to reprint my book about the AMIA for the twentieth anniversary of the bombing and I want to include a little paragraph on Iosi, with just a bit of information," he told me one day in March 2014.

He was no longer asking for my opinion, which had not changed. It was now a fact that he was going to make use of the information that Iosi had trusted him with only because Horacio and I had vouched for him. There was no sense arguing professional ethics. We had no time to lose.

We had to accept the fact that we wouldn't find support to help Iosi testify abroad. Iosi was disappointed. He knew there was no way to avoid going into hiding. Once again, he'd have to rebuild his world. And given that he now had to testify quickly, it would be difficult to find a court qualified to deal with his sensitive testimony. For the past ten years, the same prosecutor, Alberto Nisman, had been in charge of the AMIA case. This was the man Cristina Kirchner had recommended we see years prior. He had been in the background as part of the prosecution team that included Mullen and Barbaccia, both of whom would later face trial themselves, accused of cover-up. I'd seen these prosecutors in the hallways of the federal courthouse. They were young, attractive, and friendly. They had an excellent relationship with the press, and off the record they expressed disagreement with Justice Galeano, who they claimed to have a tense relationship with. They accused him of ignoring their requests to advance with certain lines of investigation, filing away evidence.

Galeano, on the other hand, was a man who preferred to remain shrouded in mystery. He was distant with the press in general and talked only to a few select contacts who he'd hand-picked to parrot his theories. It was these contacts he called upon when he wanted to spread information. The doors to his office were always closed. At first, it was believed that his discretion implied a responsible work ethic. No one suspected that his reserved nature was instead hiding million-dollar payments for false testimonies, hidden camera videos, destruction of evidence.

Twenty years after the attack, when Iosi finally testified, the truth seemed further out of reach than ever. There were many people responsible for that, even within the Jewish community, such as Rubén Beraja, the president of DAIA, for example. In 1997, during the commemoration of the third anniversary of the attack, many booed and turned their backs on Beraja, who received the criticism with a furious, bitter expression. There was general disapproval of the direction the investigation was taking and the excessive friendliness between Jewish community leadership and the national government. Beraja was later said to have apologized to Carlos Menem for the harshness of the speeches given by families of the victims demanding justice at that event. Beraja denied it, but by that time the lie about the Buenos Aires Police had already been fabricated by Justice Galeano's office. And that was the supreme betrayal.

In April 1994, in the period between the two attacks, I'd

traveled to Germany with Beraja, his wife Raquel Bigio, and two Argentine Jewish men of German descent. We were there to cover Beraja's visit to the Dachau concentration camp, the main Gestapo headquarters in Berlin, and the location of the Wansee Conference, where the solution to the "Jewish Problem" was signed into effect in 1942. Beraja had been invited for the first time by the German Consulate, probably out of sympathy for the bombing of the Israeli embassy. Beraja seemed like a sensitive, intelligent man, with an open mind, progressive even. During a layover at the Frankfurt airport, he jumped for joy at the reelection of the Peronist government but declared his distaste for Carlos Menem. A short time later, he was seen in one of the meeting rooms of the Casa Rosada standing beside President Menem in an announcement related to bank loans. "My friend Rubén Beraja," the president said in his speech. The Jewish community was not overly fond of Menem, and that meeting made the head of DAIA even less popular. I couldn't believe my eyes. Beraja was visibly uncomfortable but he couldn't just walk out of the frame that proved he evidently had had a price. His bank, Banco Mayo, was in trouble.

Beraja would end up in prison for twenty-two months. A comfortable, white-collar prison, part of the Anti-terrorist Investigation Unit on Figueroa Alcorta and Cavia, but a prison nonetheless. He was charged with handing out two hundred million dollars in loans to four companies over eight days in 1995 in order to empty out his failing bank. He argued that anti-Semitic sentiments held by Pedro Pou, president of the Central Bank, who had told him that there was no room in Argentina for an "ethnic bank," had been the true reason for his downfall, but Justice Norberto Oyarbide's investigation had turned up proof of criminal misconduct.

Who else had negotiated the blood of the dead? How many others had been disloyal to their community? Could we now truly trust this prosecutor, even if he was Jewish, after everyone else we'd trusted before had been mere puppets to political, international, or worse, purely economic interests? Horacio knew Nisman. The prosecutor had not made any significant advances in the case despite renewed resources and political support for his work. We both would've preferred to avoid involving him. Nevertheless, Horacio firmly believed that Iosi needed to enter witness protection as soon as possible, which meant presenting a plea to the courts.

The witness protection programs in Argentina, based on what I'd seen through my work, were not very efficient. They had exaggeratedly grand names and promised a kind of earthly paradise in hiding, but, in practice, the "protected witnesses" were more like hostages to their security detail, generally police officers who were, if not corrupt, at least opportunistic. In an investigation I once did in the late nineties a man who'd exposed a bribery scheme set up by a commissioner of the Buenos Aires Police in Palomar was trapped inside an apartment in a small beach town in the middle of winter with his wife and young children. They forced him to spend his government stipend at one specific shop that had super high prices, because his guards had made an agreement with the owner and received a kickback. He didn't have enough money to buy diapers for his baby, for basic medicine, they pushed him into despair.

Another person, the victim of sexual abuse by a priest who entered witness protection was extorted by his bodyguards. They "sold" him telephone contacts and even supposed evidence implicating the people he'd accused. It was a perverse plan to feed his paranoia and take the few pesos he had to spend. In an attempt to improve the broken witness protection system, Néstor Kirchner's government created the National Protection Program for Witnesses and Accused in mid-2003, under the Ministry of Justice and Human Rights, but I didn't know if it was working any better than before or whether the changes were in name only. We were uneasy about the idea of Iosi being cut off from us, trapped in that spider's web.

PART VI

My "exile" in Paraná, far from Eli, was difficult. The trips to Buenos Aires, which at first were every twenty days, became less frequent. Eli lost hope that they'd transfer me back. She was still living in our apartment and she insisted that I should talk to my bosses and convince them to let me come back. She accumulated resentment, slowly. She felt abandoned and saw no way out of the situation. Every time there was a family gathering she had to come up with some excuse, because we couldn't tell them that I was living in Paraná. She wanted to have kids and I explained to her that we couldn't stay here, in Argentina, that we had to leave. There was no other option. Even if I quit the force, we weren't going to be able to live in peace. The relationship, on her side, gradually grew colder. I realized that there was nothing I could do, it was impossible to row against the current. In 1999 she said needed to be alone so she could think. "Just give me some time, give me some space, I can't see a future for us," she said over and over. I didn't object. I didn't want to pressure her, but I was destroyed inside.

"I've made up my mind," she finally said. She didn't want to stay together. We got divorced in 2000. But I dreamed of getting her back, somehow. I couldn't give up. I was willing to do anything to keep her. Quit the force, admit everything I'd done, leave the country, whatever I had to do to convince her somehow. But I couldn't burn all my bridges. My plan was to get support to go abroad and testify. To share everything I knew, everything that had been weighing on me for years. In Argentina it would've been impossible.

"I'll leave . . . come with me. I'll leave everything behind for you," I said.

"How? It's too dangerous."

"I need to talk to someone who can help me. Who can I trust?"

I tried Eli's brother. He'd studied Communications and worked as a journalist. He listened intently to my story but then he turned his back on me, he didn't want to get involved. It was frustrating because he'd been my family, my brother-in-law, the best man at my wedding.

Then Eli thought of Horacio Lutzky. I knew who he was, I'd seen him many times and even invited him to give a talk, but she had a much closer relationship with him since she'd been his assistant and was a friend of Roxana, his partner at the time, who had worked at Sojnut.

LAST-DITCH EFFORT

Eli called Horacio at his office and we arranged a meeting at Tzavta. We spoke alone in a room off the kitchen. He seemed very frightened. That day I had with me an intelligence report, an internal memo, something impossible to obtain if you're not on the inside, so that he'd know I wasn't lying to him.

We began to meet occasionally, always in different places, generally cafés. We used codes. I lived in Entre Ríos but on every trip to Buenos Aires I tried to meet with him even if only once. He listened to me, he made me feel better. At first I was so nervous I could hardly speak. I told him my story little by little. He asked me questions, curious, naturally, but I wasn't ready to let go of the information he wanted.

Whenever we parted ways, I went to extreme measures to make sure I wasn't followed. I was meeting with a Jewish journalist from a leftist Zionist newspaper, one of my previous targets, someone I could have tailed in the past, and I was revealing things that I was supposed to keep secret. It was a last-ditch effort. I wanted Eli to know that I was taking action to try to get her back. I was doing it out of love for her. But not only that. When I looked back I realized that my mission had been a pointless odyssey; I'd joined intelligence with the idealistic notion of fighting terrorism but had ended up, unknowingly, helping aid terrorist attacks. I had to make reparations for those past mistakes, even if I couldn't bring back the dead, who appeared to me in my nightmares. I would often wake up panting and bathed in sweat.

I moved to the city, to Paraná for a year, renting an apartment to live in with my son. But it wasn't safe. The guys on the team didn't know anything about me, only that I was in intelligence, but they had no idea where I'd worked before. Precisely for that reason, my co-workers—two sergeants and two captains—took a long time to warm up to me. They kept me at a distance, because they didn't know who the hell I was. They might've thought I'd been sent by Internal Affairs, to investigate them for who knows what corrupt schemes they were up to.

Even if they'd been friendly, I would've still felt isolated, tremendously lonely. I didn't know what to talk about with those guys. I was in intelligence, and they were in security; we had different codes, we used different language. The only people I felt comfortable around were the people in the community I'd left behind. Sometimes I would call them. The excuse I gave for leaving Tzavta, leaving Buenos Aires, had two versions. One, Eli's version, was that we'd separated because of an infidelity on my part. Out of respect for her, no one asked too many questions, although there must've been a lot of gossip among the women. Several of her friends, in fact, gave me the cold shoulder.

THE BIG LEAGUES

The other version of my disappearance from Buenos Aires wasn't something I said explicitly, but left implied: that'd I'd been called to play in the big leagues, abroad, even, by Mossad. I never came out and said it, but I let it be inferred, giving vague answers when people asked where I'd been. That generated respect and allowed me the possibility to reappear as often as I wanted without anyone daring to ask about my absences. They looked to me with admiration, they accepted my silences. I even sent some guys e-mails that made it seem like I was in London or Paris. I was a god to them, especially the guys from bitajon, who were proud that one of us had risen so high.

I missed Eli. Especially at night. I would wake with a start and stretch out a hand to touch her curls, like I'd done before. I missed her even more during the Jewish holidays. Passover, Rosh Hashanah, Yom Kippur, which we always spent together, with her zayde, her bubbe, her entire family. They weren't very religious but they knew the ceremonies, they repeated them rotely. Eli, who had studied Hebrew and was more religious, started to explain the religion to them, even her grandparents, with that sweetness of hers. It was touching to see.

At first, when I was studying to go undercover at the Library of Congress, or in Hebraica, I would repeat the prayers and the rituals like a parrot, without absorbing any of it. But when I fell in love with Eli something shifted inside me, very deeply. The prayers and songs began to make me emotional, moving me to tears because I felt them so deeply.

"Why is this night different from all other nights?" Eli asked her zayde, survivor of the concentrations camps, at Passover. And then we'd read: *Baruj ata adonai eloheinu melej haolam ha motzi lejem haaretz*: Blessed are You, Lord our God, King of the universe, who has brought forth bread from the earth. *Baruj ata Adonai eloheinu melej haolam, boré prí agafen*: Blessed are You, Lord our God, King of the universe, *who creates the fruit of the vine*.

The wine would come, the matza, the unleavened bread and the bitter herbs. The Afikoman, the piece of matza that had to be hidden so the kids could find it at the end of the meal. When I heard: "We were *slaves* to *Pharaoh* in the land of Egypt. And the Lord, our God, took us out from there with a strong hand and an outstretched forearm," and I saw her zayde with his prisoner number tattooed on his arm, it made me want to cry.

When I traveled to Buenos Aires I always asked after Eli. So I knew when she was still single and I found out when she started dating the man who is now her husband. I still knew a lot of people at Tzavta, where I'd left a girl in charge of bitajon in my place, and they told me everything. I always found an excuse to visit, not only to be near Eli's acquaintances, but because I felt comfortable there. It was a space where I felt free. The only place I had real friends, where no one questioned me. I was incapable of making friends who weren't part of the collective. I was unable to rebuild my personal life.

The secretary of Tzavta, for example, was one of the people that told me who Eli was with, where she went. And she added quietly: "I know I can't ask you what you've been doing." A friend, who'd gotten married more or less around the same time as Eli and I, told me that she couldn't believe we were no longer together. I felt the same way and, even as time went on, I never lost the hope of rekindling our lost love.

In Paraná I had some other missions, with varying degrees of importance, but none of them were related to the Jewish community, of course. They sent me to discreetly collect evidence in seven towns along the coast in Paraná. I also uncovered the theft of glyphosate from Monsanto being sold in the town of La Paz. And a few clandestine ports, where they brought in drugs from Paraguay.

I liked the work, because I could easily blend in as a local, hitching rides from town to town with my backpack, never raising suspicion. Around the time of the landowners' strikes in protest of Resolution 125, I uncovered clandestine ports sending out shipments of soy. I also investigated a shady business deal involving a congressman and a famous French water company that would come to fill up their boats with water and take it away.

SOMEONE ELSE

I continued to meet with Lutzky in Buenos Aires, with the objective of finding some way to leave the country and testify abroad. But as much as we racked our brains, we couldn't come up with a solution. I started to think about contacting an investigative journalist from Channel 13, Miriam Lewin. She'd done some important work and she seemed trustworthy to me. She'd survived kidnapping during the dictatorship, but she didn't talk much about that. Also, not less importantly, she was part of the collective. I got her e-mail address and began to write to her, over and over, until she finally responded. I imagined I wasn't the only person trying to get her attention, and I only explained my story in broad strokes: "I have information that could help solve the AMIA case." Finally, she agreed to meet me. This must've been August 2002.

We met in a little dive in Constitución. Like always, I arrived a little early to make sure there wasn't anything fishy going on. "Erev tov. Ma shlomej? At medaberet Ivrit?" I greeted her in Hebrew. But she told me that she didn't know what I'd said, that her family had spoken Yiddish. I thought she seemed frightened, like Horacio had, looking around constantly, like she was anxious to get up and leave. But in the end she stayed. I started talking but I got too upset to talk. I was sweating and shaking. I wasn't able to tell her very much that first meeting, but we agreed to speak again.

I didn't immediately tell Lutzky that I'd met with Miriam, and I didn't tell her about my meetings with Horacio until several months later. I didn't mention that I lived in the province either; it didn't matter, since, at first, I hadn't provided her with any way of contacting me. Miriam immediately began to come up with ideas on how to get support for me to share the information I had, and she managed to meet with people who seemed like they'd be able to offer me protection. I say seemed because, soon enough, every one of them, whether from the Jewish community, the government, or some political party, either put off helping us or offered solutions that we didn't trust. I was risking everything, I needed not only guarantees for myself and my family, but also a little bit of money, not a lot, just enough to begin a new life somewhere else, far away.

After a few months, I introduced Horacio and Miriam. They got along well, and I imagine that they met to come up with solutions for me while I was away from Buenos Aires. The two of them, for different reasons, were very interested in my going public with what I knew. Miriam, at least at first, wanted to break the story for the TV program she worked on, *Punto doc*, and Horacio had been investigating everything related to the two attacks from the very beginning.

They sometimes pressured me. They were anxious. They told me that the people they went to requesting help had asked how they could be sure I would provide a testimony that would contribute to the resolution of the attacks. The few people who were actually interested in helping me wanted certainties; many others didn't seem to care about what I had to say at all.

I gave evasive responses, dodged their questions. Even now, trapped here where no one can find me, I feel that if I share everything I know then I'm through. They'll be no turning back. I have to admit that they were very patient with me, they put up with my neuroses, the days that I only talked about Eli because I'd seen she was on Facebook but she hadn't even wanted to chat with me. About the times I called her but she found excuses to hang up as quickly as possible.

I've never had any trouble finding girlfriends in all this time, that's true. Some were from the collective, such as a high-up employee at AMIA. She had no idea of my true identity, she knew me as a kabat. We went on vacation together to Brazil, I felt comfortable with her. I traveled to Sweden with another girlfriend, to Gothenburg, because she was a systems analyst and they'd sent her to do a training course there. I had a good time with these other women, but no one could hold a candle to Eli.

DASHED HOPES

What got my hopes up the most was when Horacio and Miriam went to speak with Congresswoman Nilda Garré and then with Cristina Kirchner. But Cristina, who at that time was First Lady, suggested that I testify here in Argentina. I refused, it was insane, I'd get run down in the street if I did that. And then, incomprehensibly, Cristina sent them to speak with Jaime Stiuso, a heavyweight at the SIDE, telling them that he knew more than anyone about the AMIA case. They went to meet him at the SIDE headquarters on 25 de Mayo. Cristina had sent them so they had to go through the motions even though they knew nothing good would come of it. Stiuso sent SIDE agents to tail us but they were like the three stooges, like a thief who rings the doorbell before they break in. Luckily, we were able to lose them immediately, thanks to my experience, but it was a shocking situation for Horacio and Miriam.

I got my hopes up again in late 2004, when Prosecutor Alberto Nisman was assigned exclusively to the AMIA case, granted all the resources he needed, and a bigger staff than ever before. Cristina had told Miriam and Horacio that she trusted Nisman, and that we could trust him too. While I had some doubts and reservations about his actions, and especially about my own safety, it seemed like a sign that those in power were finally taking the case seriously. But that only led to more disappointment.

Then, when Miriam went to Washington to interview Santiago Cantón, the executive secretary of the Inter-American Commission on Human Rights, I briefly thought that all my problems were solved. We couldn't get any higher than that. This was the first time I agreed to meet face to face with anyone, but it didn't make a difference in the end. On one of his trips to Argentina we met in a café in Belgrano and Cantón suggested I testify abroad, like I'd always wanted to, and said he could extend the IACHR's protection, which would make me untouchable. But just then my mom was sick and she died of leukemia a short while later, so I had to be there for her and my father. When he finally called me to testify in Central America, just two days before the anniversary of the attack, Horacio, Miriam, and I all thought it was suspicious. It seemed like more of the same political propaganda they always trotted out every year around July 18, a smoke screen. So I refused.

The second time that I met someone at Miriam and Horacio's suggestion was Gabriel Levinas, a journalist who, like Horacio, had written extensively about the AMIA attack. Miriam and Horacio told me it was important to meet him and I trusted their advice. That was the biggest mistake I made in all those years. We met in a boutique hotel near Plaza Serrano, in a little back garden where he ordered himself a Campari. To get on my good side, he told me how his family had helped catch Adolf Eichmann, the Nazi war criminal. I thought he seemed to be well informed on the investigation into the attack and sincerely committed to solving it. I was mistaken. Miriam and Horacio had wanted me to be in touch with Levinas because he had contacts at the American Jewish Committee and he did in fact go along with Miriam to speak about my case with a director from the Committee who had come to Buenos Aires. But then the businessmen from the collective who, with the AJC's approval, would finance my exit from the country, backed out, and we were once again left with nothing.

Over time I realized that in addition to political agreements, there were business dealings between the police and powerful members of the Jewish community. Like Gustavo Dorf, once head of the Department of Institutional Security for DAIA who later managed funds for the Shared Dreams Foundation started by the Mothers of Plaza de Mayo and ended up defrauding them, along with Sergio Schoklender. Then there were others who partnered with the police in security companies and raked in the dough, I can assure you.

THE TRAP

Levinas wanted me to record a video telling my story, just in case, and the three of us agreed that it was a good idea. We planned to travel to Punta del Este, Uruguay, on a long weekend, so as not to draw any suspicion, and the video film there. Then one day I received a call from Levinas inviting me to his house. It was near Pasteur and Corrientes, in Once, and it was full of art, because he was an art dealer. I'd assumed we'd all be at the meeting, but Horacio and Miriam weren't there. He was alone. He made up some excuse for their absence, filmed me, and kept the tape for safekeeping. I was hesitant at first, but I ended up talking about where I'd come from, and I answered all of Gabriel's many questions. I'd say the interview lasted about two or three hours.

When I left I called Horacio Lutzky. He was highly concerned. He told me I should've never agreed to record that video without himself and Miriam present. He smelled something fishy. Every once in a while, Levinas would call me to tell me that he could get the money for me to leave the country, but I was never convinced by the conditions he offered. After a while, I stopped hearing from him. Miriam told me that he'd occasionally ask after me, and that he tried to convince her to publish my story without my permission. But she stood firm and said that she would never do something like that behind my back.

INTERNAL AFFAIRS

For a few months in 2004, they sent me back to Buenos Aires. Miguel Colella, was put in charge, for a while, of Internal Affairs, and he brought me along. This was the only period in which the division fulfilled its true function, which was to investigate any kind of crime committed by officers within the Federal Police Force. Never before or after did the department work so efficiently. Colella did a surprise raid, because up till then they'd always picked up the phone to let everyone know who they were going to investigate.

With Colella at the helm, we had the chance to finally take down the powerful, corrupt Fino Palacios, the commissioner so fiercely defended by Jewish community leadership. Palacios had always upheld Justice Galeano's explanation of the attack, the story about the involvement of the Buenos Aires Police. This investigation into Palacios resulted from the kidnapping of Axel Blumberg, in March 2004, when it was discovered that some of our officers were involved. Miguel told me that Palacios was said to be linked to the group that had kidnaped and murdered Axel, and that he was also involved in a car theft ring, as proven by a wiretap from 2001. I had to find the chop-shop they'd supposedly set up to take apart the cars. It was in Bajo Flores, near where I'd grown up, and I found it. It was run by someone from the force, a sergeant. This discovery caused a major uproar, and Kirchner fired both men: Colella and Fino as well. They claimed that Colella was just out to get Palacios, his rival, and that he was protected by Cristina, but that wasn't true. I know for a fact that he did not know her personally.

I continued, meanwhile to gather evidence that the Police had either participated directly in the attacks on the embassy and the AMIA, or at least in the cover up. One time, when I entered the Federal Police headquarters at Moreno and San José, I ran into officer Pereyra, who had been in the POC, Protection of Constitutional Order. He was in his fifties or sixties by then, short, graying, with a mustache, and, if I remember correctly, a beard as well.

"So you're Polak," he said straight out. Then he told me that in the period after the AMIA attack they'd obtained wiretap recordings, Telleldín's agenda, and other documentation that they'd confiscated in searches, and that they'd been given the order to "burn" everything. He was laughing as he said it, like he was proud of it, and my stomach was twisting with rage. Castañeda, head of the POC, was later charged with "losing" evidence, but it was clear that he'd done it to cover up for someone, and they never found out who.

A little while before, at one of the barbeques Colella organized every Friday for the staff of Internal Affairs, I sat beside one of his drivers, by the last name Imbrogno. We started talking and he told me that the day of the attack on the AMIA in 1994 he had been assigned to guard Pasteur and they'd warned him to move away from the door. He was deafened by the explosion, and in compensation he'd received a special assignment, the force looked out for him by giving him light duties. I didn't dare to ask any more.

That year the force gave me several postings around Buenos Aires. One was in the San Isidro delegation. Jorge Sagorsky was detained there, under investigation for his alleged connection to the sale of stolen vehicles. His family would visit him as well as his girlfriends. He treated the cops like his servants, like cadets. I imagine those types of privileges weren't free, beyond the fact that he was close to Fino Palacios. He wasn't the only one who enjoyed such treatment, there was a woman who had a luxurious incarceration as well, ordering the officers around and allowed to do things unimaginable for the regular inmates. Once again I felt like an unwilling witness. Maybe it's my destiny.

In each new office, I had to explain that I needed to remain practically hidden. Not all the bosses took kindly to me. For some, I was a live coal that burned their hands. In the best case scenario, they kept me on the fringes, like a piece of old furniture to be pushed aside, someone practically useless except for paperwork or an occasional menial task.

I was posted for a while at Lomas de Zamora, where I'd

worked before, and the situation was no different. The most important job they tasked me with there was tailing Raúl Castells, the blockade organizer.

PÉRES WITH AN "S"

I was sent back to Entre Ríos and in 2006 or 2007 a man named Darío Mendoza, a deputy commissioner I'd met before, took the position of second in command at the Paraná delegation. He was one of the ones who'd said sarcastically: "You're Péres, with an 'Sssss,'" drawing out the pronunciation. "You're a true Jew," he would insist. On internal communications he'd even misspell my name on purpose.

"I'm Roman Catholic," I'd reply. But he was convinced that I was playing for the other team. One day he said to me: "You can't ever mention your undercover work, because if you talk, everyone will blame you for the bombing."

I'd never told him anything, so if he knew that I'd been undercover in the community it was because someone in the agency had been talking about me. It was clearly a threat. I had to stay on my guard and have eyes in the back of my head. I fulfilled my orders and tried to pass unnoticed. I knew that among my colleagues there were some open Nazi sympathizers who were also responsible for deaths during the dictatorship. One night they sent me to stand guard in the Paraná cemetery, an exhumation being done by the forensic anthropology team to identify bodies of persons killed by the military government. It was terrifying to think that the next day I could run into one of the people responsible for those deaths at the office, still there, without anyone knowing what they'd done.

In 2008, during the landowners' protests against the government due to Resolution 125, they sent me to tail Alferdo De Angeli, the director of the Agrarian Federation. It was easy because my family was part of the Rural Society of a town in the area; I took to it like a fish to water. "Stay there in Entre Ríos and go wherever he goes," were the instructions they gave me. So I followed De Angeli everywhere. I was with him at road blockades, assemblies. De Angeli even visited my parents' house. We have a framed picture of him with an arm around my dad. The guy is clever, sly, but he never suspected a thing. At that time the feds had a very good relationship with the Intelligence Department of the Entre Ríos Police, even with the SIDE, but there were a few meetings of people from the country that they couldn't get into, and I could.

I was at the La Paz blockade. When you drive from Corrientes down Route 12, the first city you come to is La Paz. A blockade there, on that route, was strategic because the cars had to detour onto Route 14, and that was some seventy-five miles. And then when they got to Route 14 there was another blockade. I was also at the Subfluvial Tunnel blockade. I could put names to everyone there with De Angeli and that made the bosses trust me: it was my cousins, my friends, people from the country, who of course never imagined I was there to pass on information. Even when I was in Paraná, at the headquarters, if they let me know about a blockade in such and such place, I could show up and say I was coming from any town along the route, because I knew everyone. Afterward I would return to the office, write the report and fax it to Buenos Aires.

All this was ordered by Commissioner General Néstor

Vallecas, on his own initiative, not something handed down from above. I don't think that the ministry knew what I was doing. The Federal Police answered first to the Ministry of the Interior and then the Justice Department, until the Ministry of Security was created. Vallecas's order was totally anti-democratic. It went against the Intelligence Act. It wasn't supposed to happen, but it happened.

AN UNBEARABLE BUZZ

I began to suffer a permanent buzz in my ears. It's hard for someone who hasn't experienced it to understand. I couldn't sleep, I couldn't concentrate, it was miserable. I put in a request to travel to Buenos Aires to see some specialists. I thought the symptoms would improve with treatment, but after running a bunch of tests the doctors concluded that the damage was permanent. They diagnosed me with an internal lesion of the ear canal—the Organ of Corti—with perceptive hypoacusis in both ears accompanied by tinnitus. All a product of my work, to be certain. I decided to file an administrative complaint. In March of 2009 I wrote a letter detailing my career, the infiltration, and my ailments, meticulously; I raised it with Commissioner Vallecas, the head of the Federal Police force, knowing that it was going to cause an uproar. And that's what happened. "You can't hold us responsible for this," they told me. If anything could make me more of a pariah, this formal complaint was the tipping point.

By this time Eli was remarried with two sons. It had been difficult for her to get pregnant and she'd done fertility treatment. They told her she had a psychological block. The second of the two boys is the first one's twin, despite the fact that they're several years apart, because they used a frozen embryo. She gave him the name we'd picked for our son, if we ever had one. That destroyed me.

I ran into her a few times, by chance, and I asked her if she was in love. "I'm happy," she answered. I swear that if she'd told me she was in love, if she could've looked me in the eye and said those three words: "I'm in love," I would've been able to forget about her forever, but I couldn't. I still can't. I dream about her, I think constantly about our life together.

Eli is very decisive and that's why when she made the decision to leave me, I knew she'd never change her mind no matter what I did or how much I yearned to get back together. It must've been very hard for her to get over it. Because, like me, she couldn't do therapy. Who could she talk to about everything she went through with me?

Due to all my health-related issues I took a medical leave and moved back to Buenos Aires. That also helped me get away from Deputy Commissioner Mendoza, who had it out for me. I never went back to work in Paraná again.

BACK IN BUENOS AIRES

The force sent me to an anti-terrorism course led by Daniel, a guy from those meetings of undercover officers that Laura held in Retiro. It had been a long time since I'd seen him, because after the La Tablada insurrection we stopped having those meetings. Daniel had been undercover in the Radical political party and went by the last name Andrada. He didn't know me by my real name, Pérez, but as Jorge Polak.

I sat in the back, trying to pass unnoticed. Daniel now worked for the Anti-Terrorist Investigation Unit and the class he had to give was on the Middle East. At one point he showed a photo of Moshe Dayan, Yithzak Rabin, and Uni Narkis entering the old city of Jerusalem during the Six Day War. He got Narkis's name wrong, but I'd met the general when he'd come to Argentina and I had his personal business card. When the class ended, I went up to him.

As soon as he saw me he gave me a hug. "Oh, hey, Jorgito, how are you doing!" he greeted me warmly.

"What's up, Dani!" I answered.

We immediately struck up a conversation and I told him I was in the Lomas delegation.

He knew, of course, that I'd been undercover in the Jewish community. "You already know everything there is to know about all this, what are you doing in this class?" he asked, surprised.

"Well, I know a little I guess. For example that the guy in the photo is General Uzi Narkis, I've met him," I corrected him quietly, so that he wouldn't be embarrassed.

He told me he was going to talk to his superiors and have them bring me on to work with him. He called me to a meeting with his boss at the Alcorta Mall, next door to their office, and he said: "This kid spent ages undercover in the Jewish community, he knows a lot about the Middle East, the relationships between the different groups, the conflicts."

The boss asked me several questions to verify that what Daniel was saying was true, and when he finished, he asked: "Do you want to come on with us?"

Obviously, I said yes. It was my ticket out of exile, my

chance to be around people who could really appreciate what I had to offer. But my vacation days were coming up and between my medical leave and meetings with different offices, they never assigned me any position. Daniel and I became close anyway. We thought similarly on many things, we had the same criticisms. He was an honest guy. Or at least I thought so. But it would be a while before we were able to work together.

WORKING FOR THE MINISTER

Shortly before the end of 2010, the Ministry of Security was created and President Cristina Kirchner appointed Nilda Garré to head it. Garré had previously been director of the Ministry of Defense, managing the military men, hundreds of whom were being tried for the crimes perpetrated during the dictatorship. Doing this job as a woman, and one known to be a "leftist," from the left-wing of Peronism, was no easy feat but she'd led with a firm hand, and I wanted to help her now in her new post. Without someone to advise her, leading blindly, she wasn't going to get far.

I told Miriam and Horacio my idea. Garré had already heard about me from them so she knew some of my story. I told them that I'd like to offer my services to help her in whatever she needed, from my area, intelligence. I also talked about it with Daniel, and he wanted to approach her as well. Miriam tried to get in contact with Cristina Caamaño, a prosecutor who had investigated the murder of Mariano Ferreyra, a Communist militant assassinated by thugs from the

Railway Worker's Union. Caamaño had brought charges on José Pedraza, the union's secretary general, a very powerful guy, without batting an eye. And Minister Garré had called Caamaño in to be her right hand.

But before we could nail down a meeting, Daniel ran into Minister Garré by coincidence in Cariló. He told me how he waited for her to leave a shop where she was buying a ring and he asked for a meeting with her in Buenos Aires. Later on he joked with her and said that if Minister Garré took as long to make a decision as she did to pick out a ring we were toast. But he said it in jest, because he had enormous respect for her.

Garré soon set up a new area of the ministry, the Department for Intelligence on Organized Crime, and she put Daniel in charge. He chose me, along with some other guys, to help him. Before we started work in the new department, Minister Garré invited me to her house to get to know me and hear the story of my undercover work firsthand. The conversation left an impression. She made me feel safe and free to tell the full truth without fear. When I finished, she told me that she was personally going to guarantee my safety. And up to now, I can assure you that she did not let me down.

The period in which I worked with Daniel for the Ministry was probably the most comfortable I'd been. The department had its offices at San Juan and Catamarca, but I didn't work there. I worked alone and met Daniel at places around town. I also sent weekly reports to Nilda. Daniel seemed highly professional and transparent about his work, insisting that everything had to be done within the law. He never moved forward with any procedure, never tailed anyone in an investigation if it wasn't first ordered by the judge assigned to the case.

There were internal conflicts between different groups

within the Ministry, people who had come from other areas and didn't agree with Daniel or who disliked his influence on Nilda. I knew they would try to get rid of him if given the chance and I'd warned Daniel to be careful with his computers. He told me he had it under control, that he had specialists advising him, but in the end it happened. They hacked his e-mail and they sent his wife some messages he'd exchanged with a woman he was having an affair with. They also turned him in to Minister Garré. The effect was catastrophic. Because when Nilda had met with Dani for the first time, she'd said: "First off I want to know everything about your life. I don't want anyone to be able to come to me saying something I didn't hear from you, is that clear?"

She felt betrayed and she let him go. I don't know if the accusations were true or not, but they included financial matters as well, because they even claimed he owned racehorses. What I do know is that he made a mistake and he paid for it. He was relieved of his duties, although he continued to receive his salary.

Meanwhile, I had taken advantage of my return to Buenos Aires to show up for as many Jewish community activities as I could. I never missed one. It was good for me to be reunited with my old friends, I felt comfortable. I even went back to the new AMIA offices on Pasteur, which had been rebuilt with a security pavilion in front of the main building. They never searched me, I was still considered part of their security force.

But, in addition to participating in the protests demanding justice for the bombings, which I fully supported, I went hoping I might run into Eli. One time, I met Lutzky at a café on the corner of Suipacha and Santa Fe so that we could go together to a protest at the Israeli embassy on the anniversary of the attack. We began walking toward Arroyo, where there were barricades with security checkpoints and Eli was there, in her role as secretary for the second-in-command at the Israeli embassy. I don't know why, but I was armed that day and I told her this. Of course, it wasn't allowed. She spoke with the chief of security and explained that I was a friend.

"I'll let you in, but if anything happens, don't pull out your gun, because you're not authorized. I don't know you," he told me, but he let us in.

That was the last time I saw her. Later on, she helped me get medication for my father and she was very nice, but we never again met in person.

I ran into Miriam at a demonstration on the anniversary of the bombing, at Pasteur. She was standing on the stage, to one side, transmitting live for the TV station she worked for and holding the microphone for the speakers. I waved to her from the ground, subtly, with a complicit smile.

It had been a long time since I'd heard from Gabriel Levinas, to the point that I imagined he'd forgotten about me. But one night in winter of 2012, I think it was August, I received a call from Miriam. She told me that Gabriel was beside himself because his teenage son, who was visiting Buenos Aires from Holland, had disappeared. He wanted to know if there was anything I could do. I got in touch with Daniel and told him. He immediately sent out two search brigades and they located the boy. Levinas was so grateful that he wanted to give Daniel a gift to thank him, but Daniel wouldn't hear of it. He told him he was just doing his job.

WRONG TIME

I was working in Garré's new ministry and I continued to meet with Horacio and Miriam. They believed there would never be better circumstances under which to testify, and I was in full agreement. Under Nilda's wing, as she swept all the filth from the force, nothing could touch me. Also, from that first conversation I'd had with her I'd made it clear that I wanted to testify, that I felt it was my responsibility to share everything I knew so that those responsible for the attacks could be brought to justice. I'd also said that I wanted to do it soon, with the necessary support, of course. Nilda had been in agreement. But for some reason that neither Horacio, Miriam, nor I could understand, once I made up my mind and I wrote her a message saying that I felt ready to speak out, she responded simply: "It's the wrong time for it."

Horacio, Miriam, and I spent ages analyzing those words, but none of us could come to any conclusion. Who knows what she meant. Because, afterward, I don't remember how long later, Nilda was asked to resign and they replaced her, in June of 2013. I only have good things to say about her, because she never let me down, never failing to answer a single one of my e-mails, phone calls, requests. Without Daniel, without Nilda, I was left at the mercy of people within the agency who wanted to wipe me off the map. Cristina Caamaño was still there, although only for a few more months because she was going to return first to the DA's office and then later to be named head of the Wiretaps Office, on Avenida de los Incas, which had previously been run by the SIDE State Intelligence and we called Ojota: Judicial Observations.

The unit that Minister Garré created was dismantled and

I, at Nilda's express request, went to work for a time under Commissioner Roque Luna in the Superintendence for the Interior and Complex Federal Crimes, which had been previously called Federal Coordination.

My problems started when they sent me to work at Judicial Observations. Problems I surely wouldn't have had with Cristina Caamaño as boss, but unfortunately it all fell apart for me about a year before that, which I'll explain. It was impossible for me to work there, as bad as being at headquarters on Moreno and San José, because there was staff everywhere and I was totally exposed. There were people from Chaco, from the provincial police forces, who came in to do wiretaps for specific cases they were investigating. The order was for me to track the communications from several military officers who had fled when faced with charges of crimes against humanity. They told me I could do it without headphones, because of the buzzing in my ears, but it was impossible, ridiculous.

And then, one officer, a woman who was an eternal rival of Laura by the last name Rojo, figured out who I was and tried to trap me when she discovered that I'd asked the office for information so I could reconnect with an old flame, something everyone did even though it was prohibited. She filed an administrative complaint and even asked them to arrest me. It was an old grudge that she wanted to take out on me.

In the meantime, Horacio and Miriam continued to come up with theories on why no one, not Israel, Jewish organizations, community leaders, the government, or the Justice Department seemed interested in the local connection for the two attacks. I had a very clear hypothesis of my own that could be summed up in one word: money.

MONEY, MONEY, MONEY

When the kabatim Israeli security course ended, in 1995, two army coronels moved to Argentina from Israel. One of them was named chief of security for DAIA by Rubén Beraja. His name was Amir Eshet. He immediately began to set up a sophisticated security structure; he'd even brought in equipment to sweep for microphones. They gave him a list of everyone who'd completed the kabatim course and he called us in one by one; he wanted to select three men to be Beraja's bodyguards. They called me and I went to an interview with Amir himself in the Banco Mayo building. This was Beraja's bank, at Sarmiento and Maipú. Amir asked me a series of questions and a few days later I received a call telling me I'd been selected and asking for some more information.

So I had been chosen as a personal bodyguard for the president of DAIA, the federation of Jewish organizations, the community's highest authority. I knew that it was an important achievement for my mission, but, personally, with the doubts that had begun to plague me about my agency's role in the attacks, I didn't want anything to do with it. I told Red the news and, luckily, she gave me the order to turn it down. "You can't guard Beraja," she told me. She hadn't even wanted me to do the kabatim course in the first place because she was convinced I would stand out and raise suspicions. In this case, of course, I didn't argue.

One afternoon, when I wasn't home, Eli answered the phone in the apartment. Someone named Nardi was asking to speak with me. I later found out he was a retired Commissioner Major of the Federal Police who came from the Superintendence of the Interior. He was partnering with

Amir, the Israeli coronel, to set up a security company, for which the presence of a former superior official of the armed forces or police was a necessary requirement. So they'd already gone into business together, the Argentine cops and the Israelis. Nardi knew about Jorge Polak, the undercover agent, and he could've accessed my file, my real identification.

I let Laura know that I was once again at risk. The guy probably wondered why I'd rejected the post, he was sniffing around. He looked everywhere for me for two or three weeks. Two of my friends had been selected for the security team Amir was setting up. One of them was the kabat for the Maimonides Institute on Nazca and Avellaneda, and the other was head of security for Ioná. They resigned from their posts and went to work with Beraja. When they asked me why I'd turned the job down, I told them I'd been "summoned" to work somewhere else, implying that I was "above" it. And they didn't probe any further.

The other coronel who moved to Argentina to help with security in the community was much more of a pirate than Amir. He'd come from Israel with an authorization from SIBAT, the Department of Exterior Assistance and Exports, part of the Israeli Ministry of Defense, fully official. Not just anyone can say that they were in the Israeli army and that the State of Israel then sponsored them as a marketing tool. He was named Amar Salman, and he opened an agency called SIA. The local version of Black Water, a security company that absorbed former members of the Israeli army and used them as mercenaries, hired by anyone from narcos to human traffickers. Salman was in Angola, and now lives in Argentina, like Amir, but he brokers multi-million dollar deals with companies, offering them assistance to help "grow business in complex environments." But he also works with governments, because the agency gives courses on krav maga, hand to hand combat, and even intelligence systems for prisons. And that's just what they advertise openly.

Then there was Gustavo Dorf, who I'd met in his role as head of Institutional Security for the Jewish community. He was the top boss of bitajon, responsible for guaranteeing the safety of all activities held by the collective, supervising all security systems in place across the different social, sports, and educational complexes. Dorf ended up working with Commissioner Roque Luna, the last of my bosses in the force, in security for a session of the International Olympic Committee held in Buenos Aires. There were sheiks and presidents in attendance, even Prince Felipe of Asturias. It was like two presidential conferences in one because of the complexity. The whole surrounding area was barricaded off, there were scanners, GPS systems for all phones, cameras, the rooms were swept by anti-explosive experts and the food was even monitored. More than 180 guys were working under him at the Hilton in Puerto Madero. At that time, Dorf had already been charged for defrauding the Mothers of Plaza de Mayo. Together with Sergio Schoklender, they signed several multi-million dollar contracts for armored cars for their company, Armoring Systems, and that caught the eye of the prosecutors.

Another former Israeli military man who landed in Buenos Aires around the time of the attack was Meir Zamir. I must've run into him more than once among the rescue workers. For some reason he decided to stay on in Argentina and partnered with Brigadier Andrés Antonietti, a friend of Menem who'd started out as an aide and ended up as secretary of security. Zamir sold Israeli weapons to the Paraguayans and ended up being—like Antonietti—close with Lino Oviedo, one of the generals who had been responsible for the military coup.

They were in Asunción, Paraguay, when Oviedo's rival, Luis Argaña was assassinated. They say that Zamir was kidnapped by Paraguayan police and forced to give up Oviedo's bunker in Greater Buenos Aires but was saved by a timely call from a Menem government official.

As a sampling, I think that's more than enough to demonstrate that, with the excuse of the AMIA case, a bunch of people from the Jewish community partnered with members of the Federal Police to start successful businesses, and many are now millionaires. Meanwhile, no one was interested in the truth about the local involvement in what happened. And I continued to be bounced around like a rubber ball.

PART VII

It was a relief to have Miriam join the effort to aid Iosi. He introduced us, in another meeting like so many others, and we immediately hit it off. From then on, Miriam and I took turns meeting with the spy and each other as we feverishly ran through all the options we had at our disposal to secure favorable conditions for Iosi to testify. She had the same reservations as I did, identical fears. Together we walked the surprising paths that led us from Nilda Garré to Cristina Kirchner. We went into the SIDE headquarters and met face to face with Jaime Stiuso. We joined forces, temporarily, with Gabriel Levinas, who put us in touch with the American Jewish Committee. We prepared a proposal for a television production company and argued a request for asylum with the Inter-American Commission on Human Rights. Then one day Miriam told me that Levinas was going to publish an article about Iosi; there was no way to persuade him to wait. We set up a meeting so we could give Iosi the news.

"You no longer have a choice," I told him at a table in an old, spacious café on Montevideo Street.

"Levinas is going to give you up," Miriam nodded worriedly.

Iosi went pale. "He can't do that, he knows that what I told him, because you guys vouched for him, wasn't meant to be published, it was for safety reasons. I'll be exposed and defenseless, my family too!"

"He told me he was only going to publish a paragraph, without any details about who you are or any identifying information," Miriam said.

"But we don't know how far he might go," I added.

"Whatever the case, Iosi, it's an enormous risk," Miriam said. "I think you should leave the country as soon as possible and then we can try to set something up."

"And what about my dad? He's old and sick and he depends on me. Who's going to take care of him? And what about my son?" Iosi put his head in his hands, more desperate than we'd ever seen him, cursing over and over.

Time was running out, so I was direct with him: "You have two options: leave the country or enter witness protection. Think about it."

EXIT STRATEGY

We left Iosi with a difficult decision. I knew someone who worked in the National Witness Protection Program, and I promised to reach out to him. Luciano Hazán had been a lawyer for the Grandmothers of Plaza de Mayo. Young and well-versed in issues related to human rights, he immediately made time to see me when I asked for an urgent meeting to discuss a classified matter. Luciano worked with the Truth and Justice Program on cases of crimes against humanity and had also aided the prosecution to prepare the charges for the cover-up of the AMIA case. We'd been in touch because he'd used my book *Toasting over the Rubble* as evidence. Miriam knew him as well and felt, as I did, that he was trustworthy and committed to revealing the truth about the bombings.

He listened intently as I sat in his office explaining the situation, but he asked me not to give him any details on the person in question because it could compromise his role as a government employee with the obligation to bring charges. It was enough for him to know that it was an individual who was at risk and who could have information related to the AMIA case.

"We have the resources to protect witnesses, send them to live in remote locations, and help them change their identity," Luciano told me, "but, given the delicate nature of the issue, I'm going to have to raise it with my superiors."

Days later, the subsecretary of the National Justice Department, Juan Martín Mena, opened his office on a holiday to listen, along with Hazán, to what Miriam and I were asking on Iosi's behalf. That April 2, 2014, Mena had just come from the Casa Rosada where he'd attended an official event in commemoration of those fallen in the Malvinas War. On his desk were photos of Cristina and Néstor Kirchner. He sat down in shirtsleeves on one of the brown leather sofas in his office, and the rest of us followed suit. He showed sincere interest—and shock—as we summed up the story for him. He assured us that he could safeguard the lives of Iosi and his family, so that the spy could share what he knew.

"We have cases of police officers who reported internal crimes within the force and we've had to move their entire family into protection, a large group of people. We can do that," he told us.

He also assured us that the witness protection system had been completely revamped and now functioned properly. Iosi could give a statement that would open an investigation and from that moment on he would remain hidden and protected. His case would probably be led by one of the judges previously involved in some aspect of the AMIA case, after Justice Galeano was charged with coverup.

Miriam and I felt like we were finally close to obtaining an appropriate level of security that would allow Iosi to reveal his story safe from the media circus that characterized every supposed revelation in the AMIA case. When we said our goodbyes, we asked for as much speediness as possible in the decision-making process so that we could coordinate the testimony and secure the evidence that the judge deemed necessary before the story made its way into the public eye. After that, Iosi's life could begin to run serious risk.

But days went by and there was no response. It was mid-April of 2014, and we were certain that the information on Iosi would be published in late June or early July at the latest, to land right on the eve of the anniversary of the bombings on July 18th.

MESSAGING

We began to grow impatient. In the following weeks I sent countless messages to Luciano asking for news. But they were always waiting on final approval from "higher up," which he promised would come through soon. This went on until the last week of June when, at a social event, Miriam found out that Levinas's book had already gone to print, although it had not yet been distributed. For some time, Google had been digitizing books and making some pages available to be read online. I had the idea to search for the new edition of Gabriel's book and there it was. Among the pages that could be read, was the "little paragraph" on Iosi. Just as I'd suspected, he had not held back any identifying information or taken any consideration for the safety of his source: he told Iosi's story at length, over several pages, using his real name. He included many confusing direct quotes taken from the video, full of errors but enough to convert Iosi into a walking target. He even used Eli's real name, although they'd been divorced for years and she'd remarried and had children with her new husband. Her brother's name was in there as well. When Miriam called to confront him about his lack of journalistic ethics, he responded that he'd been wrong in publishing some of the names but that he hadn't even realized it because he'd run out of time and sent the video to a transcriber. "I didn't even read it," he said by way of excuse. He also said that Iosi had more than enough time to do what he needed to do to ensure his safety.

I immediately wrote to my contact in Witness Protection: "Hello, Luciano. The guy published his book, it's going to be everywhere in a few days. The person in question is desperate for protection. Can anything be done, urgently? He'd be willing to go and talk anywhere."

We spoke over the phone and the conclusion was the same: the first step was for Iosi to testify. He could provide incriminating evidence against a long list of federal police commissioners. After Jorge Julio López had disappeared for doing something similar, it was not an action to be taken lightly.

"So, once he testifies, will you move him into witness protection immediately?" I asked.

"The judge is the one who has to ask that he be placed in witness protection. As soon as he gets in touch with us, we'll evaluate all the options."

"And what if the judge refuses? What if he doesn't ask Witness Protection to get involved?"

"That's never happened. The logical thing would be for him to request protection. Tell your guy to testify and we'll be waiting for the order."

"Can you guarantee that it will work out that way?"

"I can't guarantee it, no. But that's the way it usually goes."

Now I had to convince Iosi to appear before a judge under the assumption that they would "most likely" place him in witness protection. As the Argentine hypnotist and illusionist Tu Sam said, "It could fail." In this case, I didn't want to think about the consequences of a single misstep.

Also, even if many things had changed for the better within the Justice Department, the federal penal system was still a complex landscape. A swampy terrain littered with opportunistic political operators and intelligence agents that I was unaccustomed to navigating, given that my legal expertise was limited to trademarks, patents, and intellectual property. Justice Galeano had been stripped of his post for intentionally sabotaging the AMIA case, but the reputation of the court that held the case had been damaged, especially where everything related to the AMIA investigation was concerned.

Iosi asked me to go with him to testify, prepared to finally lift the veil that had hidden him for twenty-eight years of his life. But, first, he wanted more assurance from Witness Protection, to feel supported in the move he was about to make. I started another round of calls but days went by without any concrete answers.

It was clear that the Ministry of Justice would not intervene until Iosi took a decisive step but he needed to enter witness protection urgently. It was already July, with the anniversary of the attack looming, and the press would grab onto any news about the attacks. This time around, Levinas hoped his book would become the lead story. We knew that at any moment the alarm would begin to sound.

Thursday, July 3rd my anxiety was killing me and I had a bad feeling. I thought about how crazy it was to leave Iosi unprotected as the weekend approached. I made a decision: I called him and told him we had the green light and we had to go before the judge without a second to lose. Immediately.

"But did they give you any guarantee?"

"Don't worry. It's all under control," I lied, silently thankful that he couldn't see my face as I went red.

BLIND FAITH

Iosi was resigned. He agreed to testify if I would go with him. We arranged to meet on Friday July 4th in the Plaza Tribunales Café, near Lavalle Plaza, where I'd spoken at the Active Memory group's Monday events demanding justice for the AMIA case. We planned to meet that Friday at 11:00 a.m. to chat briefly over coffee and then take one of the buses that went to the courthouse on Comodoro Py in Retiro.

A few minutes past 8:30 in the morning I was driving down

Corrientes Avenue toward my office downtown. Like every morning for the past several months, I'd just dropped a family member off for treatment at the Hospital Italiano. I wasn't in a good place, emotionally; I was overwhelmed and constantly in a bad mood, but I couldn't abandon Iosi to his fate. I listened to one of the morning news shows as I drove, the least apocalyptic one I could find, since I was already nervous enough over the situation I was about to face. A few blocks before I reached Callao, my phone rang. It was my friend Alejandro, one of the people connected to the film production company we'd contacted a while back about the story of an undercover agent in the Jewish community. I put the call on speaker and answered as I waited at a red light.

"Hello, Horacio, did you see what Levinas published today in *La Nación*?" he asked.

I felt a blow to the gut. "No, I didn't see it, but I know what you're talking about. I'm driving, let me call you back."

I hung up and looked for a place to pull over and buy a newspaper. I read the article, hurriedly, on the street. I called Iosi on the spot to tell him the news and move our meeting forward. We met outside the café at 9:30, too anxious to go inside despite the icy wind that blew across the plaza. The article talked about a federal mole who had gone undercover in the Jewish community. The story had been twisted to somehow place the blame on Cristina Kirchner's government, making it seem like a political operation of the worst kind and finishing up with a plug for Levinas's new book. Iosi's identity wasn't printed in the article, but that information was surely only hours away from being revealed. For certain heavyweights in the Federal Police, the race to unmask the source had undoubtedly already begun.

We talked for a few minutes standing on the cold corner

outside the café and then went to get on the bus. The trip was short but charged with tension and unease. We walked up the long stairway to the courthouse, passing several TV cameras and reporters waiting to get statements from lawyers, plaintiffs, or defendants for the cases of current interest. Once we walked through the front doors of the courthouse, I felt somewhat more at ease. We were no longer outside, exposed to the elements.

In the wide reception hall, I asked for directions to the office of Justice Rodolfo Canicoba Corral, the judge assigned to the AMIA case, as Iosi waited at a prudent distance. The security guard told me how to get there and which elevator to take, never imagining the story behind the man I was escorting. We passed several more uniformed federal officers as we moved through the building. I didn't dare to leave Iosi waiting alone downstairs. We got on an elevator surrounded by lawyers, paralegals, and clients. On the way, we overheard a woman say to her lawyer: "I hope the guy rots in jail." It wasn't the kind of comment we wanted to hear at that moment.

I walked hurriedly down a long hallway, and then another, to the offices of the court, as Iosi waited near the stairway. I wouldn't have him come in until I had some minimal guarantee. I approached the secretary, anxious and praying that everything would turn out all right. "I need to speak to His Honor Canicoba Corral about an urgent matter; it's a witness linked to the AMIA case and he's in danger," I said, as I presented myself as a lawyer and journalist. I was immediately greeted by the court clerk assigned to the case.

"It's a spy who was undercover in the Jewish community, mentioned today in an article in *La Nación*," I told her, trying to be brief and concise. "His life is in danger."

The woman listened sympathetically, but immediately let

me know that the judge would not be able to hear the testimony. I imagined that the excuse would be his absence or some circumstantial obstacle.

"The AMIA case is being handled by Prosecutor Alberto Nisman, and he's the one who has to receive the testimony," she told me, without leaving any room for arguement.

I left the office disoriented and unsure of what to do. I knew that the judge had placed Prosecutor Nisman in charge of the case but I'd supposed, erroneously, that he would want to take an initial statement from Iosi if he showed up at his chambers. Luciano had not warned me of this possible hurdle.

It was getting closer to the court's closing time and Iosi and I were still wandering the Kafkaesque hallways of the enormous building, trying to think of a way out of the situation. We couldn't let the courts close and the weekend begin with the most wanted spy in Buenos Aires out wandering the streets. We sat down on a bench to go over our options. There was only one choice left: pay a visit to the prosecutor.

I knew Alberto Nisman; I had criticized his work on more than one occasion and did not trust him. On November 9, 2005, at a press conference surrounded by lawyers and the administrators of DAIA and AMIA, he'd held up a picture and claimed that the "suicide driver" had been identified, the man who—he said—had blown himself up behind the wheel of a van turned car bomb. This was based off the report that had been drafted in January of 2003 by the SIDE, headed by Miguel Angel Toma, with input from US and Israeli intelligence services. The front pages of all the newspapers the next day ran the same headline: "Suicide Bomber in AMIA Attack Identified."

After reading Nisman's very weak evidence to support his announcement, I published a satirical article in *New Zion* that enraged him: "Perpetrator of the Embassy Attack Also Identified." Using the same kind of forced logic as Nisman, I "proved" that the attack on the embassy had been perpetrated by "Mingo," referring to "Minguito Tinguitella," the character popularized by actor Juan Carlos Altavista. I concluded the article with a parody of the press conference: "A FIFA informant who has joined the case testified that at one point—weeks or months before the attack—'Mingo' walked slowly past Carlos Pellegrini and Arroyo, less than sixty meters from the embassy, and subsequently stayed in the vicinity, supposedly to buy cigarettes at a kiosk from which he could view the terrorist target, despite the fact that his family members confirm that at the time 'Mingo' had once again quit smoking. The investigators have obtained the terrorist's clinical history, which clearly states that he had been advised to quit smoking. Faced with the overwhelming evidence, the judicial clerks, along with lawyers, Jewish community directors, journalists, PR specialists, singers, artists, poets, and building co-op administrators are all rushing to share the photo of the terrorist, reproduced here, with which, after fifteen years of patient effort, this investigation is brought to a close." Below, I included a comical photo of Mingo.

It was ridiculous, just like the prosecutor's conclusion, which was grossly mistaken and was discredited shortly thereafter. To my surprise, Nisman called Guillermo Lipis, the then director of *New Zion*, to express his anger over the article. A few years later, when I was gathering information for my book, I went to see him at the DA's office. In *Toasting over the Rubble* I once again criticized the official explanation of the attack upheld by the prosecution and Jewish community leadership. I sent Nisman a copy through the publishing house, as he'd asked me to. He called to thank me for sending it and promised he'd let me know his thoughts; I never heard them, but I can imagine. Now I had to go and ask him to save a man's life.

TESTIFYING WITHOUT NISMAN

Iosi and I went back out onto the street. The icy air in that area near the port whipped our faces but we could hardly feel it. I stopped a taxi to take us to Plaza de Mayo, where the DA's office was located. Time was of the essence and traffic was terrible. I tried several times, with no luck, to reach Nisman on his cell phone. I wanted to give him a heads up about the reason for my visit and check that he would be available. It went straight to voicemail every time. I hoped that he hadn't decided to leave Buenos Aires that Friday. Between each call to Nisman, I received anxious messages from Miriam, but all I had time to tell her was that everything was under control. I couldn't give her more details, it didn't make sense to worry her needlessly. Also, there was nothing she could do, as much as she wanted to help.

We got out of the taxi on the corner of the old building that stood just steps from the Cabildo and the historic plaza, an area crawling with police presence. We decided it would be best for Iosi to wait nearby for news from me. After passing through the building's security, I got off the elevator on the floor of the DA's office and had to explain to more guards that I was there to see Prosecutor Nisman on an urgent matter. I didn't have an appointment, but it was urgent. I waited, impatiently, in the small reception area. One of the guards told me that the prosecutor's secretary would be with me shortly. A while later, the door opened.

"Who's looking for the DA?" asked the slim assistant.

"I'm Dr. Lutzky, the DA knows me, it's about an important matter that I can only explain to him."

"Dr. Nisman is out sick today."

Unbelievable, I thought. "There's no way to get in touch with him? It's very urgent."

She told me that she was going to call him and that they'd let me talk to him through a secure line. Minutes later, she led me through to a large meeting room that I'd been in before and she offered to turn on a TV to create background noise. I agreed. She brought in a cell phone and left me on the line with the DA before she left.

"I have a terrible flu that really did me in, I'm destroyed. But they have me on antibiotics now so I suppose I'll be able to get back into work on Monday. Tell me what this is about."

"Did you see *La Nación* today . . ."

"Yes, the thing about the spy," he said, interrupting me. "I'm already on it. I want to call Levinas in. They told me he's out of town."

"Forget Levinas. I have the guy, Iosi, waiting nearby. He wants to testify. But only if you can put him immediately into witness protection. They're already aware of the situation, but you're the one who has to put in the request."

"Don't worry, I'll take care of it. You bring him in, my two assistants can take the statement with me on videoconference. They have my total trust. I'll supervise everything."

"I need reassurance. To know that he'll be protected as soon as he comes in," I insisted.

"Yes," he answered. "Tell him that as soon as he sits down, I'll formally request he be placed under witness protection. I can do it by phone, all it takes is a call to the ministry. We'll do it while he's testifying. It won't be a problem. But you're not going to be able to stay for the testimony."

I went downstairs to get Iosi and returned to the DA's office with him. He was pale, exhausted. We'd been under a lot of pressure for the last several hours. But also, the spy knew that from this moment onward his life would be dramatically different, and that he was going to have to disappear from all the places he frequented. To leave his home and cut all his affective ties. I walked him to the door of the DA's office and left him with one of the secretaries, who offered to let me wait in reception. But she warned me it would probably be a while. I left.

Moments later, Iosi would begin to reveal his story. A part of it, only a small part. Because, like so many other times, the Justice Department employees charged with investigating the AMIA case stayed only on the surface. The spy planted in the Jewish community, who carried out the bulk of his undercover work during the Menem government, was immediately manipulated for political means. Over the following days, Nisman—in parallel with Gabriel Levinas—twisted Iosi's testimony into a criticism of Nilda Garré and, by extension, Cristina Kirchner. Just a few months later, Nisman would present formal charges of cover-up against President Cristina Kirchner, an accusation he claimed to have been working on for a year and a half before our visit to the DA's office.

I went back to work but returned several times in the seven or eight hours that Iosi's testimony went on. Meanwhile, I exchanged anxious messages with my contact at the witness protection program. Nisman had put in the formal request, as promised, and Iosi's protection measures were being arranged. It was now nighttime and the director of the National Witness Protection Program was on his way to collect Iosi. They told me that he was exhausted, but doing fine. That he sent me his thanks. He was soon going away to live in a secret location and we wouldn't be able to speak again. Only then was I able to call Miriam and leave her with the assurance that the situation was under control. And that unforgettable Friday was finally over.

Just as I'd suspected, that weekend, Levinas published another article, announcing the new edition of his book and including a photo of Iosi along with his personal information. There were no longer any doubts who the mole was and many members of the police force would be surprised by the news. The article, in the Sunday edition of *Perfil*, bore the title "A Spy Inside AMIA." It included extracts from the video that Levinas recorded of Iosi, which would be republished days later in the journal *Noticias* and on Levinas's personal webpage as well. In order to cover his ass, the author—or the editors of *Perfil* at his insistence—added a caption under Iosi's picture, reading: "The interview was conducted with *Pérez's consent.*" *If* we take the term "interview" as a journalistic genre, then the statement was false. Levinas, the next day, not only recognized in a radio interview that he had not been authorized to share the video, but he also admitted to having gone against his source's will.

In his interview with the Miguel Steuermann, on Jai Radio, Monday July 7, Levinas had no idea that I'd taken Yossi (the spelling Levinas chose for his name) in to testify, stating that the spy could not testify before the Argentine justice system. "This is a man who is a member of the armed forces; he was doing the job he was hired to do, and there are internal protocols within the Federal Police that have to be complied with. He didn't do anything that the Federal Police isn't all but authorized to do." And to another question, he admitted: "He doesn't even want me to tell his story." All that mattered to Levinas was the media coverage, days away from the anniversary of the bombing, and most of all he wanted to dump charges of espionage onto Nilda Garré and the Cristina Kirchner government, as he expressly stated in interviews and numerous tweets.

Prosecutor Nisman attempted to give the spy's testimony the same political spin. In his first statements to the media, Nisman took aim at Nilda Garré. Then, in a matter of hours, a copy of Iosi's testimony had been leaked to the press, and some excerpts of it were published, making a huge scandal out of something that should've remained a strict secret in the DA's office. Beyond the brief media uproar, which formed part of the chorus of complaints against the government, the investigation into the Federal Police's role in the attacks did not move an inch, just as Miriam and I had feared.

For the past ten years, Nisman had done absolutely nothing to identify the local connection to the attack; why would he change course now? If he dug down even just a little bit, he'd have easily uncovered agreements and connections between leaders of the Jewish community and members of the Federal Police that should've been investigated. Iosi's testimony was a clear signpost pointing in that direction but it was ignored because it did not serve the DA's working hypothesis.

The issue soon lost steam. What was worse, we also got our hands on a copy of Iosi's testimony and we were able to verify that, once again, falsehoods plagued the AMIA case. The official record stated that DA Nisman was present, which was not true. Because he did not even participate by teleconference. The entire interrogation was carried out by the DA's assistants. But the minutes read: "In the city of Buenos

Aires, on the fourth day of the month of July in the year 2014, appearing before District Attorney Nisman sits an individual who has been made aware that they are about to provide a sworn statement." And, at the end, it closes with "after reading this statement aloud and ratifying it, the witness provided their signature in the presence of District Attorney Nisman." So the events described did not match the reality. More important than the accuracy of the procedural minutes was their utilization to political ends, another characteristic of the AMIA case.

Days and weeks went by with no news of Iosi. His testimony on the Federal Police and Intelligence Services' involvement in the attacks had disappeared from the newspapers. The big issue on debate was the memorandum of agreement with Iran, hastily drafted and signed by minister of foreign affairs, *Héctor Timerman*, as well as his Iranian counterpart and passed through Argentina's Congress with the reported objective of making it possible to take statements from the Iranian terrorists on Interpol's red list accused of the bombings. A "Commission for Truth" would be set up to examine the evidence but the constitutionality of this commission was challenged in court by Jewish entities, after an initial display of support. The issue was the center of public debate, a polarizing topic, with the Kirchner government and its supporters generally in favor, and the opposition, against it.

DA Nisman spoke out against it. The political climate at the time was quite tense and Nisman's mentor, the dark purveyor of evidence for all of the prosecutor's rulings, Jaime Stiuso, was finally removed from his post as "de facto" head of the SIDE in December 2014. Stiuso had entered the state intelligence services in the seventies, before the military dictatorship, and his removal caused a true firestorm. Everyone expected some reprisal from the most powerful spy in the nation.

On the morning of January 14, 2015 a huge story was splashed across the pages of newspapers across Argentina and the entire world: the district attorney for the AMIA case, Alberto Nisman, had presented formal charges of cover-up against President Cristina Kirchner, Héctor Timerman, and other minor players, accused of negotiating the removal of Interpol's red alerts on Iranian terrorists in exchange for business contracts. The impact was major. That night, Alberto Nisman appeared on the TN station news and swore that Jaime Stiuso had nothing to do with the charges he'd presented. And that if he had requested Stiuso's help in the investigation into the attack at all it was because the Kirchners told him that Stiuso "knew more about the AMIA case than anyone." The same phrase, word for word, that Cristina had said to Miriam and I when she sent us to see him.

That following Monday, Nisman was scheduled to present evidence for his charges against Cristina before Congress. Hours before dawn that morning, the sound of a message on my cell phone woke me from my dreams. Alarmed by the hour, I checked it. It was Miriam and I couldn't believe what she was telling me: Nisman was dead.

The bloody scene in the bathroom of Nisman's apartment suggested suicide by a weapon Nisman had asked his assistant to obtain. A large swathe of the public, however, believed it to be a murder ordered by the government. A few hours later, the scorched body of a woman was discovered directly across the street from Nisman's apartment in the luxurious Le Parc Tower in Puerto Madero, probably the most well-guarded building in all of Buenos Aires, and the one most squarely in the eye of the media at that moment. She was found lying against a small building of the electric company, in the center of the boulevard. Incredibly, no one ever identified her; none of the parties involved in the investigation seemed to think it relevant. Days passed amidst a growing state of social unrest, which included a massive demonstration under the torrential rain, convoked by a group of fellow prosecutors "in favor of justice" with a markedly oppositional and accusatory tone toward President Cristina Kirchner.

Miriam sent me another worrying message: "In the midst of this storm, it would be easy to toss in another body . . . have you heard from Iosi?"

It was several days before we heard from him. He was fine. Anxious, but safe. Nisman's death had shaken us. Miriam and I began to follow the stories related to our old SIDE acquaintance, Jaime Stisuo. The most keen analysts suspected his involvement in the elimination of DA Nisman and, even more so, in the charges against Cristina Kirchner. Nisman had tried several times, unsuccessfully, to communicate with one of Stiuso's cell phones in the last hours of his life. The former spy was called in to give a statement. Shortly thereafter, Stiuso left the country.

The star prosecutor for the AMIA case and the spy who supposedly knew "the case better than anyone" were both gone. Forensic experts insisted that all evidence pointed to suicide as the cause of Nisman's death, but many people were skeptical. The federal officers assigned to guard him had shirked their duties immediately before the tragedy occurred. Sounded familiar.

Stiuso had been stripped of his control over the Secretariat of Intelligence, but he still held onto secrets surrounding the deaths of more than a hundred people in the two unsolved terrorist attacks, and, probably, the secret of DA Nisman's death as well.

Stuck in the middle of all this was Iosi, with truths that no one seemed to want to hear.

PART VIII

What's important to know is how I got here, buried alive in this place. It was my own fault. My fault for trusting someone I shouldn't have. The biggest mistake a spy can make.

In April 2014, Miriam told me that Levinas was going to publish a new edition of his book about the AMIA attack for the twentieth anniversary of the bombing, and he'd warned her that he was going to include a "little paragraph" about me. But it was more than a little paragraph, it was all my personal information and information about people close to me, including Eli. Miriam found out when, at Gabriel's birthday party, he gave a copy of the book, hot of the presses, to another friend and he said to her with a little smile: "Better if you don't read it."

I was furious. Horacio and Miriam had to calm me down to keep me from doing something crazy. I couldn't even begin to imagine telling my son what had happened. How to talk to Eli. She had a family, children, her job at the embassy. At that time she was secretary to the second in command; I'd placed her in a delicate position. She wouldn't even see me, she'd made an effort to keep her distance, to cut off all contact.

I was so upset I couldn't think straight. Horacio and Miriam both tried to convince me that the only way out was to enter the national witness protection program, after testifying. Horacio took me and I let myself be pulled along; I didn't even know where I was going. I think we met in Tribunales, on Lavalle, we went first to the courthouse on Comodoro Py in Retiro and finally landed in the office of DA Nisman, across from Plaza de Mayo. Nisman had left, they told us he was out sick, I think it was the flu. I never spoke with him; I never saw him. But Horacio, in spite of the fact that he didn't trust him, told me that I had to testify, and I listened to him.

I talked. I talked and talked to those three strangers, probably secretaries, I don't know. They typed into their computers the whole time and every once in a while would ask a question. I wasn't in the best mood, that was obvious. I felt like I was standing on unstable ground, that the earth would open up and swallow me. At the end, they told me to verbally request to enter the witness protection program, because that was a requirement to set the process in motion. They said I couldn't see Horacio again, even to say goodbye. Miriam hadn't come that day because she had to work, she was in touch via cell phone.

I don't think that Nisman thought my testimony was at all valuable, because he never got back in touch with me despite the fact that I could've obviously contributed much more than I said that afternoon, overwhelmed as I was. My testimony could've altered the entire course of the AMIA case. But nothing changed at all.

A while later, they took a statement from Laura as well as another of my superiors. Red must've lost it when they summoned her to testify, it was the worst thing that could happened to someone like her. She must've felt exposed, but she is great at keeping it together. Not for nothing she was a spy handler for so many years. I know that both of my bosses who testified tried to downplay the importance of my work, they wanted to make me look like a small fry, like someone who didn't matter. All you have to do is look at my report to see how I excelled. If that didn't count for anything, why did they keep me undercover for twelve years? The notion that my work didn't matter to them is absurd.

Now, six months later, alone in a forgotten town with no one to talk to, I got the news that Nisman has been found dead in the bathroom of his apartment, with a bloody .22 in his hand. The man who'd ordered my protection got a bullet to the head. A lot of people are saying he was murdered, that they forced him to commit suicide. It's quite possible it was a suicide, that he couldn't take the pressure, but I can also assure you that the people in my line of work are capable of absolutely anything.

DEFENSELESS WITNESS

I'd always imagined that the day I testified I'd feel an enormous weight lifted, but it was just the opposite.

It was getting dark by the time I finally finished my testimony and signed the formal petition to enter the witness protection program. They kept me waiting another hour or so, until a lawyer for the program came to introduce himself. I had to wait a little longer, while they completed the paperwork. Then the two of us went down alone in the elevator. It must've been past 7:00 p.m. The lawyer led me across the plaza which was now dark and almost deserted. We walked down Reconquista and then turned. I was afraid someone would step out of the shadows at any minute and stab me, or a car would appear out of nowhere to run me down.

I was dumbfounded. I never imagined they would just walk me out of the prosecutor's office on foot, totally unprotected. We got to a building and went inside. Another employee was waiting for me there, a friendly guy. They had me read some pages that described what the program supposedly guaranteed me in terms of material and emotional support, in addition to my obligations, which meant completely erasing my past. I had to go home and pack. The next day I was going to disappear from my world.

I'd begun, a month prior, a new relationship with a girl who lived in a small town, not far from where I'm now in hiding. She knew that I was with the agency, but not much more. The next morning I went to talk to her. I told her that I had a serious problem, that I'd reported corruption within the agency and that I had to go into witness protection with a new identity. She didn't ask any further questions. She agreed that we should rent a house together on the edge of town. And the people in the program thought it was a good idea.

I had to leave all my belongings, everything I had in my house. I was allowed to take only clothes. I didn't have any luxuries, but I'd been comfortable there. I'm a tidy guy and I'd kept the place up. I only returned once, after it had been emptied out. I looked around thinking: "I lived here, my home was here." It was like a wasteland. That's the way I felt inside.

In the end they allowed me forty-eight hours to pack. I stuffed whatever I could into backpacks, suitcases, bags. I put it all in my car and they escorted me in another vehicle. I'd expected them to take care of the move for me, but that's not what happened. They didn't want me to bring my car, but I said that I wouldn't be able to get around without it. That night I couldn't sleep.

Before leaving, I gave a friend the key to my apartment and he went in and emptied everything out. He gave all my stuff away to his friends, with my permission. Washing machine, TV set, refrigerator. I settled in a house on the edge of a small town, near the river. Anyone else would've thought it was paradise, but not me. My new life consisted of being constantly on guard. I did my Russian lessons, as well as German, which I'd recently begun studying. I was alone all day since my girlfriend left early for work. Sometimes I went on walks, visited the three or four pastry shops in town. Within a week I knew the place like the back of my hand and everyone waved to me. I bought a cap, I tried to blend in, I grew a beard and long hair.

I wasn't paranoid, just the opposite. I moved around freely. I felt active, alert, with all my senses heightened. But I was a prisoner, even if they tried to convince me otherwise. "Why, if I'm not a criminal?" I asked myself over and over. I couldn't contact anyone in my family, not even by phone; if I had to make a call it could only be from a pay phone in another town. I visited every town in the area one by one.

I did meet, from time to time, with the representatives from the program at a general store. "You can't leave the area, you can't go through any toll booths, you can't be picked up on any camera," they told me.

I felt like I was suffocating. I collected maps that I bought or downloaded off the internet and started to look for all the roads that didn't have toll booths. I drove around in circles and then returned to the town. If I got caught in the rain on one of those dirt roads I could end up stuck in a ditch, lost, in the middle of the night.

Things with my new girlfriend quickly soured. We lived together for just two months. She wasn't from the collective, but she was similar to Eli in a lot of ways. She was vegan, mentally healthy, a member of an organization that protected animals. It was a virtue, but in the end it was too much. I didn't want to change her. But she had eight dogs. Eight. Added to the stress I was under, the constant barking was unbearable. I never explode, I never get aggressive. I'm more likely to go out on a walk to unload my rage. Then the arguments started. We talked, but there was nothing for it. She wanted to introduce me to her friends, relatives, she called me Nicolás, which was my new name. But I didn't want to lie, I'd spent my life lying. I couldn't stand to do it anymore. I said to her: "How are we going to make this relationship grow? I'm going to have to live a lie again . . . I can't do it, don't you see that?" All that, added to other conflicts, meant I had to move again.

The people in the program told me that they left me on my own because I was a professional and I knew how to take care of myself. No one guarded me, they trusted in my abilities. The truth is, I could've done whatever I wanted, even traveled to Buenos Aires. When I broke up with my girlfriend, I stayed for a few nights at a hotel in another town.

They were still paying me my salary from the force, as promised by the Ministry of Security. But every month I could breathe easy only after that money came in. I was convinced they were going to come up with some excuse to stop paying me. And that added on more instability, it was very stressful.

I didn't walk around armed like before, I felt confident enough in my abilities. If someone tried to come for me I would be able to get away as long as the other person was within reach, even if they had two guns or tried to run me down in a car: I'd done an anti-kidnapping course with the Israelis. I'm trained in krav maga, but the way it's used in the Israeli army, not the commercial version that only serves as defense, to keep from being robbed. It's a version that they can't teach anyone who's not Israeli. It's designed for when you run out of ammo and you're unarmed, for example, in a trench. They teach you how to strike with all your force, quickly, in precise places, to kill the enemy, because they consider you the last obstacle, an unbreachable barrier.

ADRIFT

The witness protection program accepts three kinds of cases: drug trafficking, human trafficking, and terrorism. I fell into that last category. I think I was the only one, and that wasn't a fact that made me feel safer.

I decided to move to the coast. At first I felt like I was on vacation. I got a pit bull, who I trusted to alert me if anyone tried to enter my house while I was away or while I slept. Winter came. The cheerful sunny days were few and far between. The house was old and unheated. The few possessions I owned were ruined when the roof leaked. The dog I'd begun to think of as my only companion got sick. I took her to a vet, who charged a fortune. I ran into neighbors I didn't know in the shared patio and I felt watched; I had no privacy.

I got permission to move again, because nothing had worked out as I'd hoped.

After that I rented an apartment where I started to feel a little better, mostly because after a little while spring came and the weather improved. I went jogging on the beach every morning. Things were okay, but not great. Then, like everything, it ended. We're not supposed to spend too long in one place.

I have regrets, I feel helpless. I lament all of my mistakes. If I'd been able to plan my exit, I'd have tried to make it so that no one else had to suffer through any fault of mine. I also beat myself up over my previous life, my undercover work. I'm tormented by all the information I obtained that was used for evil. I think, I'm almost certain, that my spot was occupied by another agent after I left. Maybe more than one. It's naïve to think it didn't happen.

I remember one time Horacio and I, in a sad game, tried to make a list of all the irregularities that had been committed in the AMIA investigation. Every time we thought we'd gotten to the end, we remembered another one. Now they've assigned new prosecutors to the case and have finally begun to look into Kanoore Edul, a Syrian man close to Menem. That, and the payment of a $400,000 bribe to Telleldín for false testimony that placed the blame on the Buenos Aires Police. Menem has been charged, along with the chief of the SIDE, Hugo Anzorreguy, Beraja himself from his time as president of DAIA . . . and two feds, Castañeda and Fino Palacios. But it's hard to believe that it might lead to anything all these years later.

In truth, I'm still trying to figure out who I am. I think I know. The Talmud states that a man has three names. The first, given to him by his father and his mother, which in my case is José. The second, given to him by his peers, Jorge Polak. And the third, the most precious, is the one he gives himself. That name, I'm certain is Iosi.

I don't have anything else to say as I pack my bag and once again seek safe harbor. There is no peace for me. I'm nothing more than an inconvenient piece of evidence. As I've said a thousand times, life, my life, is worth nothing.

EPILOGUE

The story of Iosi, the spy who infiltrated the Argentine Jewish community under democratic rule, raises a lot of disquieting questions. Some are obvious. How much did political authorities from the multiple administrations know about the espionage activities carried out after democracy was restored in 1986, going against citizens' fundamental constitutional rights? Was the government monitoring the actions taken by its intelligence services, or was it these services, to the contrary, controlling government power? Was Iosi the only spy? When he was removed from the field, did another agent move in to replace him? Did the intelligence departments of other security forces or armed forces, or the SIDE, have spies undercover in other social, political or religious organizations? Do they still?

Do active police officers today still have prejudices against those who are different from them? In the Tragic Week of 1919, a journalist for the Jewish media named Pinie Wald was arrested and taken to Precinct 7 (the same station that decades later would fail to protect the AMIA). He was then savagely punished by the Central Police Department, accused of leading a "maximalist" Russian plot to install a "Soviet" in Argentina. During the last military dictatorship, in 1977, the journalist Jacobo Timerman was tortured in custody by Ramón Camps, chief of police for the Province of Buenos Aires, who wanted Timerman to "confess" to his involvement in the "Andinia Plan," the supposed Jewish conspiracy to take control of the Patagonia and create an Andean Republic, a second Israel. That lie was spread by Nazi sympathizer Walter Beveraggi Allende during the dictatorship. But democracy had been restored by the time Iosi was planted in the Jewish community to investigate these same ridiculous claims. Has the intellectual and professional training of the police forces really changed?

Other questions. Two bombings—with evidence of police participation in the perpetration and cover-up of the crimes—took the lives of more than a hundred people in Buenos Aires. Nevertheless, the existence of a key witness with a front-row seat to the moments leading up to and immediately following the tragedies drew no real interest from leaders of the Jewish community nor those tasked with obtaining justice for these crimes.

Iosi was asked to gather detailed information on two institutions that were later targeted by terrorists. And he did so under orders from his superiors at the Federal Police Intelligence Department who considered the Jews to be a threat. He provided them with everything: the characteristics of the buildings, layout, access points, weak spots, the ways of getting in and out undetected.

In the moments before the two attacks, all the federal officers who could have been victims or who could have prevented the crimes disappeared from their posts because they were warned to leave. It was no coincidence: this wasn't one or two officers but a dozen between the two attacks. And, after the massacres, it was the same federal police—among others—who destroyed the evidence. Meanwhile, they continued to spy on the community, not to protect them from within, but to find out whether they had uncovered evidence of the crime. Iosi was tasked with this job.

But the leaders of the Jewish community looked the other way. Rubén Beraja, president of DAIA, his successor José Hercman and others that followed, as well as the Israeli ambassador Itzhak Aviran, defended the official explanation of the attacks, praised the Federal Police, and aligned themselves with the Carlos Menem government.

We now know, thanks to the Wikileaks files, that the United States embassy put pressure on District Attorney Alberto Nisman, urging him not to investigate the cover-up of the bombings and Galeano's flawed investigation. Why were these power players in Argentina and abroad all working to keep the truth obscured?

The lawyers for DAIA and AMIA, as plaintiffs in the case for the attack on their headquarters, unlike the families of the victims, defended Justice Juan José Galeano's scandalous mishandling of the case and its numerous irregularities, which delayed any chance of obtaining truth and justice. Together with the SIDE, the State Secretariat of Intelligence, Jewish community leaders jealously guarded the covert and often illegal activities of the spies involved in the supposed investigation.

Against all logic, a few days after the AMIA attack, the local investigation was aborted, despite mountains of evidence and suspicious actions such as those of the Argentine citizen of Syrian descent Alberto J. Kanoore Edul, with ties not only to Carlos Telleldín but also another central suspect: the cultural attaché for the Iranian embassy, Mohsen Rabbani, who appeared in Edul's list of personal contacts. On August 1, 1994, orders were handed down from the Casa Rosada to immediately clear Edul, whose family was very close to Menem, along with another central suspect: the Lebanese miner Nassib Haddad, explosives expert and owner of the dumpster parked outside the AMIA minutes before the detonation, after stopping by a vacant lot that Edul used. Both of the men were sent home after only a few hours in questioning. Then, the investigation into them was closed and the evidence collected was systematically destroyed (cassettes, transcripts, and confiscated items). This line of the investigation, referred to as the "Syrian lead," although it also included Iranian suspects, directly implicated Carlos Menem.

How much did the personal business gains by Jewish community leaders and government officials come into play? Or is it all part of a larger conspiracy at the international level? Could the massive ring of weapons and explosives trafficking from Argentina to Croatia and Bosnia, which Menem's government was known to have taken part in through Syrian and Iranian intermediaries, be the reason for all the smoke and mirrors? But that operation was not arranged by Menem alone; it was secretly approved by the United States, in spite of a UN ban on selling weapons to the region that went into effect in 1991. For the Serbians, who had an entire arsenal left over from Tito's Yugoslavia, the embargo wasn't that dire, but for the rest of those involved, it was. Israel, for its part, from the 1970s onward was known to collaborate with the Argentine military and US agents in supplying weapons to Iranian buyers. This market was very active in Argentina in the nineties. The backdrop for these operations was the port of Buenos Aires. There, shipments piled up by the ton in warehouses where the cargo was inspected by intermediaries and buyers, mostly Croatians, Bosnian Muslims, and Iranians. All that contraband, destined for the Balkans, was held just minutes away from the AMIA headquarters. Steps, in fact from the warehouse owned by Nassib Haddad, the same warehouse where the dumpster deposited outside the AMIA originated.

Menem officials, Carapintada right-wing extremists, government repressors from the military dictatorship, SIDE agents, and heads of the military industries from several countries including Argentina all got a cut. It has been proven in court that they went as far as to cause the explosion of Río Tercero to hide their arms trafficking operation. And this operation had to remain hidden, without interference, in spite of the bombing of the Israeli embassy and the AMIA. No pesky investigation could expose these illicit dealings; it would have to be halted by any means necessary.

Why was the SIDE tailing Mohsen Rabbani, the Iranian diplomat suspected of involvement in the attack, as well as members of Iranian terrorist cells, before the AMIA bombing? If the Iranians were responsible, as the prevailing theory maintains, and the nation's top intelligence service was watching them, why didn't they stop the attacks from happening? Also, what role did the helicopter play as it lit up the rooftop of the AMIA on the night before the bombing? Why were all warning signs ignored and certain testimonies thrown out? Why was Iosi asked to gather such plentiful and precise information and what was it used for?

Until now, these questions remain unanswered. The agents of darkness are winning the game. But Iosi is living proof that there's another story waiting to come to light. The true story.

GLOSSARY

TERMS IN HEBREW, YIDDISH, AND NAMES OF INSTITUTIONS

aliyah: To emigrate to Israel. In its original usage it means to ascend Mount Zion, in the foothills of which Jerusalem was built.

Baath Party: Syrian political party that combines Arabic Socialism, nationalism, and pan-Arabism.

Bar and Bat Mitzvah: Bar Mitzvah for a boy, "son of the commandments" or Bat Mitzvah for a girl, "daughter of the commandments." Jewish ritual which considers B'nai Mitzvah children who have reached personal maturity and can be seen by their community as responsible for their actions. Held at age thirteen for boys and twelve for girls. Generally celebrated with a ceremony.

Betar: Right-wing Zionist youth organization.

Beteinu: Meaning our house. Home for children in at-risk situations.

bitajon: Security.

bubbe: Grandmother.

breira: Meaning alternative. Broader leftist Zionists affiliated with the Zionist Organization of Argentina.

CISSAB: Jewish community country club located in Tristán Suáerz, in the province of Buenos Aires.

Frai Shtime: Meaning free voice. Militant leftist worker's association, made up mainly of immigrants who were very active in the Buenos Aires union scene in the early 1900s.

FUSLA: Latin-American Zionist University Federation.

Gadna: Military training course for teens held in Israel, before their obligatory military service.

ganenet: Nursery school teacher.

Guili: Informal education center for small children run out of Tzavta.

Hacoaj: Nautical Club and sports complex with branches in the Buenos Aires neighborhood of Almagro and in Tigre, in the province of Buenos Aires.

Hamakom Shelí: My place. Hebrew school for children and teens with differential educational needs.

hasbara: Clarification.

Hashomer Hatzair: Youth guard. Socialist Zionist movement with characteristics similar to the Scouts, founded in Poland in 1913 and popular in Jewish communities around the world. One of its leaders, Mordecai Anielewicz, led the Warsaw Ghetto uprising against the Nazis in 1943.

The organization was responsible for founding dozens of kibbutzim in Israel.

hatzeira: Youth.

HaTzionim HaKlalim: General Zionists. Centrist group within Zionism.

Hertzliah: Temple and school within the Jewish school system of Buenos Aires located in the La Paternal neighborhood. The school's name is taken from Theodor Hertzl, founder of the Zionist political party who was a writer, lawyer, and journalist.

Herut: Meaning freedom. Right-wing organization formed around the principles of a major Israeli political party that went by the same name until it fused with the Likud party.

Habad Lubavitch: Hassidic Jewish Orthodox religious movement founded in the late eighteenth century in the Russian village of Lyubavichi. There are an estimated two hundred thousand members worldwide; headed in Argentina by Rabbi Tzvi Grunblatt.

Ivrit: Hebrew.

Jaim Weitzman: Jewish school in the Floresta neighborhood named after the Zionist leader and scientist who became the first president of Israel.

Jativá: Zionist student organization with conservative leanings.

jinuj: Education.

Kabalat Shabat: Ceremony held with family to celebrate the arrival of Saturday, the sacred day of rest and spiritual enrichment, beginning with the lighting of candles when the first stars come out on Friday night and followed by a celebratory dinner.

kabat, kabatim: Singular and plural; security guard, person who provides protection.

kadish: Prayer for lost loved ones.

ketubah: Jewish marriage contract.

Kibbutz: Self-sustainable community with Socialist principles of shared property, equality, and social justice, mainly based around agriculture in its origins, which played an essential role in the formation of the State of Israel.

kipa, kipot: Singular and plural; the ritual cap that should be placed on a man's head in religious spaces as a sign of submission to God.

kita: Class.

klita: Absorption.

krav maga: Israeli discipline of fighting and personal defense.

Likud: Right-wing Israeli political party founded in 1973 by Menachem Begin.

Macabi: Macabi Hebrew Organization, social and sports club with branches in the Buenos Aires neighborhood of Abasto and in San Miguel, in the province of Buenos Aires.

machane: Campground.

Mapam: Israeli Socialist party, later fused with the Meretz party.

Martín Buber: Jewish school in the Palermo neighborhood, named after the writer, philosopher, and cultural Zionist who was a fierce proponent of dialogue between Jews and Arabs in Palestine.

Max Nordau: Progressive community center with a branch in the city of La Plata named after the Hungarian Jewish writer and activist.

mazquirut: Secretary general.

menorah: Candelabra with seven arms, one of the most ancient symbols of the Jewish people.

Meretz: Leftist, pacifist Israeli political party.

moadon: Club, clubhouse, meeting room.

moalim: Plural of mohel; person authorized to perform a circumcision.

mora, morim: Singular and plural; teacher.

Mossad: Israeli secret service for operations outside Israel.

Natan Gesang: Jewish school in the Once neighborhood, named after the Polish-born community leader and founder of several Jewish institutions in Argentina.

Ofakim: Horizons. Name of the university group started by Iosi.

olim: Emigrants to Israel.

OSA: Zionist Organization of Argentina.

Pesach: Celebration that honors the freedom of the Jewish people from slavery under the Egyptian pharaoh, characterized as the festival of freedom, in which families gather to celebrate with a dinner of specific foods and read aloud extracts from the Haggadah (the story). It usually coincides more or less with Easter on the Christian calendar.

Rambam: Jewish school named for the philosopher Maimonides, in the Once neighborhood of Buenos Aires.

Ratz: Israeli political party, integrated into Meretz.

sabra: Person born in Israel. It comes from the Hebrew term tsabar, the name given to a cactus native to the region, spiny on the outside but sweet inside.

Schlijim: An emissary.

sheliah, shelihim: Singular and plural; envoys or representatives of an Israeli movement.

Shin Bet: General Intelligence and security service within Israel.

Shinui: Israeli political party, integrated into Meretz.

shofar: Traditional wind instrument made from a ram's horn and used in religious ceremonies for the past three thousand years.

Sholem Aleijem: Jewish school in the Villa Crespo neighborhood of Buenos Aires whose name is taken from the artistic name of a popular Russian Jewish writer and humorist in Yiddish.

Sojnut: Jewish services agency whose office processed the paperwork for emigration to Israel.

Tagar: Challenge. Name given to the anthem of the Irgun, the Jewish paramilitary organization that fought against the British rule of Palestine.

Talmud: The book of Judaism that includes laws, traditions, stories, and sayings.

Tarbut: Jewish school in the Buenos Aires neighborhood of Belgrano and in Olivos, in theprovince of Buenos Aires.

Tzavta: Meaning together. Name of the secular, progressive Jewish community center in Almagro neighborhood of Buenos Aires. The Tzavta building also housed for a time the offices of the *New Zion* newspaper.

Vaad Hajinuj: Jewish education council.

Yamim noraim: Meaning terrible days. This is the name given to the ten days between Rosh Hashanna (Jewish New Year) and Yom Kippur (Day of Forgiveness). Considered a period of deep introspection and reflection on the mistakes made during the year.

Yiddish: Language spoken by European Jews in the diaspora.

Yom Ha'atzmaut: Israeli independence day.

zayde: Grandfather.

BIBLIOGRAPHY

"Argentine Jews Sad and Wary at First Anniversary of Bombing," *J Weekly*, July 14, 1995. Accessed August 12, 2015. http://www.jweekly.com/includes/print/1292/article/argentinianjewssadandwaryatfirstanniversary-ofbombing/.

Bar-Zohar, Michael, and Nissim Mishal. *Mossad: The Greatest Missions of the Israeli Secret Service*. New York: Ecco, 2014.

Beris, Jana. "Shabtai Shavit: 'Tras los atentados, las fuerzas de seguridad no ayudaron.'" *La Nación*, March 5, 2015. Accessed April 30, 2015. https://www.lanacion.com.ar/politica/shabtai-shavit-tras-los-atentados-las-fuerzas-de-seguridad-no-ayudaron-nid1773442/.

Bermúdez, Norberto. *La pista siria*. Buenos Aires: Ediciones de la Urraca, 1993.

Caballero, Roberto. *AMIA: La verdad imposible*. Buenos Aires: Sudamericana, 2005.

Dan, Ben. *The Spy from Israel*. London: Valentine Mitchell, 1969.

Delfino, Emilia, and Rodrigo Alegre. *La ejecución: La historia secreta del triple crimen*. Buenos Aires: Sudamericana, 2011.

Di Nápoli, Carlos, director. *AMIA, la causa*. 2011.

Fayt, Carlos S. *Criminalidad y terrorismo sagrado: El atentado a la Embajada de Israel en Argentina*. La Plata, Argentina: Editorial Universitaria de la Plata, 2001.

Goddard, Jim, director. *The Impossible Spy*. 1987.

Goldman, Joe, and Jorge Lanata. *Cortinas de humo*. Buenos Aires: Planeta, 1994.

Goobar, Walter. *El tercer atentado*. Buenos Aires: Sudamericana,1996.

Gordon, Thomas. *Gideon's Spies: The Secret History of the Mossad*. New York: St. Martin's Griffin, 2015.

Juvenal, Carlos. *Buenos muchachos*. Buenos Aires: Planeta, 1994.

Levinas, Gabriel. *La ley bajo los escombros*. Buenos Aires: Sudamericana, 2015.

Levitt, Matthew. *Hezbollah: The Global Footprint of Lebanon's Party of God*. London: Hurst and Company, 2013.

Lifschitz, Claudio. *AMIA, porqué se hizo fallar la investigación*. Buenos Aires: Dpto. Editorial, 2000.

Lipis, Guillermo. *Nueva sión, periodismo crítico: De lo comunitario a lo nacional*. Buenos Aires: Milá, 2004.

Lutzky, Horacio. *Caso AMIA: La deuda interna[*. Buenos Aires: Fundación Mordejai Anilevich, 2003.

Lutzky, Horacio. *Brindando sobre los escombros*. Buenos Aires: Sudamericana, 2013.

Perednik, Gustavo D. *Matar sin que se note*. Buenos Aires: Planeta, 2009.

Salinas, Juan José. *AMIA, el atentado: Quiénes son los autores y por qué no están, presos*. Buenos Aires: Planeta, 1997.

Slutzky, Shlomo, director. *El tercero en camino*. Channel 1, 2008.

Spielberg, Steven, director. *Munich*. Universal Pictures, 2005.

Timerman, Jacobo. *Preso sin nombre, celda sin número*. Buenos Aires: El Cid, 1982.

Young, Gerardo. *Código Stiuso: La SIDE, la política desde las cloacas y la muerte de Nisman*. Buenos Aires: Planeta, 2015.

Wald, Pinie. *Pesadilla*. Translated by Simja Sneh. Buenos Aires: Ameghino, 1998.

ACKNOWLEDGMENTS

We would like to thank all those affected by the attacks on the Israeli embassy and the AMIA headquarters for their enduring commitment to justice even after two decades have passed. They are living proof that all hope is not lost. To the activists and honest members of the Jewish community who refuse to negotiate, who are not afraid to challenge the official explanation of the bombings. And who want the truth, above all else.

To the Argentines who still feel like those attacks were an attack on us all.

In the long years that our relationship with Iosi lasted, we crossed paths with many people who we thought very highly of and who, after an initial display of interest in his case, ultimately let us down. But thankfully, we also had many friends and colleagues who continued to lend us their support in many different ways despite our stubborn reservations. They know who they are. To those who never lost their capacity for shock and indignation when we were able to speak with them.

Finally, our thanks to Isidoro Gilbert, maestro of all maestros, for his erudition, his enthusiasm, and his sharp observations, to Ana Laura Pérez for her understanding and dedication, and to Mercedes Sacchi for her outstanding work.

—THE AUTHORS

Bs As, 19 de Septiembre de 2005

Sigla /Y.T.O.H.
LP. 1633

Manifiesto que me encuentro prestando servicio en la Delegacion Parana de la Policia Federal Argentina siendo los responsables de mi persona los siguientes funcionarios:
Comisario General Valleca - Jefe de la PFA.
Comisario General Pardal - Jefe de la Superint. del Interior
Comisario Mayor Masaferri - Director General de Delegaciones

Comisario Pujol - Jefe de la Delegacion Parana
Subcomisario Costantini - 2° Jefe de la Deleg.
Como asi tambien a los Jefe y 2° Jefe de la Delegacion San Isidro
Comisario Filgueiras - Sub Comisario Lucero

Copy of Iosi's Federal Police credential and a hand-written statement explaining his position and naming his superiors, provided to the authors in September of 2005, during one of the periods that he felt unsafe.

Certificate of Participation in the Department of Anti-terrorism course on international terrorism in 2010.

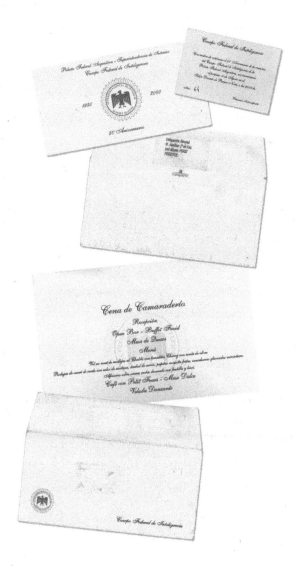

Iosi's invitation to a dinner celebrating the 50th anniversary of the Federal Police Intelligence Agency.

```
|CUA.|JER.| LEGAJO| AFIL...| SIGLA |  FECHA  |  ALTA   | DEST.|
  A   709   01633   061770  Y.T.O.H.   3/92    11/03/85   05
```

COD.	CONCEPTO	CANT.	HABERES	DESCUENTOS
1	BASICO	0.00	111.81	
2	BONIFIC. COMPLEM.	0.00	260.89	
3	SUPL.RIESGO PROFES	0.00	115.25	
30	SUPL. POR ANTIG.	7.00	68.31	
64	REINTEGRO O.SOCIAL	7.50	41.72	
	TOTAL DE HABERES :		597.98	
101	APORTE JUBILATORIO	8.00		44.50
110	ASISTENCIA MEDICA	10.00		55.63
120	SEGURO VIDA OBLIG.	0.00		1.88
121	SUBSIDIO SOCIAL	0.00		2.10
144	AYUDA GTOS.SEPELIO	0.00		2.54
	TOTAL DE APORTES:			106.65

```
                                      597.98      106.65
                        | NETO $   491.33 |

        FIRMA RESP.PAGADOR

    SE RECUERDA LA OBLIGATORIEDAD DE
    PRESENTAR CERTIFICADOS DE ESCOLA-
    RIDAD AL COMENZAR EL AÑO LECTIVO.
                                      FIRMA REC. CONF. NETO

    *** HABERES DEL MES DE MARZO DE 1992 ***
```

Iosi's receipt of services rendered for the month of the attack on the Israeli embassy, with his secret identification code, Y.T.O.H.

BUENOS AIRES, 28 de Septiembre de 1992

PARA SER PRESENTADO Y DIFUNDIDO ANTE LA OPINION PUBLICA Y LAS AUTORIDADES
DE LA EMBAJADA DE ISRAEL.

DECLARO que yo PEREZ JOSE ALBERTO nacido el 29/5/60 en CAP.FED. divorcia-
do y con domicilio en R.S.ORTIZ 467 7mo. piso dto. 18 de esta capital, hace
8 años que pertenesco a la SUPERINTENDENCIA DE INTERIOR de la POLICIA FEDERAL
ARGENTINA,con el cargo de AUXILIAR 4to.DE INTELIGENCIA sigla Y.T.O.H. legajo
personal 1633, habiendo ingresado en la misma en marzo'85 en la ESCUELA DE
INTELIGENCIA sita en la calle Gral. URQUIZA 556 altos de la Cria..8ª y tenien
do los siguientes destinos:
Dto. ASUNTOS LABORALES.-MORENO 1417
Div. OBRA SOCIAL.-P.ZANNY 289
Div. AGRUPACION.-Av. de los INMIGRANTES 2550
Dto. ASUNTOS EXTRANGEROS.-MORENO 1417
Dto. PROTECCION al ORDEN CONSTITUCIONAL.-MORENO 1417

En 1986 se me dio la mision de infiltrarme en la COMUNIDAD JUDIA por lo cual
se me instruyo en los aspectos de historia, tradiciones y costumbres del pue-
blo judio e incluso el idiomatico;creando luego una historia ficticia para mi
insercion en la misma,lograndolo a mediados del mismo año.
Asi logre infiltrarme en los siguientes lugares:

JATIVA UNIVERSITARIA SIONISTA
TNUAT ALIA
TAGAR
BREIRA
CONVERGENCIA
ORGANIZACION SIONISTA ARGENTINA

Ocupando diferentes cargos e informando todos los hechos que estuvieran rela-
cionados con los intereses de ARGENTINA y los intereses de ISRAEL hacia la //
misma.
En ningun momento perjudique con mis informes las buenas relaciones, autori-
zandome incluso a proteger o neutralizar cualquier tipo de atentado a los //
miembros de la comunidad, como lo realice en todos los actos de IOM HAATZMAUT
durante la GUERRA DEL GOLFO y despues del atentado a la EMBAJADA.
En 1990 estando en CONVERGENCIA conoci a ▓▓▓▓▓▓▓▓▓▓▓▓ de quien me enamore
y con la cual pensamos casarnos y formar una familia, por ello en caso de su-
cederme algo a mi o a cualquiera de mis padres e hijo incluso a algun familia
de mi novia responsabiliso a las siguientes personas:

Crio.Inspec._DE LEON -JEFE DEL P.O.C.
Scrio. CASTAÑEDA
Ofic. de Intelig.(nombre supuesto) RODOLFO MIRANDA Telef.part. 775-4900
          NOMBRE REAL _ MIRAELA SUCCI - DOMICILIO JF SEGUI 4372
Dejando como prueba un maletin con diferentes elementos y documentos utiliza-
dos en misiones realizadas.
La firma que realizo a continuacion puede ser comparada con la registrada en
mi caja de ahorro de BANCO de BOSTON Suc.CONSTITUCION.

Letter written by Iosi in September 1992 detailing his undercover work as his relationship with Eli progressed.

```
POLICIA FEDERAL ARGENTINA
SUPERINTENDENCIA DE INTERIOR

           CERTIFICADO DE PRESTACION DE SERVICIOS

          La División ADMINISTRACION de la Superintendencia de /
INTERIOR de la POLICIA FEDERAL ARGENTINA certifica que José Al-/
berto PEREZ, revista en ésta repartición bajo la jerarquia 708 y
con Legajo Personal Nro. 1633, habiendo ingresado el día 11 de /
noviembre de 1985 y percibe a la fecha la siguiente remuneración
mensual de PESOS UN MIL DIEZ CON 45/100 ($ 1.010,45).-
          Se extiende el presente a pedido del interesado y al /
sólo efecto de ser presentado ante la SOCIEDAD MILITAR SEGURO DE
VIDA. Dado en BUENOS AIRES, a los 30 días del mes de marzo de /
1994.-
          Se deja constancia que el causante no se encuentra suma
riado, ni embargado, ni en trámite de baja o de retiro y que al/
dia de la fecha tiene afectado el 00,00 % de sus haberes brutos.
```

Iosi's proof of entry into the Federal Police Force in 1985.

```
FEDERACION SIONISTA ARGENTINA
      KINUS TERRITORIAL Y
   CONVENCION LATINO-AMERICANA
     DE SIONISTAS GENERALES

   PERES    YOSEF

Buenos Aires, 19, 20 y 21 de Septiembre de 1986
```

Iosi's name tag for a Zionist convention and his business card as kabat.

Certificate of completion of the first and second year of extended Hebrew studies at the Argentina-Israel Institute for Cultural Exchange.

Iosi's invitation to an event in October of 1990 on the occasion of a visit from the Israeli minister of tourism to AMIA.

Buenos Aires, junio 20 de 1995

Organización Sionista Argentina

Atn.: Sr. Oscar Hansman - Presidente
H.C.D.

Estimados javerim:

Por la presente les solicitamos tengan a bien poner en funciones a nuestro compañero José Alberto Perez en el puesto de Pro-Secretario, que quedó libre a raíz de la renuncia de nuestro compañero Jorge Fraiman el año pasado.

A la brevedad les informaremos el próximo compañero de nuestro partido que ocupará el lugar correspondiente de José Alberto Perez en vuestra institución.

Les agradecemos desde ya y rogamos informar a la Comisión Directiva y a las instituciones comunitarias y medios judíos que Uds. consideren apropiado.

Aprovechamos para saludarles con nuestro cordial

Shalom!

David Grinberg
Secretario

Dr. Noé Davidovich
Presidente Mapam Argentina

Iosi's official designation as representative of the Mapam Party in his role as sub-secretary of the Zionist Organization of Argentina.

Part of Iosi's original call list to create the first university group at Tzavta, which would function in tandem with the Convergence Youth.

Pay stubs for Iosi's work as security guard for the AMIA.

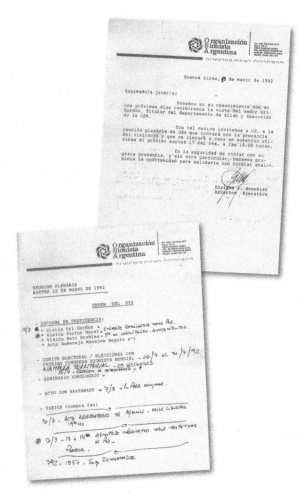

TOP: Invitation to a meeting with an Israeli government employee on March 17, 1992, the day of the attack on the embassy, signed by the executive director of the Zionist Organization of Argentina, who, days later, Iosi would accompany to the morgue to identify bodies.

BOTTOM: The Zionist Organization of Argentina's schedule of activities for the week prior to the attack on the Israeli embassy, with notes taken by Iosi, including a meeting planned for the day of the attack, March 17, 1992, which he did not attend.

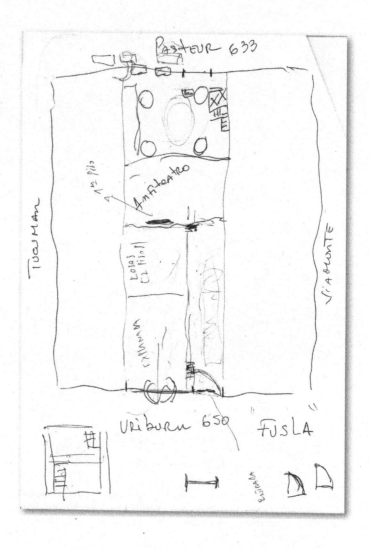

Floorplan drawn by Iosi showing entrances and access points to the buildings at 650 Uriburu (FUSLA offices) and 633 Pasteur (AMIA headquarters).

TOP: The future spy as a child, with his bicycle in Parque Avellaneda in the Floresta neighborhood of Buenos Aires.

BOTTOM LEFT: Iosi as a young man, taking his first steps into the world of spies.

BOTTOM RIGHT: Certificate of merit from the Federal Police, given to José Polak Pérez, AKA, Iosi.

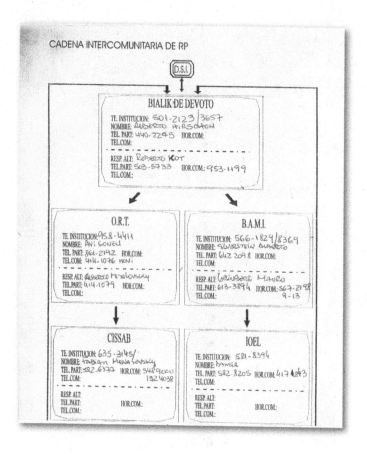

List of contact information and chain of command for the Jewish community security organization in the case of a threat, which included Iosi as representative of Tzavta.

Security protocol for Tzavta designed by Iosi.

First and last pages of Iosi's testimony at the prosecutor's office assigned to the AMIA case headed by Alberto Nisman, who was not present for the testimony but signed as if he were present.